Welcome to the Mrs B stories. I hope you enjoy them.

This book is dedicated to my family, who have put up with me being distracted. More than that, they have cheered me on! They are the reason that I write. More than that, they are the best part of me.

1.

Mrs B and The Keen Gardener

"Oh my, those flowers are a sight to lift anyone's spirits. The fragrance is a balm to the soul." Mrs B. pushed her bicycle along the garden path and rested it against the wall by the back door. In the basket on the handlebars was her bag, in which she kept all the keys for the places she cleaned, safely labelled and zipped in. Her apron, in a floral print, was washed and ironed and folded over the top of her bag. Her work day was about to start.

She let herself into the house and started with washing up the dishes in the sink. Mrs Appleby had waved in response to her comment on the flowers, but she was a quiet soul, and Mrs B had noticed that she found conversation uncomfortable. In truth, the cleaning lady rarely missed anything. If she had come from a family with more money, perhaps she might have completed her education, and gone on to do more, but cleaning paid her bills, and her natural curiosity was fed by the homes she cleaned and the customers she met. She kept her nose out of people's business and her hair neat and tidy under her hat. Unless, of course, there was something that she could help with.

She might be old-fashioned, but she believed in doing things the right way. She disapproved of the young girls running around without a hat or gloves, for goodness' sake.

The dishes were always piled high in the sink in Mrs Appleby's house, usually covered in congealed gravy, which Mr Appleby was very partial to. Mrs B. was what people referred to as a 'treasure.' She worked hard, and always left the houses spotless, and she kept her mouth shut. Gossip was not her way.

The water was hot and soapy, soon the sticky plates were washed and dried. Today was the day for a good clean of the kitchen, and Mrs B. scrubbed the kitchen table before giving it a good polish. The table and the floor were littered with pieces of flowers and leaves. She washed all the shelves and the cupboard fronts, before giving the floor a good mopping. Her time was nearly up, but she had long enough to give the bathroom a short clean and dust the living room. She checked her watch. Five minutes left. She usually did Mr Appleby's study every other week, but she might just get it done now.

"Mrs B?" Mrs Appleby's voice filtered through the

sunbeams in the hallway. "Mr Appleby is working in his study he asked me not to disturb him."

"Thank you, Mrs Appleby." Mrs B would not have liked to barge in unwanted. Mr Appleby could be quite particular. She had heard him shouting at his wife on more than one occasion.

"The kitchen looks wonderful. Thank you so much, Mrs B." Mrs Appleby passed over an envelope, a muddy fingerprint on the side. "Sorry, I've been planting the late lettuce crop." She smiled widely and with real joy. "I should have come in earlier and made you a tea."

"Not at all, Mrs Appleby. Perish the thought of the late lettuce being delayed." Mrs B smiled across at her employer. A cup of tea would have been nice, but she had another job to do and she knew she would have tea there, and an iced bun, which was her favourite.

The weather was positively balmy, and cycling through the village was a joy. There was a proper place to park her bicycle, too. The local police station was a twice a week job, and one she truly loved. Her curiosity was fed and watered by the constant stream of information that surged through their doors. She had become invisible to the officers; she was there so often. Sometimes she laughed to herself that her apron was better than camouflage.

Before she started, she called into the canteen

and ordered a much-needed cup of tea and that iced bun. Kathleen had worked behind the counter there for years, and joined her for the treat. They were still there five minutes later when Sergeant Harrington rushed in. He found the young detective nursing a cup of coffee, and, Mrs B. imagined, a hangover. He propped up the bar in the Dog and Duck more evenings that he was at home, or so people had told her.

"Come along. You can't sit there with a face like a wet weekend lad. There's been an unexplained death. No time to waste!" They hurried out.

"A body?" Kathleen tutted loudly. "Whatever next?"

Mrs B. made her start in the CID offices, where they were discussing the surprising demise of Mr Appleby. She listened carefully to the details, discovering that he had only been found when his wife had brought his lunch. It appeared to be a heart attack, according to the doctor. There was no evidence of foul play. Her duster flew over the desks, and she positively whizzed through the toilets and the corridors. In less than an hour, she was back on her bicycle and pedalling through the village. The heat of the day was finally cooling a little, but she was still glad of the fresh air.

The back door stood open. "Mrs Appleby?" The kitchen smelled rather delicious. A cake of some kind was in the oven, and the radio was on. It was a little disrespectful for Mrs B's taste, but everyone reacted differently to grief. Her employer turned away from the kitchen table.

"Mrs B?" Her face was a picture of confusion.

"Yes. I just heard. I thought I would pop in to see if you were alright." She reached the table and sat down.

"Shocked, obviously. I had been telling him to slow down, but he would push himself to work so very hard. They think it was a heart attack." She did not meet Mrs B's eyes.

"Now that is a very sad thing. Do you have anyone staying with you tonight? You shouldn't be alone." The timer that had been ticking away on the table pinged, and Mrs Appleby brought out a perfectly risen sponge.

"I'm fine on my own. Perfectly fine. Thank you for thinking of me though, Mrs B." She patted the older woman on the back of her hand.

"Mrs Appleby? I need to have a chat with you." He filled the back door frame. "Oh, Mrs B. it's probably good that you're here. She shouldn't be alone." The detective was wider around his middle than he should be, and his face was friendlier than his reputation.

"Come in, detective." Mrs Appleby stood up, pushing her chair back.

"Your husband appears to have suffered a massive heart attack. I am so sorry, Mrs Appleby. I know that you told the attending officer that he had been overdoing it for some time. Is that right?" He ran his finger around the inside of his collar. "Perhaps this heat was unhelpful, too."

"Yes. I kept telling him to take some time off, but he wouldn't listen." She dabbed at her eyes with a handkerchief.

Offering his heartfelt condolences, he made his excuses, and moved faster than a man his size should be able. The scent of the flowers drifted in through the back door. Mrs B. was absolutely certain that Mr Appleby had not died of natural causes. Even more so that the detective would not listen to her. He was already halfway back to the police station and would be hoping that the canteen would still be open. The unexpected death would be written up as a terrible tragedy.

Mrs B. boiled the kettle and poured the hot water over the tea. She patted Mrs Appleby gently on the shoulder, noticing the younger woman flinch.

"I know that you were unhappy, Mrs Appleby, and in many ways, this is a relief. I understand how you did it, and actually I understand why, too. He was not a pleasant man. I have noticed the bruises far too often for them to be accidental. You must have been terrified when you mixed the paste from the foxgloves into his drink." The younger woman gasped and pushed back from the table. "No, please don't be afraid. You really have spent enough time being frightened. I do not agree with what you did, but the detective would no more take my word for what happened than I could learn to fly. We will have to settle for natural justice. Ironically, I cleaned away all the evidence this morning. All those broken flowers and leaves from the foxgloves. He would have tasted nothing out of the ordinary with his favourite bitter coffee. It was very clever of you. Digitalis, such a powerful drug, and so readily available in foxgloves." She patted Mrs Appleby's hand. "I think we should stick to tea, don't you, dear?"

"Mrs B. You won't tell anyone, will you?" Genuine fear filled every feature of the young woman's face.

"Perish the thought." Who would believe an old busy-body like me, anyway? "Those flowers are beautiful, though. Drink your tea dear."

DEBBIE HEWSON

2.

2.

Mrs B and a pig in a poke

Mrs B. had started her day as she always did, cycling from her home with her bag and an ironed apron in the basket on her handlebars. Her mind was on an expected visit from her nephew, Arnold. He had written to say that he would be passing close by for work and she was looking forward to seeing him. Perhaps she would buy some pork chops, as they were his favourite.

Her first call of the day was to the police station. The hustle and bustle of the place gave her such joy. If she had been born a boy, perhaps she might have entered the police force. No point in regrets, though. Her life was a happy one.

The car park was empty, usually the two police cars, and three bicycles were parked there until later in the day. Something must have happened. A fizzing excitement filled her stomach. She loved a puzzle.

"Morning Kathleen." The canteen was entirely

empty, and she was glad to be able to sit down and have a cup of tea and an iced bun with Kathleen.

"Big kerfuffle today. A child's gone missing!" Kathleen's wide set blue eyes opened wide in her chubby face.

"Which child?" Mrs B watched Kathleen carefully.

"Molly Peters. Lovely little thing. Only six months old." She shook her head, surprised again at the wickedness of the world. "What sort of person would take a child? Is she in danger, do you think?" Her hand fluttered around her neck.

"Perish the thought, Kathleen." Mrs B. reached across to her friend, trying to calm the worry.

The CID office was all business, shouting and organising a search. Down in the general office, the uniformed officers were writing up their reports. Mrs B. dusted and listened. Oh, how she wished that they would listen to her.

She knew Molly Peters. She was a pretty little thing, blonde curls and pink cheeks. Her mother had always been a nice-looking child. A little spiteful, as Mrs B. remembered.

The only thing left in the pram, which had been parked outside the village shop, was a pink blanket. It was slightly grubby. The officers had folded it and placed it in a box. She cleaned the desk it sat on, bending low towards the box to clean the legs of the chairs.

Very soon the whole police station was empty, except for Mrs B. Everyone was out searching. They had left with declarations about leaving no stone unturned.

Mrs B. cleaned her way through the station with her brain ticking away. She had never believed in coincidences, and three strange things had happened already that morning. First of all, she had arrived at the house she should have been cleaning. She had let herself into the kitchen as usual, through the back door. One of the things she always admired about Mr Pendle was his speed and accuracy with the crossword. Mrs B. herself was no slouch, but she had never, until that morning, found the crossword incomplete. She had accepted Mrs Pendle's explanation that the couple were both very unwell, and perhaps Mrs B. might come another day, in case of spreading the illness. She had left, of course. In all the years that she had known the Pendles, neither of them had ever been unwell, let alone at the same time. That was the second strange thing. The third was very odd indeed. Mrs Chambers had been holding onto a wall as though she would blow away, and was as white as one of Mrs B's bed sheets. She had stopped to enquire after Mrs Chambers' health and been met with a stoic, thin lipped nod. All of that before she had arrived at the police station.

Of course, the truth behind the disappearance was clear to see. If only she could tell the detective in charge. She knew, however, that he would not listen.

She pedalled through the village to the vicarage. The Reverend Chambers was outside checking on his roses, which were under attack from aphids again. "Good morning, Mrs B. It's not our day today, is it?" He peered over his half-moon glasses at her. For a younger man, he had very poor eyesight.

"No, not today, Vicar. I just popped in to see if I could catch Mrs Chambers." She leaned her bicycle against the wall.

"In the kitchen I believe." Released back to his roses, he had lost all interest in the conversation.

Mrs Chambers was indeed in the kitchen, a cup of tea in front of her, and her face was white and sweating. "Mrs Chambers. Are you quite alright? Are you feeling unwell?" Red-rimmed eyes met Mrs B's gentle enquiry.

"I feel so sick. Must be something I ate." Her hand shook a little, and the cup rattled back into the saucer.

"Shall I make you a ginger tea? Best thing in the world for an upset stomach." Mrs B. filled the kettle with fresh water and busied herself around the kitchen, finally placing a cup of steaming liquid in front of Mrs Chambers. "My sister swore by it when her three were on the way."

"Oh, Mrs B. Please don't tell anyone. It's early days and I haven't told my husband yet." A tear slipped from her eye. "I'm not certain how happy he will be."

"I will tell nobody, but I imagine he would be delighted. Has anyone else guessed?" She covered Mrs Chambers' hand with hers and watched while she sipped the tea. It must have made her feel better because a little colour returned to her face.

"Mrs Pendle made a very harsh comment. I wondered if she had guessed. She said I looked like I was in farrow, as though I was one of her pigs." She sipped the ginger tea and looked a little stronger.

"Well, your secret is safe with me. I would suggest you stay on the ginger tea and look after yourself." She checked her hat was on straight with a swift pat of her hand.

"You won't tell my husband?" There was a waver in her voice.

"Perish the thought that I would ever betray a confidence, my dear." She patted Mrs Chambers gently on the shoulder and bustled out of the house.

If Mr Pendle was surprised to see Mrs B peddle

into the farmyard, for the second time that morning, he hid it well. "Morning Mr Pendle." She called and let herself into the kitchen.

"Mrs Pendle? Are you here?" The kitchen was empty. Mrs B. poked her head around the door frame and called again.

"Hello Mrs B. Was there something you needed?" Mrs Pendle joined her in the kitchen.

"I just wanted a chat, if you have a minute." Mrs B. sat down at the table, leaving Mrs Pendle no choice but to join her. "I know that it has been a difficult time for you lately. You are surrounded by so many females who are constantly producing piglets, or babies. Mr Blandford and I were never blessed with children, and I have spent many days filled with regret over it. Of course, losing my husband young gave us less time, I suppose." No reply came, but Mrs Pendle's head hung low. "I've seen the tender care you give to the piglets who are rejected by their mother. You will be a wonderful mother if you are given the chance." She reached for Mrs Pendle's hand. "Was that what happened? You saw Molly Peters, not being looked after properly by her mother? You knew you could do a better job, so you took her?" A sob escaped from the other woman.

"I knew it was wrong, but I couldn't help it. Even that Mrs Chambers is expecting. Everyone but me. Veronica Peters left that lovely baby outside the shop, while she was chatting and laughing with the shopkeeper." She sniffed. "I'll go to prison, won't I?"

"I think it's a case of all's well that ends well, don't you? Of course, we will have to take the little one home." Her voice was gentle, and she squeezed Mrs Pendle's hand to soften the words. The other woman nodded and pushed herself up from the table. "I will keep your name out of it. If I can."

Mrs B. arrived back at the Police Station, her bag over one shoulder, with her apron squashed inside. In the large basket hanging from her handlebars sat Molly Peters, laughing and waving her hands, thoroughly enjoying the ride. The sturdy basket supported her chubby frame. The explanation that Mrs B had found the child near the bridge on the way out of the village was not universally believed, but as the detectives had failed to follow the clues that Mrs B. had seen, they had no way of disproving it.

The only thing that mattered really was that Molly would be back with her mother before lunchtime, and the secrets of the village were safe and sound.

"I hope you are going to stay for a cup of tea, Mrs B. Can't have you rushing off without a thank you." Sergeant Harrington smiled down at the little girl who was smiling up at him.

"Perish the thought." She smiled at the child, too. "I'll pop in and see Kathleen in the canteen. Oh, and I'll take the child's blanket and give it a wash. We don't want her poor mum to have to deal with that on top of the day she's had." The pastel pink blanket with the stain that smelled of the pig farm disappeared into her bag and would be washed and smelling fresh when it was next seen.

3.

Mrs B and Rainy Days

The weather had taken a turn for the worse. Mrs B looked out of the window and shook her head. She pulled on her long beige mackintosh rain coat and tied her rain bonnet under her chin. Her galoshes were in the cupboard next to the back door, just as they always were. Once upon a time, when she was younger; when she had a husband instead of an empty chair at the table, she had worn shoes and boots that made her ankles look attractive. She leaned her hand against the back door, pushing her feet into her galoshes. Her thoughts taking her back to a time when his laugh filled the house, and his smile warmed her heart. Now the ticking of the clock kept her company, and she kept her mind busy by working out puzzles. She enjoyed the crossword, and more than that, the puzzles that she found around her in the people that she met, and the mysteries in their lives. In Little Mellington, where she had lived her whole life, and knew almost all the residents, there was always something to consider over a cup of tea. Not gossip. Never that. Concern and interest certainly; never gossip.

The lean-to roof over the back door protected her from the rain while she climbed on her bicycle, but the rain found the gaps between the collar of her coat and the rain bonnet. She arrived at her first job of the day a little damp, and was glad that she had been careful to pack her apron inside her bag.

"Good morning, Mrs Caldecot. It's a dreadful morning out there." She shook her rain bonnet over the sink, and hung it, and her coat on the hook by the back door, slipping her feet out of her galoshes and retrieving her slippers before she ventured any further into the house.

"Oh, Mrs B. I am so pleased you are here. I went out early this morning, the paper boy was late, and you know how my husband likes the paper when he gets up. I went down to the village shop and fetched it, and when I came home, someone had been in here. The whole house was topsy-turvy. I went to ask my husband what had happened, and he was still fast asleep. The police are in the living room having a look at the moment." She rested her hand against her face and sank into a chair at the kitchen table.

"Oh my, I'll make a cup of tea for you. At least the kitchen seems to be untouched." Mrs B boiled the kettle and poured it into the teapot on the table. "Come on now, you need a hot drink and a biscuit."

"Thank you. You hear of these things, in the big cities, but not in our little village. I have always felt so safe here." Her hair was wet from the rain, and hung limp around her face. She dabbed at her face, missing the tears that were falling.

"I'm sure that there is a reasonable explanation. The police are here, everyone is well, and I will tidy up. Life will go back to normal again. You've had a terrible shock, I know." She rested her hand on the table, her head tipped to one side.

"Mrs Caldecot? We have had a look around and made all the notes we need to make. We will be in touch as soon as we know any more." Constable Briggs smiled his most reassuring smile. "It will be fine to tidy up now." He nodded to Mrs B, and he was gone.

While she set the living room to rights, she took note of which items had been moved around. She knew the room well, after cleaning it for years. Mrs Caldecot was looking more like herself, but her husband was still nowhere to be seen.

"I've made some lunch for both of you, Mrs Caldecot, and I will pop in later on my way home to see if you need anything." The weather meant that she still had to pull her rain gear back on before she pedalled to the police station. It was not her day to clean there, but she could at least pop her head around the door and see her friend Kathleen for a cup of tea in the canteen.

She left her galoshes by the back door and slipped inside. Kathleen had made her a cup of tea in less time than it took to take her coat off. "Oh goodness, this weather. You'll have your work cut out tomorrow. These floors are in a terrible state with all this rain and mud. I brought you over a flapjack. I've run out of iced buns." Mrs B. stared at the well-intentioned substitute, and ran through Mrs Caldecot's house in her mind, as it had been before she cleaned it. Something niggled at the back of her mind, and it was nothing to do with the flapjack.

"It's a terrible thing about Mr and Mrs Caldecot. Imagine someone going into their house. I suppose we can only be grateful that nothing was taken, and nobody was hurt." Kathleen sipped her tea. "Don't fancy the flapjack? I've a piece of battenburg left."

"It's fine. I should be getting on my way. Thank you for the tea, Kathleen." Mrs B. slipped her feet into her galoshes and pedalled her bicycle back to Mrs Caldecot.

"Mrs B? You were quick to come back." She tucked her handkerchief back into her sleeve.

"I have been thinking. These burglars of yours, they were very considerate." Mrs B. sat carefully, facing Mrs Caldecot.

"In what way is what they did considerate?" Mrs Caldecot's bluster was all the confirmation that Mrs B. needed.

"They took their shoes off before they came in. I cleaned the floors, and there were no muddy or even wet footprints. Either that, or whoever threw everything around in your living room, came from inside, not outside." Mrs B. softened the words with a smile and a gentle pat on the back of Mrs Caldecot's hand. "Someone was looking for something, and angry. Am I right?"

"She came round last evening. Some young flibbety-jibbet from his work. She thought I ought to know what has been going on. Behind my back. He was out at the Dog and Duck. She waited until he came home. He was furious. It seems strange to say it out loud, but he was angry with me. He pulled the living room apart, looking for his savings book. All the while, he was insisting that he was taking his money and leaving me." She dabbed at her eyes. "She left before midnight, but he was still ranting after three. I just watched him. Not once did he apologise to me. He stomped off to bed and left me downstairs. I thought about it and decided to let him explain it." She shrugged. "The paper boy is always late. I took the opportunity and left him to sleep. Selfish, selfish man."

"Will you be able to forgive him?" Mrs B. tipped her head to one side.

"I have no idea. I do know that he won't get far without

his savings." She pulled a small maroon coloured book from inside her blouse. A giggle wrapped around a sob escaped from her lips.

"I think Mr Caldecot needs to learn some manners, and I have a feeling he will be taught them whether he wants them or not." Mrs B. stood up and wrapped an arm around her customer. "You're going to be fine. You and I will keep what happened under our hats. Or perhaps our rain bonnets." She chuckled.

"You won't tell the police? I wasted their time." Mrs Caldecot chewed her lower lip.

"Perish the thought." Mrs B. smiled, pulling her coat on and tying her rain bonnet tightly. "This rain looks like it's set for the week! See you on Wednesday."

She pedalled her bicycle up the hill to her cottage, where she planned on putting her feet up and enjoying the iced bun she had picked up from the bakery with a proper cup of tea.

4.

Mrs B finds it Shiny and New

"Good morning, Reverend Chambers. It's going to be a lovely day, I think." She pushed her bicycle to the church and leaned it against the wall.

"Mrs B? Yes indeed, a lovely morning. Did you need to see me?" Reverend Chambers was always a little absentminded, but he seemed positively dithery. His glasses had sunk to the end of his nose, and his hair had not seen a brush or comb that morning.

"I do need to check with you about the flowers. I was thinking we might use some of the pinks that are looking so lovely at the moment." She had been on the flower arranging rota at the village church for years. The vicar had always seemed interested before in the choice of flowers, but he was nodding as though he had not heard her suggestion.

"Yes, yes. Whatever you think, Mrs B." He pushed the sleeves of his cardigan up to his elbows.

"Are you quite well, Vicar?" She reached out to

him, but stopped short of touching his arm.

"Yes, of course. Just a little worried." She tipped her head to one side. "Mrs Chambers is unwell, and I am, I confess, at a loss without her help. On top of that I have found that the church candlesticks have gone missing, and the bishop will be visiting at the end of the week. I am very concerned." The dark circles beneath his eyes suggested that he had been losing sleep as well.

"I'm so sorry to hear that Mrs Chambers is unwell. Perhaps spend the morning with her. I will have a look for the candlesticks, they have probably just been put away in the wrong place." She ushered him back down the path and opened the door to the ancient building. Her steps rang out in echoes around the rafters, and she stopped in front of the altar to bow her head in respect.

The door to the vestry was stiff as it always was, and she had to push with her shoulder to ease it open. Inside, she searched through the cupboards, where all the silver should have been. The rest was there; just the candlesticks were missing. She huffed a breath out. The rest of the cupboards were filled with hymn books and one held washed and ironed surplices and cassocks for the vicar to wear. There was a cupboard for vases, and flower arranging equipment, which she used herself, and a desk for dealing with any correspondence that the vicar might receive. This lay unused, since he preferred to use the study in his own home.

Mrs B sat in the chair and caught her lower lip between her teeth. Nobody would steal the candlesticks, that was certain. It was a church, for goodness' sake. The world was changing, a fact of which she was very much aware. One only had to look at the papers to know that. In cities, she had read that churches now had to be locked against the threat of thieves. Progress was all very well, and now that they were in the 1950s, perhaps it was inevitable, but nobody knew where it would end up. Whatever was wrong with things staying the same?

There was a cleaning rota, running alongside the flower arranging and the cake and tea rotas. Whoever cleaned the candlesticks last might have put them away somewhere different. She checked the list. Mrs Chambers. Oh dear, she was unwell. It really was not a good time to ask her about the cleaning. Mrs B looked around the vestry, but there was no other way. She had never, in her life, shirked a responsibility and was not about to start.

Mrs Chambers was in her kitchen, sitting at the table. "Hello Mrs B." She smiled over the rim of her cup. "Would you like a cup of tea?"

"No, not at all. I think, though, if you have a moment, I need to talk to you." She gestured to a chair and Mrs B. sat down. "It's none of my business, but your husband is terribly worried about you. He thinks you're ill. This is good news. Please share it with him, so that he can stop worrying and start celebrating." She reached across and held Mrs Chambers by the hand. "It's wonderful news. A new human being, a wonderful gift."

"Yes. You're right, of course. I have been worrying in case something was to go wrong. I would have made him happy only to dash his hopes." She wiped a finger under her eyes, pushing the tears away.

"Given the choice, I would rather have the happiness and lose it than never have it at all." Mrs B. patted her hand.

"Thank you for not telling him." The tears fell faster, but she was smiling too.

"Perish the thought that I would ever betray a confidence." Mrs B. smiled and turned away. "Oh, I meant to ask, do you know where the church candlesticks are?"

"Of course, the smell of the wax burning was making me feel so sick. I put them behind the altar when I went in there to clean." She sniffed. "You're right, I'll go and have a chat with my husband. Thank you, Mrs B."

"My pleasure, Mrs Chambers. If you could let your husband know that I will put the candlesticks back, where he can find them. Take care of yourself." Mrs B. pulled her coat on.

"Home now?" Mrs Chambers stood up, too.

"Just a couple more things I need to do." Mrs B. smiled and let herself out of the back door.

A quick stop at a house in the village to pick up what she needed, and Mrs B. was back on her bicycle. Mr and Mrs Pendle were in the kitchen when she knocked on the back door. "Hello?"

"Mrs B? Is everything alright? Nobody found out about the baby?" Mrs Pendle came to the door to meet her, wringing her hands.

"Oh yes, everything is fine. I just thought that you might be able to help me out." Mrs Pendle lifted an eyebrow. "You see, I know your skills with animals, and I know how hard it is when you have to say goodbye to the piglets that you have raised. I thought you might like a little something that you could keep, and love." She reached into the basket on her bicycle handlebars and brought out a tiny kitten. "She's in need of a good home, and I don't know of a better one."

Tears filled Mrs Pendle's eyes. "She's beautiful. Oh love, look at you." She lifted the tiny fluff ball to her chest. "Thank you. She's beautiful. Thank you so much."

"My pleasure entirely. I know she will be safe with you, and she has big ears. I believe that is the sign of a good mouser." Mrs B. hopped back on her bicycle. She knew that Mrs Pendle wanted a baby. That was what had pushed her to take little Molly Peters, but that had all been resolved. Mrs B. could do nothing to help, but love was love. Mrs Pendle needed to love, and the kitten would probably be the most spoiled animal in the village. The thought brought a smile to Mrs B's face.

Once the candlesticks were polished and back on the altar, she bowed her head. Another day done, a puzzle solved, and some worries and sadness relieved.

Tomorrow the sun would bring a new day, and it could start shiny and new. She climbed back onto her bicycle, knowing that she would have earned a cup of tea and an iced bun.

5.

Mrs B and Arnold's Visit

"Three of the pork chops please, if you will." She knew they were his favourite. He liked the way that she cooked them, and she was buying one extra because he was her only nephew, and she loved him. From the first moment, when she had visited her sister in the maternity home, and had held him in her arms, she had known that she would love him for the rest of her life. Not that she would say it out loud. She said it with pork chops, and with mashed potatoes.

He had sent her a letter, as he did every three weeks. She replied the day that she received his letters, every time. His latest letter had told her that he would like to visit, if she would be available. She would. If she had to move the whole village of Little Mellington four feet to the left to make herself available.

The chops and the potatoes were safely in the basket on her bicycle handlebars, and the runner beans were ready to be picked in her garden.

Pudding would be, as it always was when Arnold came to visit, a raspberry trifle.

Arnold was her sister's son. Although Mrs B. did not see eye to eye with her sister on many subjects, on the subject of Arnold, they were entirely in agreement. He had a great deal in common with his aunt. They both loved puzzles and were extremely good at solving them.

Mrs B. made lunch. One thing that she knew for sure was that her nephew would be on time. He had said a quarter to one, and she fully expected the knock on the door that announced his arrival exactly as the hands on her kitchen clock turned to a quarter to.

"Auntie!" His smile was wide and his eyes sparkled with joy.

"Arnold!" She held open her arms and offered a cheek for him to kiss.

"I smell my favourite dinner. If I am not mistaken, it is pork chops and mashed potatoes." He clapped his hands together with undisguised joy.

"It will be ready in twenty minutes. I thought we might sit and chat for a while." She led the way into the living room.

"That suits me. I have a puzzle for you." He chuckled. This had always been the way between them. She sat in her favourite chair and watched her favourite person in the world, who was busting with wanting to challenge her ability to solve the puzzle. "First clue. How many pork chops did you cook?"

She tipped her head to one side. "Three pork chops. One for me, and two for you."

"Second clue. Is clear to see right through." He laughed, watching her puzzle it through.

"Glass? A window, a glass of water? Water?" She shook her head.

"Those are all clear. You're right." He patted his hands on the arms of his chair. "Third clue. You know how my mum is? I love her, but she can be a little difficult at times." He shrugged, and she nodded a little. They both knew what he meant. "Which is why I am bringing this to you first. I need you on my side. The clue is this." He reached inside the bag by his feet and pulled out a bouquet of flowers, which he passed to his aunt.

Mrs B. took the flowers and ran her finger over the blooms. The gypsophila and cream-coloured roses were beautiful, but not for her. These were flowers for someone else. The soft, velvet texture of the rose petals reminded her of flowers she had carried herself many years before.

"I believe that someone is waiting in your motor car, which is why you did not park outside my house, as you usually do. I think that's why you wanted to know if there are three pork chops in my oven. One is for the extra person. Am I correct?" She watched his face split into a smile. His nod was almost imperceptible.

"These flowers are almost exactly the same design of bouquet that I carried when I married. I think your mother carried pink roses." She stroked the petals again, resting the flowers on the occasional table next to her chair. On her feet, and moving, she crossed the room and looked out through the window. "Oh, I was hoping to see something through my window. Clear to see through. I wonder what that might mean." Her fingers tapped on the window frame. They were not the same as when she had last carried a bouquet of roses. The knuckles were a little more pronounced than they had been. Dark age spots sprinkled their way across the back of her hands. The lines on her palms were deeper. The rings she wore were the same, though. Her wedding ring, a thin golden band which she had never removed since the day her husband had slipped it on her finger in the village church. There was also her engagement ring, a gold band with an opal that glowed with a fire and a life of its own. She knew it was old-fashioned now, but it meant the world to her. Girls had different expectations now.

"Did you work it out?" He shifted his weight from one foot to the other.

"I think you are going to be married. I expected to

see a girl outside my house, but from the first and third clues, there is a wedding coming up." She turned towards him. "Soon, maybe in a month?" For the first time, he looked uncomfortable. "You are going to be a father, Arnold, unless I have misjudged the clues."

"How did you get that from the clues?" He ran his finger around his collar.

"You're worried about your mother, and she is more worried about appearances and propriety than anyone I know." Her smile had him relax back into his chair. "Of course, the gypsophila is beautiful, but it's known as baby's breath. That's a clue and a half!" She turned away from the window. "I suggest you go and fetch her, or dinner will be spoiled, and she is eating for two, after all." He rushed from the door while she put dinner on the table. The next few weeks would be uncomfortable for Arnold, while he negotiated with his mother and came to an agreement. Mrs B. hoped with all her heart that the girl involved was sensible. More, she hoped that they would be friends.

Over pork chops and mashed potatoes, she saw the reason for the second clue. The tiny diamond on Barbara's finger was clear to see, as was her nephew's obvious affection for her.

"You won't tell Mum, will you? I mean, about the baby?" Arnold held out his bowl for a second helping of trifle.

"Perish the thought. You know that anything you tell me in confidence goes no further. Congratulations to you both. I wish you a long and happy life together." Mrs B. raised her glass of water, and they clinked together. Three glasses instead of two.

Later, when the kitchen was clean again, and Arnold and Barbara had left her with kisses and hugs, and the promise of a wedding invitation; she sat with a small glass of sherry. Usually she saved it for Christmas, but that night she raised it in a toast to her husband. Gone too soon. A smile lifted her lips when she imagined how her sister would react to the idea of becoming a grandmother, and she chided herself for being uncharitable. There was a wedding to look forward to, and a new baby too. It had been a most extraordinary day.

6.

A call for help

The iron was hot, and the scent of the steam rose up from the sheet that she was ironing. Most people told her that they disliked ironing, but Mrs B. had always enjoyed it. She found it gave her time to think, and the steam cleared her mind just as it cleared the creases.

The knock on her front door was a surprise. She was not expecting anyone. Through the glass, which was rippled, she saw a wobbly outline, only blobs of colour, really. She slipped the lock open, and if the knock on the door had been a surprise, her visitor was a complete shock.

"Mrs Lennet?" The woman on her doorstep lived in the manor house just outside the village. She was effectively the lady of the manor.

"Mrs B. I have come here to ask for your help. May I come in?" She checked over the shoulder of her soft pink jacket.

"Of course, I am so sorry. Come through. I was in the kitchen, doing my ironing, but perhaps the living room would be more appropriate." Mrs B. stepped back to open the door and closed it behind her guest.

"Not at all. Please carry on ironing. We can chat while you are busy. I had no intention of interrupting you." Mrs Lennet sat at the kitchen table, running her fingers over the folded linen. "Beautifully ironed."

"I was going to stop and have a cup of tea in a minute, anyway. Will you join me?" The nod she received sent her to fill the kettle at the sink. She moved the pile of sheets from the table onto a chair and replaced them with a teapot and a plate of biscuits. "You said you needed help?"

"Yes. I did." She nodded, perhaps to herself. She sipped from her tea. "You have something of a reputation for helping people, finding missing items, solving puzzles." She raised her eyes to Mrs B. "I am in something of a pickle."

"I'll help you if I can. Perhaps if you can tell me a little more?" Mrs B pushed the plate of biscuits a little closer to her guest.

"When I married my husband, I inherited several quite valuable pieces of jewellery which had previously belonged to my mother-in-law. Family things, you understand?" Mrs Lennet worried at the small lace-edged handkerchief in her hand, embroidered with her initials. "There was a pair of earrings and a matching necklace which were really very beautiful, particularly lovely. I only wear them very occasionally. It's a family tradition that I would wear them on my husband's birthday, which is two weeks away. The earrings are safely in my jewellery box, but the necklace is nowhere to be found. I have pulled the house apart." Her voice rose a little.

"Have you called the police?" Mrs B. sipped her tea.

"No. The thing is, that I should really have put them in the safe, but I had forgotten the last time I wore them, I think. If it were possible, I should like to keep my husband from finding out." She caught her lower lip between her teeth. "I would be embarrassed, look foolish in front of the family, and there are some members of my family who would enjoy that a little too much for my comfort."

Mrs B. considered the whole matter for a few moments. "What would you like me to do?"

"Will you come with me to my house and see if you can work out where they are, or what happened to them?" She moved to the edge of her seat.

"Will your staff not think that strange?" Mrs B. was well aware of the gossip in big houses.

"I thought of that." She looked very pleased with herself. "I shall say you are helping with the preparations for the village fayre." Mrs Lennet's eyes snapped wide open. "You should join the committee. You would be a breath of fresh air. You've no idea how stale it can be." Her eyes were rimmed with red.

"Well then, we should go and take a look. I'll finish my ironing later." Mrs B. set the kitchen to rights quickly and slipped her feet out of her slippers and into her shoes.

The manor house was huge, and very grand. Mrs B. had been to the gardens before for the annual village fayre, but never inside. Upstairs in Mrs Lennet's dressing room, surrounded by what seemed like a thousand dresses, compared to Mrs B's meagre wardrobe, Mrs Lennet opened her jewellery box. "They're gone. My earrings are gone. They were here this morning." She slumped into a small chair. "I must be the stupidest woman on the earth. Even after the necklace went missing, I neglected to put the earrings in the safe."

"Oh, my goodness. Perhaps we should alert the police." Mrs B. listened to the tiny creaks of the house. It was an old building, and she imagined creaks were perfectly normal, but it suggested that someone was outside the door, and possibly listening to their conversation. "When did you last wear them all together?"

Mrs Lennet thought for a moment. "Last Thursday. We had a reception to go to for the

Mayor. My son and his wife came down from London in the afternoon. They're here for the Easter Holidays with my grandchildren, which is a delight. We went out in the evening, and then on Friday morning, I was rushing to take the children out. I should have put everything away first. How I wish I did now." She ran a hand over her face. "My son is very like his father in many ways. He is a straight talker, and I know he would be disappointed by my stupidity."

"And your daughter-in-law?" Mrs B tipped her head sideways.

"She's very beautiful. I worry she's a little too lovely. Sharp witted, unlike me, I suppose." Mrs Lennet shrugged, but the thin line of her compressed lips gave away her worry.

"Do you lock the dressing room when you're out? I noticed you unlocked it when we came in."

"Oh yes, the key lives in the cupboard by the door." She shrugged. "I suppose that's a bit pointless, isn't it?"

Mrs B. ignored the comment. Clearly Mrs Lennet trusted her household, and it seemed likely that the thief was one she trusted, not an outsider. Nothing else had been touched.

"Any ideas?" Mrs Lennet's hands fluttered at her throat. "I shall be entirely humiliated if I have to admit I have lost them."

"Perhaps that's the purpose." Mrs B. thought carefully through everything she had heard.

"We had better have a cup of tea and pretend to talk about the fayre for ten minutes." She straightened herself up, raising her jaw as though she faced a firing squad. Not her own home.

Tea was served in the drawing room, which was painted in a delicate yellow, the windows showing a wonderful view across the gardens and the valley beyond. The door opened and in marched a beautiful younger woman. "Oh, sorry, I had no idea you had company. I'll come back later."

"Not at all. Mrs B. this is my daughter-in-law, Patricia. Mrs B. is here to discuss the village fayre. We have to start planning so early. Do join us for a cup of tea, Patricia." Mrs B. watched the interaction between the two. Patricia was clearly trying to think of a reason not to join them, but nothing came to mind and she sank into a sofa, crossing her elegant ankles.

"It's a pleasure to meet you, Patricia." Mrs B. smiled the most open and joyful smile she could muster.

"Yes. You too." No smile from Patricia. Her dress was pale blue and quite tight. Mrs B. spent a moment deciding if it was quite appropriate, but no longer than that.

The door opened again and a young girl came into the room carrying a handbag over her shoulder, and walking with a swagger which she would need a few years to grow into. She had applied lipstick a little haphazardly, too. "Hello Granny. Hello Mum. I wondered if you might let me have a few pennies to put in my handbag so that I can go pretend shopping?" Mrs Lennet smiled indulgently and stood to fetch some coins. Patricia had other ideas.

"Wash your face immediately and give me back my handbag." The child gave up the bag and left the room. "Sorry, she's at a difficult age." Patricia tucked the handbag carefully next to her feet and sat back down.

"I've always found Tabitha a delight. She's a wonderful girl." Mrs Lennet reached across to her daughter-in-law, who met the kindness with a thin-lipped glare.

Mrs B. placed her cup and saucer on a side table. "Apologies, Mrs Lennet, but may I use your lavatory?" Mrs Lennet gave her directions.

She stood and, rather than her usual brisk steps, her gait was hesitant and unbalanced. Passing the very pretty Patricia, Mrs B caught her foot in the strap of the handbag and tugged it over, spilling the contents on the thick rug. "Oh my, I'm so sorry." She bent to collect the items that had spread out. Her fingers holding out a heavily jewelled necklace.

"Patricia! How could you? I have been so worried about my jewellery." Mrs Lennet was relieved to have her necklace and earrings back, but furious with her daughter-in-law.

"You did that on purpose!" Patricia rounded on Mrs B.

"Perish the thought. I may be a little clumsy in my old age." She smiled widely at Mrs Lennet.

"You may not speak to my guests in that tone, Patricia; and you also may not steal my jewellery. You would have embarrassed me in front of the whole family if I had not had these to wear next week." Spots of crimson had risen in Mrs Lennet's cheeks.

"So, you should be. They should know what a stupid, careless old woman you really are." Patricia spat the words.

"They will see nothing of the sort, young lady. All that they will see is a kind, caring woman who trusts her family, even when they do not deserve it." Mrs B pulled herself up to her full five feet and three inches. "You can choose to see the good in people or the bad. That's the point of family. I must go and leave you to sort this out between you. It is, after all, a family matter." She pulled on her cardigan.

Patricia gaped, open-mouthed at Mrs B. "You're

walking is much better I see?" Her tone was snippy.

"Oh yes, I am quite revived. It must be the lovely tea. Thank you, Mrs Lennet." Mrs B smiled widely across the room.

"Thank you so much Mrs B. I shall walk you out." She reached out her hand. "You stay there Patricia. We need to have a conversation about this." They waited long enough until Patricia slumped on the sofa.

The massive hallway was bigger than Mrs B's house. She pulled on a light pair of gloves and opened the door. "She wanted to show the family how clever she is by making you look foolish. Perhaps she is very unsure of herself. I wish you luck." Mrs B. smiled and gently patted the other woman's hand.

"You have helped me enormously. Tripping over her bag was an absolute moment of genius. I could never have asked to see inside it." She laughed, and it echoed up the stairs.

"Are you suggesting that I did that on purpose? Perish the thought." Mrs B. laughed and opened the large front door out onto the driveway, where a car waited. She was looking forward to a brisk walk home to finish her ironing.

"My driver will drop you to your home. Thank you for your help, Mrs B." Mrs Lennet waved from the steps as the driver eased the car into gear and pulled away.

"I hear you gave that Patricia what for!" The driver chuckled. "On the day she moves in for good, every one of the staff will be offering their resignation. She's a holy horror. No idea what Mr Richard sees in her." His laughter twitched the bushy moustache he sported on his top lip.

Mrs B watched out of the window as the fields flew by, and in no time at all, she was back in her kitchen and the iron was hot enough to finish her sheets. It had been a strange afternoon. Families were always more complicated than you thought. She could only hope that Mrs Lennet would sort out whatever was troubling her daughter-in-law, or remember to put her jewellery away in the future.

7.

Mrs B and her sister

The morning was bright and clear when Mrs B left her house. She pedalled steadily. She had arranged with Mr and Mrs Gartree that she could leave her bicycle with them for a few days while she was away.

It seemed very grand to be able to say that she would be away from home. The last time she had been on a holiday had been before the war. Times were different then. The bus was due at ten past eight and once she had left her bicycle with Mr Gartree in his garden shed; she rushed to the stop to wait.

The bus driver was polite enough and took her fare. She tucked her ticket into her handbag and watched the driver lift her small suitcase onto the luggage rack. The countryside slid past the window, and by nine o'clock the houses were closer together. When the bus sailed into the station at four minutes to ten, she was starting to feel distinctly claustrophobic. Once the driver had deposited her suitcase on the pavement, he tipped his hat and wished her a safe journey, and he was gone, along with the rest of the passengers.

She found a bench and sat down to watch the people rushing around the bus station. She had always been happy to sit and watch, and the station, with all its comings and goings, was perfect entertainment. Her attention was taken by two women. One was young, wearing, in Mrs B's opinion, too much lipstick. She walked as though the world was watching, and certainly the male half was. The other woman was Mrs B's sister. Mrs B allowed herself a few moments of thinking about what her sister's reaction would be if Arnold had brought home a woman like that. She stopped; chiding herself for being mean, and returned her attention to her sister, who was wearing a hat which was probably extremely expensive, but really did not suit her. Of course, she should have stood up and waved, but her sister was a little like a splinter in her finger; irritating, and usually painful. That was harsh, but her sister brought out the worst in her. She was superficial, spoiled, but she was Mrs B's sister.

"Hello dear. I am so sorry I was a little late. I have no idea which way is up at the moment. Why Arnold is in such a hurry for this wedding is beyond me." She paused to take a breath.

"Young men are so impetuous." Her giggle was deliberately girlish and rankled with Mrs B.

"Letty. You look well." They left the station together. It was a short walk to her house, but the pavements were crowded. "Will Arnold and Barbara be at home?"

"To be honest, I find Barbara a little difficult. I think Arnold could do better." Letty pushed open the garden gate. The garden was immaculate. Not a weed to be seen, Letty was proud of her garden but had never pulled a weed herself. She led the way to her front door and slipped her key into the lock. "Come in. You must be in need of a cup of tea after your journey." She talked all the way through making tea, through drinking tea. Mrs B barely got a word in. Her sister had always been a butterfly of a woman, but this was a whole new level. It made Mrs B feel slightly dizzy.

"Letty. Please stop. I'm giddy with all this chattering. Please, will you tell me what it is wrong?" She rested her hand on the table next to her sister's. Such similar hands, except for the amount of jewellery. A simple wedding band on Mrs B's hand, and shiny, sparkling rings and bracelets on her sister's. "You have always done this since we were children. Whatever it is, let me help you."

"It's Arnold. He has been so rude. So unkind. He called me…well, never mind what he called me. I am very worried. Perhaps this rush towards the wedding is putting him on edge. I really have no idea, and he refuses to speak to me about it." She wrapped her fingers around Mrs B's band. "Thank you for coming." Tears threatened in her eyes.

"Come on now. Let's finish this cup of tea, and then I will have a chat with Arnold." Mrs B. busied himself with the kettle, topping up the pot, and her sister sat back and allowed her to. Nothing changed.

"Hello Auntie!" Arnold landed a kiss on her cheek. "Lovely to see you."

"You and I need to have a quick chat. Your mum needs to drink her tea in peace, so come along. We will go for a walk, because I have been sitting for far too long on the bus. I need to stretch my legs." Despite his protests, he allowed her to steer him towards the front door.

She tucked her hand into his elbow and they matched each other's pace.

"Right, so you had better tell me what is going on." He chanced a look down at her. "You might well look like that. Your mother told me that you were very unkind. That's not like you. What on earth has you tied in such a knot?"

"I think that perhaps Barbara is not everything I believed her to be. My faith in her has been shaken." He hung his head, his chin resting on his chest. He turned to face his aunt. "I'm not sure that the baby is mine." He reached a hand into his pocket and pulled out an envelope. She took it from him when he passed it over, and she waited for his nod to take out the letter inside.

'If you marry Barbara, you will be raising another man's child. A well-wisher.'

The envelope and paper were pale blue and decorated with a small sprig of yellow flowers in the corner.

"I see. Well, you had better give me Barbara's address. I need to speak to her if I'm going to help you sort out this mess." He argued, of course he did, but he was fully aware of how determined his aunt could be, and perhaps he hoped that she would actually resolve the problem.

"Hello Barbara." The girl had clearly been crying. "May I come in? I think we need to sort this out, don't you?" Mrs B. walked through to the kitchen, which was piled high with dirty dishes. "Well. How about we talk while we clear up? I'll wash." She laid her coat on the back of a chair, moving some more dishes from the table.

"Arnold is very angry with me, isn't he?" She was drying up the same cup. Mrs B. pulled out a chair and pointed to it. It would be quicker if she did it herself. The state of the kitchen worried her. "He's not in love with me anymore." She slumped down, her head in her folded arms.

"On the contrary, dear. He's in love with you, but

he needs to know the truth. It is unfair not to tell him." Mrs B. quickly cleared the washing up and stacked the clean crockery. "The question is, the only one that matters anyway is whether the baby is his." She moved on to wiping down the rest of the kitchen. "I can wait as long as it takes." She folded the tea towel and moved a pile of clothes from the chair to make space to sit down.

"Oh hello. I had no idea we had company." The woman who stood in the doorway was a similar age to Mrs B. "Good girl, Bar. I knew you would see sense. No point sulking is there? We'll be much better off like this. Who's your friend?"

"I'm Mrs B. I am very pleased to make your acquaintance. You must be Barbara's mother?" The woman nodded; her expression wary. "Was Barbara not seeing sense earlier?" She rested her hand on Barbara's shoulder.

"Daughters can be a trial. Do you have daughters?" She sat down across the table from Mrs B.

"No, I was not blessed with a daughter. My sister, though, has a son. He's been misbehaving lately." She smiled and waited.

"My daughter has come to her senses. She was imagining that she would be going off and marrying some young idiot, leaving me alone." She sniffed. "Make some tea, Bar."

"Barbara, I need to talk to you. It's important."

Mrs B. turned in her seat, pulling the young woman to sit up. "Do you love him?" Barbara met her eyes and nodded. "Has he any reason to distrust you?" Tears fell from the younger woman's eyes, but she shook her head.

"Oh, for goodness' sake. Barbara, none of that is important. You've seen sense and tidied up like I told you, and that man is off looking for another foolish woman. Make the tea, there's a good girl. You're better off here with me that with some man." The woman pulled a cigarette out of the handbag that was lying on the table, on top of a writing pad and a pack of envelopes, which seemed familiar to Mrs B. She pulled out a small bottle of gin along with it. She lifted the bottle to Mrs B, her raised eyebrow an offer.

"No, thank you. I like a sherry as much as the next person, but I have never enjoyed gin." Mrs B laid her hand on the table next to Barbara's. The younger woman's hand was clenched into a fist, but the thing that Mrs B noticed first was that she was no longer wearing the engagement ring she had shown off so proudly when she had been eating pork chops at Mrs B's cottage only a few weeks before. The slump of her shoulders, the redness of her eyes, told a story on their own.

Barbara pushed herself up from her seat, as though the weight of her body was more than she could lift. She clattered the cups and saucers and put the kettle on.

Mrs B leaned on the table so that she could lower her voice. "Barbara is a lovely girl, hardworking and kind. You must be very proud of her."

"Some man came around here, sniffing around." She poured herself another tot of gin. Her eyes were glazed, and her words were starting to run into each other. "I soon saw him off. Men are fools and women who rely on them are worse."

"How clever of you. I suspect you rely quite heavily on her. She's a helpful girl." Mrs B held her hands flat on the table.

"Are you sure you don't want a gin?" She raised the bottle to pour herself a little more.

"No, thank you. I expect I shall be having a sherry at my nephew's wedding next month, but I shall refrain until then. Far too much to do, I fear." The gasp she heard behind her made her turn towards Barbara.

"But the wedding's off. Arnold believed what he was told." The kettle boiled, and Barbara moved it off the gas cooker. A snore drifted across the kitchen, making Mrs B and Barbara turn.

"Your mother lied to Arnold, and he was fool enough to be swayed by her. The letter he received was on this writing paper. She picked up the pad and showed Barbara. She has some problems, but they are not your responsibility. I suggest that you and I clean through this house, so that she has somewhere clean to live, and then you come and live with me until the wedding. Perhaps we can ask Reverend Chambers to conduct the service." Mrs B reached for Barbara's hand. "There's something missing from your hand."

"I can't leave her. She needs help." She heaved a huge sigh. Clearly, she had been carrying this weight for a long time.

"If you stay, she has no reason to get better." She lifted her mouth into a smile, but her eyes were sad. "Pack your things. I will straighten things up down here. Come along."

Outside on the pavement, Arnold was busy wearing out the concrete slabs. "Auntie? Barbara?"

"Arnold. For a clever person, you are not very bright. Her mother has some problems and lied to you. If you were thinking clearly instead of acting like some sort of neanderthal, perhaps you would have seen it." Mrs B shook her head. She could not hide her disappointment. She held out her hand, which held a piece of the writing paper which she had taken from the pad where Barbara's mother had left it.

"Thank you for trying, Mrs B." Barbara held her hands out. "Arnold is not going to listen. It's all ruined."

"No. You will call me Auntie. Barbara is coming to stay with me for a while. When you come to your senses, you can come to visit us and I will make pork chops." She smiled and kissed her nephew on the cheek. "The last bus leaves in a little under half an hour. We should hurry." Mrs B checked her watch.

The ride in the car was tense, with none of the three talking. At the station, Arnold stopped the car and looked straight into Barbara's eyes. "I should have been more sensible. Stupidity and the fear that you might not love me are no excuse, but they are all I have."

"You couldn't just believe in me?" Barbara shrugged. "I will never feel entirely safe with you."

"We are going to miss the bus." Mrs B leaned through from the back seats.

"No need for the bus. I'll drive you both back to Little Mellington. It will give me a chance to convince Barbara that I am still worth marrying." He turned in his seat to smile at Mrs B. "Thank you, Auntie. I should have had more trust, more faith."

"Indeed, you should. You also owe your mother an apology." She looked out of the window, but she was smiling. "Perish the thought that my sister might be left unhappy." The two in the front were chatting, and neither of them heard her, which suited her just fine.

8.

Mrs B and the Gartrees

Barbara was still asleep when Mrs B let herself out of the house and walked through the morning sunshine to collect her bicycle. She had left it with Mr Gartree, imagining that she would collect it when she came back by bus, but Arnold had been kind enough to drop her home in his car.

The morning was a little fresh, and the sky that impossible blue that promised fine weather for the rest of the day. There was something though, a tang on the air, just the slightest aroma. Mrs B lifted her nose a little higher. Yes, someone was having a fire. Perhaps a bonfire in one of the gardens. Unusual for anyone to have a fire this early in the day. She shrugged.

The smell grew stronger, until she reached Mr and Mrs Gartree's home, to find smoke billowing out of the back of their house. "Mr Gartree? Mrs Gartree? Are you inside?" She banged on the door. "Oh, my." The back gate was open, and she rushed through and found the garden hose. The smoke was coming out of the back door, and she pointed the hose through the opening, hoping to have some effect on slowing the fire.

A cough made her turn around, and she found Mrs Gartree sitting on the grass. Her hair was a little dishevelled, and she had a few smudges on her hands and face, but otherwise, she seemed unharmed.

"Mrs Gartree, I am so pleased to see you safe. Is Mr Gartree at home?" The woman shook her head. Perhaps she was suffering from shock. Her eyes were a little wild, but that was understandable in the circumstances.

"I left the pan on. Completely forgot about it. Silly me." A tear slipped down her face. "Mrs B? Why are you here?"

"I came to...never mind me. Are you hurt?" She shook her head. Mrs B breathed a sigh of relief, and took a good look at the woman she had known well enough to say good morning to for many years, but not much more than that. She had a pretty face, but her expression was closed. Mrs B could not remember ever having more than a passing conversation with her.

More people arrived and soon put out the fire. The kitchen was blackened, and there was some damage, but it could have been much worse. A neighbour brought tea and consolation. Mrs B was about to ask if she might take her bicycle when Mr Gartree arrived home.

The neighbour rushed to tell him that the damage was superficial, but he was not in any way soothed or calmed by this. He was red faced with fury. Mrs B watched his wife's reaction. She shrank further into the folds of her cardigan. The fear came from her in waves.

"Mrs Gartree, perhaps it would be sensible for you to go next door to your neighbour for a while. I can clean the worst of the soot from the kitchen, and Mr Gartree will have some time to assess the damage." She felt the woman flinch away from her touch when she helped her to stand, but the neighbour was already leading her away, before she could argue.

"No need to trouble yourself, Mrs B." Mr Gartree was trying and failing to reign in his temper.

"No trouble at all. Goodness me, we shall have to set to, will we not?" She ran the tap at the kitchen sink, glad to find that there was hot water, and soon she was wiping down the cupboards and saving what could be saved.

"Pointless destruction." Mr Gartree raged. "She's a stupid, thoughtless woman." His mutterings were endless and angry. Some were inaudible, for which Mrs B judged herself grateful.

"Did you enjoy your evening out, Mr Gartree?" Her voice was sharp.

"I, yes, thank you." She could see he was wrong-footed, and that was good news.

"You were coming home this morning, after a night out. That must be the modern way. Mr Blandford, God rest him, never went out overnight." She paused, cloth in hand, to watch his face, then returned to cleaning the kitchen table. "Maybe she was worried about where you were, and distracted enough to leave a pot on the stove." He sank into one of the chairs she had cleaned.

"Since the children left home, she wanders about like a lost soul. I have tried, but in the end, I have made a life elsewhere. We grew apart when she gave all of her energies to the children. I suppose there was not enough of her left for me." He swiped his hand over his forehead. "I was lonely."

"So, you have another woman somewhere?" Mrs B considered whether she was shocked, and decided that she was not.

"Yes. I come home here. I try to keep everything on an even keel, but she is driving me away." He breathed deeply, clearly brought to the edge of his emotions by the situation.

"You come back here, hit your wife a few times and then go off to your other woman. I am surprised she has not set fire to the house before." He gasped, his face snapping up to meet her stare. "Yes. I know that you hit your wife.

She has bruises, careful ones that are hidden, but I helped her up, and hurt her by touching old bruises. I saw the fear in her face that there would be new ones." Mrs B wiped the table with more vigour than might have been required. "I remember your wedding. We came to the church. You promised each other."

"Yes, she promised to love me. To obey me." The spark of anger was back in his eyes.

"You promised, if I remember clearly, to love her, to honour her, to cleave only unto her as long as you both shall live. To worship her with your body. Those are the words. Those are the promises. You have broken every single one. Worse, you have hurt her. Physically, and emotionally. If you are going to leave, then it would be better if you went. What you are doing is torture." Mrs B leaned on the table, wet cloth in hand, and stared him down. He left the room, returning with a suitcase and a hangdog expression.

"You're right. I know that. I was hurt, and I lashed out. It was stupid." His shoulders slumped. She watched him go into the hallway and soon afterwards, he came downstairs with two more suitcases. "I will not stay. Not after what has happened. I have found happiness elsewhere. This is the kindest way forward for all of us." He rested his hands on the back of the chair. "Please, could you keep this to yourself?"

"Perish the thought that I would ever gossip." Mrs B shook her head and went back to cleaning. The kitchen was looking a great deal better than it had, and the air smelled a little sweeter.

Mrs Gartree came home when the cleaning was finished and peered around the door. "He's gone, love." Mrs B put a sandwich in front of her. "You need to eat."

"Gone for good? To her?" There was a waver in her voice.

"For good is a long time, but gone for a while. No more fighting. You both need some time for yourselves, perhaps. Feel free to pop up and see me, you know where I am?" Mrs B nodded, and fetched her bicycle from the shed.

The tang of smoke hung on her coat, but as she pedalled through the village, the fresh air blew it away. Not for the first time, she considered how lucky she had been in her husband.

That was, she reflected, the thing about life. She could spend her life bemoaning her widowhood, the short time that she had been granted with her husband. Or she could choose to be grateful for what she had been given and remember her husband with love and with happiness.

9.

Mrs B has a visitor

The sky was overcast when Mrs B set off. She had hung out the washing and asked Barbara to keep an eye open in case it rained. She had been trying to find a chance to speak to the Reverend Chambers. Once she had left her bicycle outside the church and pushed open the heavy wooden door. "Reverend Chambers, I am so pleased to have caught you."

"Mrs B? Lovely to see you." He was beaming.

"I left a short letter through your door the other day. I hope you received it? About my nephew's wedding?" She shifted her weight from one foot to the other. "I had hoped that you might be able to marry them."

"The bride would have to be living in the parish." He shook his head, a little wariness creeping into his face.

"Wonderful. She has been staying with me for the last week and a half. How long does she need to live here?"

"Six weeks." He looked right and left, perhaps hoping for a way to escape.

"That will work out just right. We need to read the bans for three weeks, and that will give us a little extra time to make all the arrangements. Arnold is coming up to visit this weekend. I shall send the happy couple down to see you, and you can book in a date. Thank you so very much, Reverend." Mrs B stopped for a moment. "How is Mrs Chambers? I must pop by and see her."

"She's grateful for your recommendation of the ginger tea." He smiled. "And your tact and discretion."

"Perish the thought that I might spread any gossip, you know that. I am only so very pleased for you both." She clasped his hands and was on her way. Her feet pounded up and down, pedalling as fast as she could to tell Barbara the good news.

Outside her house was a woman she did not recognise. Mrs B pushed her bicycle in to the garden and rested it against the wall. "Hello?"

The woman turned. "Mrs B?" As soon as she spoke, Mrs B knew her voice.

"Mrs Gartree? You look wonderful." It was the truth. The wary, frightened expression had gone, but it was more than that. She was dressed smartly, and her cardigan fitted, replacing the baggy one she used to wear.

"Thank you. I feel wonderful." She reached out and grabbed Mrs B's hands. "I wanted to thank you for whatever it was you did. I feel so much better. It should be difficult. I know the village is talking about my husband leaving, but I've never been happier."

"You look it, my dear. Now come inside and have a cup of tea. I want to hear all about this miraculous change." Mrs B led her inside.

Barbara was in the kitchen and soon the kettle was on and they were all chatting like old friends.

"Barbara and my nephew Arnold will be getting married at the village church. I just came from seeing Reverend Chambers, and he's looking forward to it." Mrs B leaned across and squeezed Barbara's hand.

"I hope that you will come to the wedding, Mrs Gartree. We'd love to have you there. I am so pleased to meet friends of Arnold's family." Barbara smiled across at Mrs Gartree.

"I'd love that. I do enjoy a good wedding. Such hope and possibility, I suppose. I wish you a long and happy life together. You will have Mrs B behind you, and that's worth having. She's a wonderful friend, and I will always be grateful for her friendship." Mrs Gartree pulled her cardigan around her thin frame. "Thank you for the tea and the invitation. Let me know when and I will be there." She hugged Barbara and Mrs B. "Thank you."

Mrs B held her at arms-length. "You are entirely welcome." She closed the door on the way out.

"She's a nice lady. I popped out to the bakery earlier today." Barbara pushed a bag across the table. "We both deserve one of those iced buns you are so fond of."

Mrs B fetched the plates. Mrs Gartree was a good woman, and she deserved a fresh start. A wedding was as good a place as any to celebrate a beginning. Perhaps better than most.

10.

Mrs B and some home truths

"Did you know?" To find Letty on the doorstep was an enormous surprise. To find her there, red faced and demanding answers, was a little concerning.

"Hello Letty. What about?" Mrs B held the door open and waited while her sister bustled past her. Letty had always been prone to excitement, and Mrs B had found over the years it was better to put the kettle on than fight fire with fire.

"Did you know about this?" Letty dug into her handbag and produced a letter. Mrs B put tea in the pot. She recognised the writing paper. She should have thought of this. It was silly of her not to have thought it through.

"You had a letter?" She fetched the cups from the cupboard on the wall. She kept her movements measured while she tried to work out the best way forward.

"Yes, I did. Read this. Poor Arnold is being taken for a fool." She pushed the letter across the table and dabbed at her eyes with a handkerchief.

"This is from Barbara's mother. She is trying to stop the wedding, because she wants her daughter to stay at home and look after her. It is untrue. It is selfish." Mrs B pushed the letter back towards her sister and fetched milk and sugar.

"There is a baby, though? This letter says there is a baby, and the father is another man. That shows you the type of girl she is." Letty's eyes beseeched her sister to tell her that none of it was true.

"Letty. Arnold and Barbara love each other, and they are going to be married. That's all there is to it." She poured the tea and let the idea settle.

Mrs B reached across the table and held her sister's hand. She had not expected Letty to be overjoyed at the prospect of a wedding prompted by a baby's arrival, but she was taking this harder than anticipated.

"You really do not seem to have grasped what is happening here. I spoke to Mrs Jenkins from the tennis club. She told me that her daughter was quite besotted with Arnold. He could have had his pick of the girls. The shame of having to be married. It's too much to bear." Letty was crying heavily, her breath coming in gasps. Mrs B shook her head.

"Letty, for goodness' sake, if he wanted to marry Mrs Jenkins' daughter or any one of the silly girls at the tennis club, he would have. He loves Barbara, and she loves him. They will be happy together." She shot a stern look across at Letty. "What could be a better start to their lives together?"

"I wanted so much more for him." Letty sobbed.

"Drink your tea, love. He's happy, and it will all work out fine." Mrs B thought back to when they were children together, Letty was always the wild one, ready to climb a tree or paddle in the stream, shoes and socks abandoned on the bank. "Whatever happened to change you, Letty?" Her sister's eyes met hers over the rim of her teacup. "You were always so much fun, you were never concerned about what someone might think. I cannot believe you're so upset by some ninnies at a tennis club."

"I have not changed. I have always viewed propriety as being very important." She glared, daring her sister to argue.

"Even when you fell in the stream and were wet through?" Mrs B sipped her tea. "You ran through the village cackling like a witch that afternoon, and the rest of us laughing behind you." She chuckled. "It was the best day."

"You must be mistaken." Her voice was so stiff, she could barely speak.

"Letty? You know that is untrue. What happened? To make you so buttoned up? We were not that way as children." Mrs B held out her hand to her sister. "You can tell me, whatever it is, you know that."

"I was pregnant when I married. I told nobody. When Arnold arrived, we told everyone he was born very early, but he was on time." She took in a deep breath. "Albert always teased me about it. Sometimes he was even quite unkind, said mean things. He could be an unpleasant man sometimes." She wiped her eyes. "I wanted Arnold to marry for love, not because he had been forced into the decision, like I was."

"Letty I'm sorry. I had no idea." Mrs B stood up and wrapped her arms around her sister. "I was always jealous of you, with your beautiful baby and your pretty clothes. Perhaps we all see the grass as being greener on the other side of the fence."

"You won't tell him?" Panic pushed her eyes open wide.

"Perish the thought." Mrs B patted her sister gently. "You have what you want, though. He is marrying for love, and so is she." The smile they shared made them both feel better. "They will be married in the same church as we both were, and we will help them. They will be fine." She thought about it for a moment. "I wish you had told me about everything. Perhaps I could have helped."

"He's gone now, and I am foolish to even think about those times, but I do. I have not missed him once. Not at all." She smiled, and this time it was more certain, less likely, to tumble into tears.

"Thank you for telling me the truth. Now, shall we go and have a look at the flowers for the wedding? There are roses, of course, and some very lovely pinks. What do you think about gypsophila?" Mrs B pushed her feet into her shoes and placed her slippers by the back door.

"Baby's breath?" Letty took in a deep breath and seemed to be on the edge of losing her temper again. She huffed the breath out. "I think that would be perfect."

Arm in arm, they walked down the lane they had often run and skipped and cartwheeled down as children. Mrs B could only hope that every problem had now been avoided. The only question that remained was whether to invite Barbara's mother. Perhaps it would all be alright as long as they kept her away from the gin.

11.

Mrs B goes to town

The car's horn blared out through the quiet of the country lane. Tutting to herself at the rudeness, Mrs B applied her bicycle brakes and put one foot down onto the road to allow the car to pass her.

The window to the rear of the car was already winding down, and she wondered who would be in it.

"Mrs B? Thank goodness. We went to your house, but you were nowhere to be found." There was more than a little irritation in the voice.

"Patricia? Mrs Lennet?" The two women were sitting forwards on the back seat. "Was there something that you needed?"

"Yes indeed. I am sorry to say that there is. Could you spare a little time?" Mrs Lennet tipped her head to one side, her tone definitely plaintive.

"I have two hours to do at the police station. Perhaps if you meet me after that, at my house?" It was clear from Patricia's expression that she had not envisioned waiting, however, they agreed and Mrs B went on her way.

Kathleen was behind the canteen counter. "Hello Mrs B. Have you time for a cup of tea? I have some very good ginger cake." Mrs B accepted the tea but shook her head at the offer of the cake.

"How are you, Kathleen? Have you enough time to join me?" It appeared that she had. Kathleen was usually a good source of information about what had been happening in the police station, but on that particular day the only thing that she could tell Mrs B was that her neighbour had been to see the doctor about her in-growing toenails. The tea was wonderful, and she was glad of it after her cycle ride.

The station was sparkling and fresh by the time she had finished, and she reached her home just as the car pulled up outside.

"Do come through, ladies." Mrs B unlocked the back door, and put on the kettle, before she shrugged her coat off and checked that her hat was still in place. The ladies sat at the table, while she set out the cups and saucers, a plate for the biscuits, and a milk jug and sugar bowl. Once the tea was brewing, she sat down with them. "Now, tell me what this is all about."

"My husband is seeing someone else." Patricia blurted it out, no tears or hurt, just anger.

"Oh, my! Whatever makes you think so?" Mrs B

poured the tea, and waited for her guests to add milk.

"I had to go into town last Wednesday for a doctor's appointment, and I saw him, with a woman. He has worked late every Wednesday for weeks now. They were sitting in a restaurant. He has been so strange lately, for the past two months, perhaps, and now this!" She took a deep breath.

"Have you asked him who the lady was?" Mrs B lifted her cup.

"I have not. I will not humiliate myself like that." Patricia's lower lip stuck out. There was something rather childlike in the action, and Mrs B wondered if she had misjudged the younger woman.

"What was the woman wearing?" Mrs B's brows pushed together in concentration.

"A brightly coloured dress, and heels, she had a cardigan, pale blue, I think. No coat." Patricia ticked off the list on her fingers.

"Mrs B. I find it hard to believe that Richard would be unfaithful. He has always doted on Patricia." Mrs Lennet shrugged. "He loves her."

"What do you imagine I can tell you about it?" Mrs B's brows were furrowed.

"It's Wednesday tomorrow. I would like you to go to town with me, and see if you can work out what is happening." The determined set to Patricia's jaw brooked no argument.

"I can go with you, I suppose, but I really am not certain that I am in any way qualified." Mrs B held up her hands, unsure how she could help.

"You caught me when I…borrowed my mother-in-law's jewellery. You're clever. I need to know the truth." If Patricia saw the look that passed between Mrs Lennet and Mrs B, she showed no sign.

"Very well. We can catch the train at eight fifteen." Mrs B was fully aware of the times of the trains. She sometimes used that train to get into town before it all became too busy.

"No, we shall take the car. We need to be there in the afternoon and evening to catch him." Patricia drummed her fingers on the table.

"Oh, dear." Mrs B was not looking forward to a long car journey and several hours watching a possibly errant husband with Patricia.

"I'll come too. We shall all go together." Mrs Lennet smiled across the table and received a somewhat weak smile in return from Mrs B.

The next afternoon, they arrived in town a little earlier than planned, and the driver dropped them off near to the restaurant where Patricia had spotted Richard.

Mrs Lennet suggested that they walk around the

block in order to use up a little time and see if there were any interesting shops along the way. It appeared that a shoe shop and a pretty haberdashery were indeed of interest.

The three women walked to complete the block, past more shops, two restaurants, and a Mrs Morris's School, whatever that was. The florist on the corner was just shutting up shop as they passed by. Mrs Lennet was keen to pop in and see if there were any bargains to be had in the florist shop, but Patricia urged her onward.

There in the restaurant was Richard. He was sitting with a young woman in a brightly coloured dress with a pale cardigan draped around her shoulders.

"I think, Patricia, that you have nothing to worry about." Mrs B turned towards her with a smile, confident that Patricia could see exactly what Mrs B was seeing.

"He is sitting at a table with another woman, Mrs B." Mrs Lennet was concerned, now that she had seen it for herself.

"Not at all. He is, I think, planning a surprise for you, Patricia." Both women faced her with complete confusion written on their faces. "Oh, very well, I shall explain. Look at her hair, that's the best clue, it is pinned back, so tidy and elegant. Look at her posture, the way she holds her neck, and how straight her spine is. I believe that she is a professional dancer, working at the Mrs Morris school of dancing. Your husband is not having an affair. He is learning to dance, so that he can surprise you. She is around the corner from her place of work, which is why she has no coat. She needs a cardigan because they have been dancing, and now she will feel cold unless she drapes it around her shoulders." Mrs B shrugged. It was all completely obvious. She wondered how they had not seen it before.

"Mrs B is exactly correct. How could you suspect me of having an affair? For goodness' sake, Patricia. How embarrassing." Richard had joined them on the pavement while Mrs B had been explaining everything to his wife and mother.

"Mrs B is tremendously discrete. She would never breathe a word about any of this." Mrs Lennet gushed.

"Perish the thought." Mrs B shook her head.

"Well, in that case, I suppose the only thing ruined is my surprise." Richard laughed. "For heaven's sake, old thing. You're quite the silliest person." He reached for Patricia's hand.

"Well, I thought you were going off me. I'm going to be awfully fat again." A single tear slipped down Patricia's cheek. The whole group turned to look at her. "I'm having a baby. That was why I had to go to the doctor; for a check-up."

"Oh my. How wonderful." Mrs Lennet threw her

arms around both of them. "How exciting."

When the driver returned, Mrs B and Mrs Lennet returned home with him, leaving Richard to take Patricia out for dinner. They were grateful to sink back into the soft seats in the back of the car and chat while every minute took them closer to Little Mellington.

12.

Mrs B and the wedding bans

She had made sure that the flowers were particularly beautiful the day before, and polished the church until every pew shone, and now, with her best blouse on and Barbara looking smart and happy, all they were waiting for was Letty and Arnold to arrive.

The walk to the church would only take five minutes, or ten, if Letty insisted on wearing shoes that hurt her feet.

When Barbara finally spotted Arnold's car drawing up to the kerb, they rushed out of the house together. "Sorry, we're a little later than planned. It took ages for me to find the right tie." Arnold nodded towards his mother.

"Appearances are important, Arnold. I was not going to allow you to go to church wearing inappropriate neck attire." Letty hung her handbag over her arm, and they set off to the church.

Mrs B slid into her usual pew, where she had

sat every Sunday since she used to come to the church with her parents and Letty when they were children. Immediately, she bowed her head to pray. Her prayers that morning, as always, were for the welfare of her family and her friends. Her particular focus was on the Reverend and Mrs Chambers. He had seemed a little strange when she had asked about the wedding, and she had barely seen him since.

Letty sat next to her, scanning the congregation for a face she recognised. Arnold and Barbara held hands, waiting for the first step to their wedding.

The usual service, hymns and prayers followed the natural rhythm of a Sunday morning. Towards the close of the service, Reverend Chambers stood to make announcements.

"There will be a sale of cakes and tea in the church hall on Wednesday afternoon to raise funds for the church clock, which, as you know, needs attention. We are all looking forward to the wonderful cakes, I know. The Sunday School has asked for volunteers to help with the midsummer picnic, which will be in five weeks' time, on Saturday the twenty-seventh. The summer fayre will be taking place two weeks after that, and Mrs Lennet tells me that there are still two stalls available. Finally, it is my great pleasure to read the bans for a young couple who are about to marry. This is a serious part of the wedding, because it allows the community to gather around the bride and groom and offer support, and help as they prepare for their big day, and also for the congregation here to consider the momentous step that marriage is. Not to be entered into without thought and consideration. Therefore, I ask, if anyone here knows of any impediment to the marriage of Mr Arnold Birch of the parish of Saint Andrew in Potterton and Miss Barbara Henderson of this parish, they should speak now or forever hold their peace." He raised his eyebrows and watched the assembled congregation for a moment. No response was forthcoming.

"They are reading the bans at Saint Andrews next week. We shall have to be there for that." Letty toiled up the hill to Mrs B's cottage. They were all looking forward to a cup of tea and Sunday lunch.

Mrs B barely had her coat off before she started cooking. Barbara made the tea and took it through to the living room for Arnold and Letty.

The knock on the back door was quiet. If she had been in the living room with the others, she would never have heard it. Mrs Chambers stood on the doorstep.

"Sorry Mrs B. I wondered if you had two minutes?" She stepped inside when Mrs B beckoned her in.

"I always have time. Do you mind if I carry on peeling the carrots while we talk?" They sat down at the table. Mrs B pushed a cup and the teapot across to her guest, and carried on peeling.

"It's my husband. He's not sleeping, he's become even more vague than ever. The bishop had to ask him the same question three times the other day. It was really embarrassing. I wonder if you can help?" She worried at her sleeve with her fingers.

"I'll pop in to have a chat with him tomorrow if that helps?" Mrs B put down her peeler and reached across the table.

"I think he doesn't love me anymore." Tears spilled from Mrs Chambers' eyes.

"I'm sure that is not the case. Let me talk to him and see what is troubling him?" She patted Mrs Chambers' hands.

"Thank you, Mrs B." She slipped out of the back door, leaving Mrs B to think about the Reverend Chambers and what might be worrying him.

Letty left her sister with promises that she would make lunch the following Sunday, and entreaties not to be late for the church service. Barbara kissed Arnold goodbye as though he would be gone for a year instead of a few days.

Monday morning, and Mrs B pushed her bicycle

out through the garden gate. The ride downhill, with fields on either side of the road, was always a joy. With her head rolled back onto her shoulders, she resisted the urge to push her feet out and shout 'weeeeee' as she had when she was a child.

The church door was open, and Mrs B was relieved she would not have to chase all over the village looking for him.

"Reverend Chambers?" She walked into the gloom of the church. "Hello?"

"Mrs B?" He was wiping his hands on the front of his trousers.

"Reverend. I wondered if you had a few minutes." He nodded. She sensed a little reluctance, but the nod was there. "How are you? I wanted to check, because I was unsure whether you were happy about the wedding, or unhappy about something else."

"I am perfectly fine. Thank you, Mrs B. I would appreciate it if you would allow me to deal with my life in my own way. I am a little fed up with you pushing yourself in to my business." His nostrils flared, and his breath came hard and fast.

"Very well, Reverend. I apologise. I meant no disrespect. My only wish was to help. I clearly have misunderstood." Mrs B backed away. Her eyes closed to hold her feelings inside. The stone walls around the church door were rough under her hands, and her vision was blurred by tears. Her hands shook on the handlebars of her bicycle as she pushed it back through the churchyard.

"Mrs B! Mrs B! I am so sorry. I had no right to say that. Please come back in. I am in such a mess, and I need to talk to someone. I owe you an apology." He looked close to tears.

"Reverend Chambers. It's for me to apologise. I get too wrapped up in things, and dive in when I should step back." She allowed him to guide her back into the church.

"I am in such a mess. Finally, I have everything I ever thought I wanted, and I am terrified that I will lose something I had not realized was the most important thing in the world." He buried his face in his hands.

"I am lost here. Please explain it to me. I'd like to help if you will let me." Mrs B leaned forwards, her hand outstretched, but the gap between them was too wide for her to reach him.

He lifted his head, and his eyes met hers. "Every morning for the last ten years, my wife has kissed me, and said good morning. It sounds like nothing much, but it was a lovely start to the day. Now she rushes to the bathroom to be sick, and in a few months, she will be rushing to look after the baby." He wiped his hand over his face. "I know this makes me selfish, but I feel that I am losing her to the baby."

"Ah, I see. You have yet to learn the lesson." She tapped him on the arm and beckoned him to follow her. Outside in the churchyard, she led him to a bench. "Take a look around." She waited, with her hands folded around each other.

He lifted his eyes and looked around the churchyard. Some of the gravestones were a little lopsided, and the grass could do with a trim.

"Did you see the grass? It gets cut down, but it grows back, pushing through the tiniest gaps. Look how the grass grows around the old gravestones. Every time it's cut back, it finds a different way to wrap itself around the stones. Look at the flowers, each one a tiny miracle, supported on a tiny thin stalk. Do you see what I'm trying to show you?" Mrs B rested her hand on his arm. "You have love, and that is a wonderful thing. The child will bring more love, not take anything from you." She patted him gently. "Your wife loves you. I bet if you found a different way, like the grass does, Mrs Chambers would appreciate it. A cup of tea in the morning, or half an hour to put her feet up and read the paper. Find a new good morning every day."

"I was letting fear stand in the way, wasn't I? Oh, you're right. Thank you. I'm going home to make a cup of tea." He jumped up and rushed through the churchyard.

"I'll close the church door for you, then." Mrs B shrugged.

"Thank you. Please tell Arnold and Barbara to come and see me at any time. I am totally in favour of their wedding, marriage in general and children." His face split with a grin. "Thank you for sticking with me, Mrs B. I was rude, and I don't deserve such a good friend."

"I hope I know my friends well enough to be there when they need me. Perish the thought I should not notice when someone is in trouble." She closed the door to the church. He was already gone. Her relief that he was not in any way unhappy about Arnold and Barbara's wedding put a smile on her face, while she pedalled her bicycle back up the hill to her cottage, where she planned to make a cup of tea for herself, and one for Barbara.

13.
Mrs B visits Potterton

Arnold collected Mrs B and Barbara early on Sunday morning. He was on strict instructions from his mother that they were not to be late to Saint Andrew's church to hear the bans be read.

Letty was almost ready to go when they arrived at her house. She just needed to change her hat and find the gloves that matched.

Arnold rolled his eyes, and they all waited patiently. Years of practice had taught them not to argue with Letty or try to hurry her.

The church was very busy, and their progress slow because Letty had to stop and say hello to everyone who was already seated. The bans were read, and the church began to empty. Mrs B excused herself and walked purposefully across the churchyard.

"Mrs Henderson?" Mrs B reached under her elbow. "Come along with me. We need to find you a comfortable place to have a sit down." Gently, she eased Barbara's mother off the gravestone where she had been sitting. "I think your house is not too far away. Perhaps we could have a cup of tea together. You might have a sit down on your lovely sofa."

Mrs Henderson had, it appeared, had a few generous gins before her visit to the church. She was leaning more and more on Mrs B, who was taking the weight, but they were making very slow progress through the churchyard. Letty would be horrified to see Barbara's mother like this, and mortified if her friends noticed.

When Arnold pulled up in his car, she had very rarely been so glad to see anyone. "Let me help Mrs Henderson into the car, Auntie. It's such a warm day. You must be quite exhausted. He took over the weight and lifted Mrs Henderson into the back seat. Mrs B almost wilted with relief. She collected herself enough to climb in next to Mrs Henderson, and hold on tightly when Arnold took the corners a little faster than was absolutely necessary.

"I'm going to tell that vicar. No wedding for those two. I'm going to stop him from taking my Barbara away. Men are like that. They always want to take women somewhere else. I'm not having it." She slumped, her head lolling forward.

"Thank goodness that we're nearly there." Arnold pulled up next to the kerb and between them they helped her out of the back seat. Arnold lifted her carefully while Mrs B found the keys. They laid her on the sofa, and Mrs B took her shoes off.

When they reached the church, Letty was almost finished chatting. "Where have you been, Arnold? Everyone wanted to congratulate you."

"Oh, I bumped into someone I haven't seen in a while. Sorry, mother." He met Barbara's eyes. "I was worried that they had been unwell, but it's all fine."

"Well, I think we should get home. I've lunch to cook." Letty bustled towards the car, with the others trailing in her wake.

As expected, Letty sat back in the living room complaining of sore feet, while Mrs B made herself busy in the kitchen.

Barbara hung her head. "What are we going to do? They will read the bans again next week, and she will be there making a scene. I've no idea how to resolve this." Arnold wrapped his arms around her.

"We'll sort it out. That's what we agreed. Whatever problems we meet, we face them together." He stepped back from her. "Now, Auntie, what can I do to help?" He rolled his sleeves up.

Mrs B passed him a pile of potatoes to peel. She watched him with pride. He had grown up into a really rather wonderful young man. She patted him gently on the shoulder. "Thank you, Arnold."

14.

Mrs B and Mrs Goffey

When she arrived home from work in the afternoon, Mrs B was very pleased to see that the washing had all been folded up in the basket. Barbara was such a help, although it appeared that she had gone out. It was such a lovely afternoon; she decided to take her cup of tea outside and sit in the sun.

"Good afternoon, Mrs B." She had to shade her eyes to make out who was standing by her garden wall. "I must say. Your sweet peas are looking wonderful this year. Have you decided if you will be entering a pie this year at the village fayre?"

"Mrs Goffey. How lovely to see you! Yes, I think I shall put a pie in. How about you?" Mrs B walked over to lean on the wall. It had been a while since she saw Mrs Goffey. Partly because she lived on the opposite side of the village, but mostly because they really did not see eye to eye on anything.

"Oh yes, I shall give you a run for your money this year, I believe. I hear your nephew is to be married in the village church. How lovely for you." She pulled her face into a smile, but it was more like a baring of teeth.

"I am so looking forward to the wedding, and the village fayre, of course. How is Daphne doing? I heard that she is doing secretarial work." Mrs B smiled, her head tilting to one side.

"Yes, she is, and enjoying it thoroughly. I'll wish you a good afternoon, Mrs B. I must press on." Mrs Goffey turned on her heel and marched back down towards the village.

A smile twitched around Mrs B's lips. Each year they both entered a pie and Mrs Goffey had yet to win a ribbon. Of course, Mrs B had only won the ribbon herself three times, but it seemed to have annoyed Mrs Goffey.

Arnold's car pulled up outside. She had not been expecting him to visit, and it was a lovely surprise. "Hello Auntie." He opened the passenger door for Barbara and the two of them joined her in the garden.

"Hello both of you. Would you like a cool drink? It has been a lovely afternoon." She stood up and straightened her skirt.

"We have something to tell you." They both looked very pleased with themselves. "After last Sunday, we talked and talked about it, and we decided to visit Barbara's mum." Mrs B pursed her lips a little, but she listened. "The house was in a dreadful state and she was in a mess. She needs help. We have decided to go and live with her once we a married. So that we can look after her."

"Well, that's very kind, but might you not want your own place? A little privacy?" Mrs B tipped her head sideways.

"That's the clever part. Arnold has thought of a way that we can divide the house into two flats Mum will be upstairs and we will be down. She was so happy; she has been very low since I moved out." Barbara sat down on the bench next to Mrs B. "Although I shall miss you. I have loved our time together. I am glad that we have a few more weeks until the wedding, if you're still alright with me staying?"

"Perish the thought. Of course, you must stay. I shall miss you when you go. You are doing the right thing with your mother, I know." She reached across and patted Barbara's hand. "Now, how about a ham salad for dinner?"

Inside, she arranged the lettuce and tomatoes on the plates, and the ham. She would miss Barbara. Tears threatened, but she blinked them away. She had been on her own before and soon would be again. In the meantime, there was a wedding to plan and so much to do. She doubted she would have time to feel sad.

15.

Mrs B goes to Arnold's wedding – Part 1

Mrs B carried a tray up the stairs, loaded with tea and toast, scrambled eggs, and a single rose. She tapped on the bedroom door and pushed it open. "Barbara?" She watched the young woman she had grown so fond of sit up slowly.

"Auntie? You brought me breakfast." She stretched her arms out and sat back against the pillows. "That is so kind."

Mrs B passed the tray to Barbara and watched her take a sip of the tea. "I have enjoyed our time together, and I will miss your company. Today is going to be an exciting day, and you will make someone who is very special to me very happy." She patted the bed, and turned away to hide the shine in her eyes of unshed tears, while Barbara sipped her tea.

"I will miss you too, but you will always be our auntie and we'll visit so often you will be sick and tired of us." She swallowed. "Thank you for looking after me." Mrs B nodded, but her throat was too tight with tears to reply.

There was no hurry. They had three hours until they had to be at the church. Mrs Henderson arrived on the bus soon after Barbara had finished her breakfast, and after a long bus ride, she was happy to discover that there was tea in the pot and a warm welcome.

"I believe I owe you an apology, Mrs B." Mrs Henderson had been practicing what she wanted to say. "I had no business behaving so badly."

"We all do things that we regret from time to time. Let's begin again?" Mrs B held out her hand. A moment passed between them, before Mrs Henderson placed her hand in Mrs B's. "Good. A fresh start is exactly what we need, and a fresh pot of tea. We are both here to support Arnold and Barbara. That's all that matters." They shared a smile "I understand that you are going to do Barbara's hair today?"

"Yes, I should get started. Thank you for the tea." She took a last sip and went upstairs to help Barbara.

Mrs B changed into the dress she had chosen. It was a deep blue. She carefully smoothed her hair with a brush and clipped it up before pinning on a hat in the same shade as her dress. Her reflection in the mirror smiled back at her. Her Arnold, her beloved nephew, the wonderful boy who had given her so much joy, was going to marry the woman he loved. It would be a fantastic day. Yes, it was the end of an era. She was losing a part of her nephew, but gaining Barbara.

She checked the slim watch that she had worn every day of her life since her husband had given it to her. It was time to go. Downstairs and with her handbag over her arm, she stood very still, whispering a prayer for Arnold and Barbara. When she opened her eyes, Barbara was coming down the stairs.

"Oh my! You look beautiful." Barbara's dress fell in soft waves, the heavy fabric pooling like liquid around her feet. Her hair fell in curls to her shoulders. Dark against the white of her dress. "I have no words to tell you how lucky Arnold is. He is lucky that you love him." A horn sounded outside. "Oh, and I have arranged a small surprise." She opened the door, and there, parked outside the house, was Mrs Lennet's car, and her driver. "I asked if we might borrow the car for an hour. Mrs Lennet was delighted to be able to help."

"Oh! Auntie. You are so kind." They shared a smile. "Thank you. For everything."

"That's enough now. You'll have me crying." Mrs B wiped her nose. "You take a moment with your mother. The driver will drop me to the church and come back for you."

"No. We can all go together. You've been a good friend to my girl. When I should have been. It's appreciated. We go together." Mrs Henderson stood on the stairs behind Barbara. "She looks wonderful though, doesn't she?"

"Indeed, she does." Mrs B smiled up at Barbara's mother before she checked her watch again. "I believe it is time to go."

The car slowed to a halt outside the church. "Here we are, ladies. May I wish you all the luck in the world, young lady?" The driver twinkled a smile, his moustache twitching. "He's a lucky man." He jumped out and opened the door for them to climb out.

Mrs Henderson stepped out and held out her hand to help Barbara. The path that led to the church lay ahead of them.

"We are in big trouble now." Mrs Henderson turned to Mrs B with fear, pushing her brows together.

The man was alone and leaning against a gravestone. "Who is that?" Mrs B turned to face Barbara and her mother.

"Tommy McKinley." Barbara whispered. Fear lurked in the corners of her eyes.

"Should I be worried?" Both of them nodded.

"Please, can you take Barbara and her mother to the other gate? I will deal with this." Both women opened their mouths to argue, but were silenced by Mrs B's hard glare. "I will speak to the gentleman. Perish the thought that you would be late for the service. Arnold will be waiting for you." They were quickly settled back into the seats. She leaned back into the car. "Tell me very quickly what you know about him."

Mrs B pushed the door closed and waved the car onwards.

"Mr McKinley?" Mrs B crossed the ground between them. "A word if you please." He turned towards her, the pistol hanging loosely in his hand.

16

Mrs B goes to Arnold's Wedding – Part 2

"Mr McKinley?" The man turned towards her slowly. "I understand that you are unhappy about the wedding, but perhaps I can help."

"What business is it of yours, old woman?" He swung the gun slowly towards her.

"That's a fair question. Barbara is marrying my nephew. I know that you were very fond of her, but that was some time ago. She is happy with him, and he will take good care of her. If you love her, truly love her, then you would want her to be happy." She looked directly into his eyes, concentrating hard on avoiding looking at the gun.

"I would have married her; she could have been a McKinley. Do you know what that means?" His face twisted with anger.

"Oh well, I've heard of your family, of course. I remember the stories." Mrs B watched him closely.

"I have been away for a while. I came out of prison last week and heard what she had been doing. She can't do this." His voice cracked with emotion.

"Barbara told me that you and she stopped seeing each other a while before you went to prison. Whilst I appreciate that your life has been on hold. Hers has moved forwards. The truth is, she's with the right man." She reached out for his hand. "You may not believe this, but I am the best friend you have here today. I am presuming that you have been here a while and watched all the big burly men arriving." Mrs B turned to face him. "You do know what my nephew does for a living?" She tipped her head to one side.

"Works for the council or something?" His forehead furrowed.

"He has just been promoted. When he goes back to work after their honeymoon, he will be taking up a post as a Detective Sergeant." She beamed at him, unable to conceal her pride in Arnold.

"She's marrying a copper? That's betrayal. She couldn't do anything worse to me." He buried his head in his hands.

"I'm your best chance. The church is full of police officers. That's why I sent Barbara and her mother inside. The best thing you can do is get yourself home." She patted him gently on the arm. "If they were to find you here, with a gun, I imagine you would be back in prison very quickly."

"I wouldn't want her. Not now she's been with a cop." His face contorted as though he had bitten into something bitter. Realisation opened his eyes wide. "I can't walk out of here with a gun." Panic rippled across his face. "Not with all those cops about. You're right, I'll be back in prison before you can say Jack Robinson."

Mrs B chewed her lip. Was this a step too far? She looked up to the top of the spire, the highest point in the village. The one place that she could see from anywhere in Little Mellington. In a slow and deliberate movement, she opened her handbag. "Pop it in here. I'll get rid of it later."

"Why would you do that for me?" He was intrigued rather than wary.

"Because you came here out of love." She smiled up at him. "Even misplaced love is still love." He reached across and placed the gun inside her bag. "Take care of yourself, Mr McKinley." She walked away with her handbag hanging over her elbow, and considerably heavier than it had been that morning.

"Mrs B?" Barbara was waiting inside the porch with her mother.

"It's all sorted out. He was very confused, but it's done now. Come along, you're supposed to be getting married." Mrs B offered her arm to Mrs

Henderson, and they left Barbara in the porch, with a gentle kiss from each.

The organ, played by Mr Phelps sprang into life, filling the ancient building with the bridal march. A rustle of excitement flowed through the congregation, and Reverend Chambers stood facing them, gesturing for them to stand.

Barbara walked into the church, down the same aisle that Mrs B and Letty had walked on their wedding days. Arnold watched her walking towards him, his face split with a grin.

They made their vows, watched over by family and friends, and finally Arnold was invited to kiss his bride. The church was filled with smiles and joy, filling the space all the way to the ancient rafters.

Mrs B turned to her sister. Letty was wiping a tear. "Look how happy they are, Letty. No more tears now." Although her own eyes were shining with unshed tears, they nodded at each other, and turned to follow Barbara and Arnold out of the church to the sound of the bells ringing out across the village and to the fields beyond.

On the road leading out of the village, Tommy McKinley stopped at the sound of the bells. He knew that she was lost to him. The woman he had met in the churchyard had made him see that. He wondered with a smile to himself what the wedding guests would say if they knew she was carrying a gun in that handbag of hers.

17.

Arnold's Wedding – Part 3

The celebration spilled out of the church hall, where a mountain of sandwiches and pork pies gradually diminished. The village green was soon crowded with friends and family, all celebrating the hope and joy of the young couple. A small band, three of Arnold's school friends who had found that playing at weddings generally earned them a few pounds and more beer than they wanted, were providing the music.

Couples danced on the village green, surrounded by children who danced too, running and chasing each other until their mothers demanded better behaviour.

Mrs B watched Arnold dancing slowly with Barbara, his arms around her, and their faces wreathed in smiles. They could have been the only two people in the world, although they were surrounded on all sides.

Her attention was caught by the sight of Mrs

Gartree, wearing a very pretty dress covered in tiny flowers. When she spotted Mr Gartree approaching, Mrs B excused herself from the conversation she was half-way paying attention to, and circled the green to stop any trouble before it began. She arrived just after he did.

"I am so sorry, my love. I have been a fool. Can you ever forgive me? I thought it would be exiting being with someone else, but it was dreadful. Fun for half an hour, but not forever. You're the only person I want in my life forever. Please let me come home?" Mr Gartree's pained and sad expression seemed to have the desired effect. His wife's frown relaxed a little. "Let's make life a little more fun, shall we? Would you do me the honour of dancing with me?"

"I'll dance with you. Let's see about the rest of it. That may take a little longer." Mrs Gartree rested her hand in his, and they shared a smile.

Mrs B stopped herself from letting out a cheer, but only just. She was glad to see that Mrs Gartree was being a little careful.

"Mrs B?" Kathleen was standing right behind her. "Thank you so much for inviting me. It has been the most wonderful day. They look so happy, don't they?"

"You are more than welcome. Perish the thought that one of my dearest friends should be excluded from such a wonderful celebration."

Mrs B smiled widely, her voice low, but her eyes sparkling.

"Are you coming to work this week? Kathleen rested her hand on Mrs B's arm and received a firm nod. "I will save you an iced bun, in that case. We can have a cup of tea together and a good chat." She stepped away to join some friends.

"Here, I've brought you a sherry, dear." Letty was standing next to her with two glasses. They sipped, able to enjoy their drinks now that all the possible calamities had been avoided. "I don't think it will rain, do you, dear?"

"Perish the thought, Letty. It's all blue skies ahead, I hope." Mrs B raised her glass in a toast to her sister, and they clinked their glasses together.

"Is your handbag very heavy, dear? The handle has left a mark on your arm." Letty reached for the bag, but Mrs B was quick to wrap her arm around her sister's waist.

"Not at all. Everything is fine. Your son is happier than I have ever seen him, and you have gained a daughter today. Nothing could be better." Carefully, Mrs B shifted the weight of her handbag and smiled sweetly at her sister.

18.

Mrs B and Mrs Tattersall

"Auntie? Are you at home?" Arnold pushed open the back door.

"Arnold? Yes, I'm here." She was halfway up the stairs with a pile of folded laundry.

"I need to talk to you." His voice, something about the urgency, or the emotion, made her stop. She carried the pile back downstairs with her. "Auntie. It's not good news."

She laid the pile down. "Tell me." She filled the kettle. If it was bad news, they would both need a cup of tea. She knew from experience that bringing bad news was as bad as receiving it.

He watched her bring the teapot to the kettle. "It's Mrs Tattersall. I know that she worked with you in the hospital during the war. The thing is, that…" He slumped into a chair at the kitchen table. "She died. I didn't want you to hear it from anyone else."

"Tell me what happened." She poured the boiling

water into the teapot. Her hands shook a little as she poured, and she watched the small droplets of water on the table.

"We're really not sure. She might have fallen, but something feels wrong. I wonder if you might be able to have a look at her house? You might see something that I've missed. Please?" He looked just like the little boy he had been. It could have been another chance at a puzzle, or a slice of cake that he was asking for. Whatever it was that he was missing, or thought he was, she would do her best to find it. She would look for him, and for her friend.

Mavis Tattersall had been a good friend. They had supported each other through losing their husbands. Neither had been interested in finding another man, though life might have been a little easier with another wage coming in. The only time she could remember seeing Mrs Tattersall angry was with the bank. She was certain that they had cheated her out of her husband's savings.

The house was as neat as a pin, just as it always was. Mrs B felt that she was intruding. They walked through the rooms together. "It looks the same as the last time I was here."

In the bedroom, she rested her hand on the polished brass of the bedstead. "I can tell you for certain that Mrs Tattersall did not make that bed.

It's all wrong. The corners are just bunched up. The pillows are facing in the wrong direction." She shook her head. "The chest of drawers has been moved too. Look where the feet made an impression on the carpet." Mrs B pointed her finger at the floor.

"Yes, you're right. Now that you have pointed it out, I can't believe we failed to spot it before." Arnold knelt on the carpet to look more closely.

"Is this how the room was when she was found?" She stood over Arnold."

"Yes. No." He shrugged. "We closed the window to secure the property. Otherwise yes."

"Did she hit her head? Was there bruising?" She ran her hand over the bedpost.

"Yes, she did. There was a bruise to the side of her head." Arnold nodded. "Her shoulder was dislocated too."

"She must have fallen with some force to dislocate her shoulder. It's possible, but she was fit and healthy, for goodness' sake. She has as many customers as I do. She's probably fitter than you." Mrs B paused; her fingers wrapped around the brass of the bedstead. "She was. Sorry, she was so very dear to me." She swallowed hard. Tears threatened to fall.

"You think she didn't fall, don't you?" Arnold watched her expression move through sad, thoughtful, and finally into weighing the evidence.

"I believe that she was not alone here. I think that she was making the bed when she was attacked, and whoever it was, they maybe hit her, so that she fell sideways into the bedpost, then she fell backwards dislocating her shoulder before she fell to the floor, about here."

"Yes, that's where she was found." Arnold nodded.

"Who found her?" Mrs B turned towards him.

"A neighbour, Mrs Penning, she was supposed to meet up with Mrs Tattersall for a cup of tea, and was worried when she failed to arrive." He shrugged.

"I need to speak to her." He fell into step behind her. "No dear, I'll do better on my own." He nodded, feeling like a child, not a detective.

"Hello? I'm so sorry to bother you. I understand that my friend Mrs Tattersall was also a friend to you. It must have been a dreadful shock, as it was to me." Mrs B leaned out for support from the door frame.

"You poor dear. You had better come in. I'll make us a cup of tea. How did you know her?" She retreated into the hallway and Mrs B followed her in.

"We worked together in the hospital during the

war." Mrs B sat in the chair that was offered to her.

"Oh, are you Mrs B? Now she told me about you. We took turns each Wednesday. She would come to me or I would go to her for tea and an hour or so of chatting. Wednesday was her early finish, so that was the afternoon we shared." She busied herself with the kettle and the teapot. "I had a key to her house. She had one for mine, too. When she was late, well, you know what she was like, so punctual. I was worried. I went around the back of the house and opened the back door. Of course, I called out, but there was no answer." She wiped the tears from her face.

"Was there anyone else about? Someone that might have seen anything?" Mrs B accepted the cup of tea that she was offered. "Thank you, very kind."

"No, it's very quiet along here. It was too early for the mums to be bringing home the kiddies from school." She sipped from her own cup and offered a plate of biscuits.

"What about earlier? Would anyone have been in the road?" Mrs B accepted a biscuit and rested it in her saucer.

"The milkman, of course, but that would be early in the day. Mrs Tattersall went out in the morning. I saw her go from my bedroom window. I was looking forward to seeing her that afternoon. Oh, of course, the window cleaner. He called round to pick up his money that evening. He would have been in the road during the day, I suppose." She sipped her tea. She sank back in the chair.

"Thank you for the tea, dear. I had better be going. I need to collect my nephew. If it is alright with you, I'll pop in next time I'm passing?" They had both lost a good friend.

"Arnold. I need to see the bedroom again." They climbed the stairs. "Yes. I believe we have a possibility."

"Auntie, please, can you tell me?" Arnold's irritation was clear.

"The chest of drawers was moved, the window was open, and someone made the bed. I think that the window cleaner came in through the open window, moved the chest of drawers so that he could climb in more easily. Mrs Tattersall must have been making the bed. I have no idea why he climbed in. Perhaps he planned to steal something. Maybe she surprised him. We might never know, but I think that he pushed her, and she fell heavily, hitting her head of the bedpost and dislocating her shoulder. I think the window cleaner tucked in the bedding." Arnold followed her around the room, nodding slowly.

"This room is exactly as you found it?" He nodded.

"I have been so stupid. I'm sorry Arnold. Now that I can see it, the whole thing is glaringly obvious. Her distrust of the banks. It all makes sense now. Help me." She put her hands on the side of the mattress, and he followed suit. They pushed. Beneath the mattress, on the springs, were pound notes. "There must be a hundred pounds here. No need to wonder what he was stealing."

"You're amazing, Auntie. Thank you. I will have the window cleaner picked up." He stopped for a moment. "Why did he leave so much behind?"

"He must have heard the neighbour coming in, and thought he could come back later. Probably just took what he could stuff in his pockets." She patted his arm. "I think it's time for a cup of tea."

"Yes indeed, you have earned it. Mrs Tattersall would be proud of you. I know I am." He smiled down at her.

"Perish the thought. It is the very least that I could do for her. She was a wonderful friend for so many years. I am going to miss her."

19.

Mrs B and the Pendle's surprise.

Mrs B started her day as she usually did with a cup of tea. A cup, sitting on a saucer and tea poured from a teapot. A little milk poured into the cup after the tea. The kitchen was a little dark that morning. The heavy clouds threatened rain sooner rather than later.

The noise outside was a surprising clatter for before six in the morning. She peered through the kitchen window to find her view of the lane obstructed by a tractor. On top of the tractor sat Mrs Pendle.

Mrs B watched her climb down from the seat and opened the back door. "Good morning, Mrs Pendle." She waited.

"Mrs B." She adjusted the bag which was hanging across her body. Each step took her closer to the back door.

"A cup of tea? I just made a pot." Mrs Pendle nodded. "Toast, perhaps?"

"That would be nice. Thank you." She sat down at the table.

Mrs B had learned long before that people who turned up in her kitchen generally would tell her why if she gave them a little time. She put a cup and saucer in front of her guest, and adjusted the knitted tea cosy so that she could pour a cup of tea. She put a piece of toast each onto two plates and placed butter and home-made marmalade between them.

The sound of Mrs B's knife scraping across her toast seemed loud in the quiet of her kitchen.

"You were very kind to me and my husband a few months back. You didn't tell the police when I was looking after baby Molly. I know that you understood." She looked at the toast on her plate, pulled off a crust, and took a tiny bite.

"Butter?" Mrs B pushed it across the table.

"I want to thank you. I know you should have told the police." Mrs Pendle sipped her tea. "A few times since, I've seen Molly in the village. I wanted to tell her mother that I was only taking care of her. I would never have hurt her." She smiled, nodding gently. "I didn't. She wouldn't understand." A slow smile spread across her face. "I was at school with Veronica Peters. Of course, she was Veronica Leason then. She was a bully, still is." She pulled another piece of crust off. "I wondered at the time if I was taking her baby to punish her, or because it all came so easy for her." She picked up the knife and spread a little butter.

"A little marmalade?" Mrs Pendle shook her head.

"I wanted to say thank you properly. Not everyone understands. But you did." She sniffed and wiped her finger under her eye. "All those months ago, you brought me a kitten. She's grown up so lovely. Anyway, she's had kittens herself now." She pulled a tiny ball of fur out of her bag and placed it into Mrs B's lap. "I thought about it. You might like something to love, just like I did."

Mrs B lifted the tiny body to look into its face. There was

a moment of appraisal on both sides. A decision was made and a commitment too. "Thank you. This is the most wonderful gift. I would never have thought that I would want a kitten, but it appears I do." She reached across to hold Mrs Pendle's hand. "Thank you. Oh, and congratulations, I believe." She smiled.

"You? How did you know?" Mrs Pendle laughed.

"You are unsure about food, pulling at crusts, spreading butter but not eating it. Refusing marmalade. You sniffed your tea with such care, as though it might bite you, then decided not to drink it. All good signs, but better than that, you look…comfortable in yourself. I'm so glad for you both." Mrs B smiled. "I'll make you a ginger tea. It will help with the sickness."

"Thank you. I think that I was trying too hard. I've always felt that working harder would get me what I wanted. You gave me something to love, and I calmed down a little. I'm sure it helped." She accepted the cup of ginger tea and sniffed it. "Oh, thank you." Her first sip brought a smile. "This is wonderful."

"My pleasure. In fact, thank you. You know my nephew was married last month. I miss him. I would not have it any other way. They have their own life and it is exactly as it should be." The kitten turned and rested his head against her. "This little one will be wonderful company. Thank you for understanding." She tickled the kitten's head. The softness of the fur making her smile, while the ginger and white stripes moved under her fingers.

"Look at us grinning like a pair of fools because of a couple of kittens." Mrs Pendle pushed back her chair.

"Nothing foolish about love." Mrs B patted Mrs Pendle's arm.

"I know you won't tell anyone about the baby. You've

already been so good at keeping my secrets." Mrs Pendle let herself out of the back door.

"Perish the thought, my love." Mrs B whispered to the sleeping kitten in her arms. "Now, what on earth are we going to call you?" She looked across the table at the half-eaten toast, the butter and the marmalade, and she smiled. "How about Marmalade? You're the right colours. What do you think, little one?" She stroked the tiny body and felt the tiny body vibrating as the kitten began to purr. "You're a good little kitten, Marmalade." The kitchen clock ticked away the minutes and Mrs B sat with the warmth of the kitten sleeping quietly in her arms. "There are going to be an awful lot of babies in this village before Christmas little Marmalade." The little kitten yawned, his mouth pink and wide open, before snuggling further into Mrs B.

20.

Mrs B has a late visitor

The news had finished on the wireless. Mrs B was in the kitchen waiting for the milk to boil on the stove. She had always made herself a cocoa before bed, and tonight was no exception. The milk came to a boil, bubbling in the pan, until she took it off the heat and whisked in the cocoa powder. Her cup was ready, and she poured the liquid in.

It was too hot to drink, but it would take a few minutes to wash the saucepan, anyway.

Marmalade the kitten was fast asleep on the little bed she had made from an old cushion and a blanket. The kitchen clock ticked all the way up to the hour. It was time she was in bed.

Only two steps up the stairs, she heard a soft tap on the door. Who on earth would knock on the door at such a late hour? She waited, imagining that she might be mistaken. The knock came again.

"Who is it?" She called out, not happy to go back

down the stairs.

"It's Tommy. I came to collect what you kept for me." The voice was instantly recognisable.

"Tommy?" She knew who he was and what he was looking for.

"Tommy McKinley. You looked after an object for me, when Barbara married your nephew. I've come to collect it." His voice was louder now, more insistent.

"Oh, Mr McKinley. I gave your weapon to the police. It was the only sensible course of action. I could not have kept it here." She sat down on the stairs.

"No, you told them it was mine? You said you were my friend." She heard something hit the other side of the door, probably his hand.

"Perish the thought. I have never betrayed a confidence. I was your best way out of the village on the day of the wedding, and if you are in need of a gun, then I have done you a great service in giving it to the police." She sipped at her cocoa, which was no longer too hot.

"Well, I…" She heard him sink to the doorstep, sliding down the door. "You might be right. I'm hot tempered. Now that I have thought about it, not having a gun might be a good idea." He tapped against the door again. "Thank you. Second time you saved me. I owe you a favour.

Remember that. Tommy McKinley owes you." She heard him shift against the door. "Good night."

"Good night, Mr McKinley." She stood up and carried what was left of her cocoa up the stairs.

Of course, she had no way to give the gun to Arnold without telling him all about Barbara and Mr McKinley, and that he had arrived armed to the wedding. That would help nobody.

Her own method of wrapping the gun in an old pillowcase; before burying it in a tub of geraniums and lobelia might not have been a perfect solution either. For the moment, however, it would have to do.

21.
Mrs B and Mrs Penning

Mrs B was already waiting by the gate when Arnold pulled up. "Hello dear, it's very kind of you to offer to take me to the funeral." She settled herself in the front seat. "How is Barbara?"

"She's very well, thank you. The baby is kicking her a lot, which is a good sign, we're told." He smiled across at his aunt.

The church was nearly three quarters full. Mostly ladies of a similar age to Mrs B and Mrs Tattersall. Some of them Mrs B recognised from her time working at the hospital.

The vicar did his job well enough, and clearly had known Mrs Tattersall personally. They sang the hymns and shed a few tears before following the coffin out into the churchyard. Mrs B stood back. She ran a practiced eye over the group. Despite her belief that the window cleaner had been involved in her good friend's death, something was niggling at the back of her mind. She rolled the facts around in her thoughts.

Some of the people at the funeral were familiar to her. She nodded to the ones she recognised. At the graveside, and dabbing at her eyes with a pretty lace handkerchief, was Mrs Penning. She had found Mrs Tattersall and had reported her sad death. Mrs B moved to the side, where she had a better view. Mrs Penning looked different. She had made a real effort for the funeral. Mrs B thought back to her visit to Mrs Penning's home. It had been clean and tidy but, without being unkind, it had been in need of some work. The walls were crying out for a coat of paint or some wallpaper. The sofa had been covered in a blanket, probably to cover wear and tear. The lady herself had been similar to the house. Clean and tidy but nothing she wore was new or in wonderful condition. There was no shame in that. Plenty of people were in the same situation. The years of rationing and austerity had taken a toll on everyone. The war might be a memory, but the whole country was still paying the price and would be for some years to come, and not only financially. Scars ran deeper than people imagined.

Mrs B moved slowly through the crowd. Arnold had stepped away, and she could see him under a tree watching the proceedings. Each step took her closer to Mrs Penning.

The hat was clearly new. Mrs B had seen it in the hat shop in town, and had been amazed at the price, yet here it was, sitting on Mrs Penning's newly coiffed hair.

Her coat was very smart, too. Another two steps and Mrs B was next to her. The vicar was reaching the 'dust to dust, ashes to ashes' part of the graveside service. "Lovely hat." She murmured into Mrs Penning's ear. The woman turned to her, a smile playing on her lips.

"I wanted to look the best for my dear friend." She whispered back. Mrs B nodded slowly.

"Will you walk back with me? We can raise a cup of tea to her memory together." The people around the graveside walked away, breaking up into groups of two and three. Mrs B linked her arm through Mrs Penning's elbow. "I miss Mrs Tattersall so much. I'm certain that you do, too."

"Of course. Wednesdays will never be the same for me." Mrs Penning pulled out her handkerchief and dabbed at her eyes again. "I looked forward to it each week. She was such a lovely, generous friend."

"Yes. Of course." They walked into the village hall, which had been booked for the afternoon. The tea was ready to be poured, and the trays of cake were waiting for them. "Would you mind getting me a cup of tea? I'm feeling a little unwell." Mrs B sank into a chair. Mrs Penning left her there and rushed for the tea. Mrs B beckoned Arnold over. "You need to go and search her house. Here's the key we found at Mrs Tattersall's. She's involved. I'm certain of it. Something was niggling the back of my mind. It was the way the blanket was tucked in on her sofa. Just like Mrs Tattersall's bed."

"I would have to get a warrant. I need to have evidence." His exasperated tone was not one he often used with his aunt, and her eyebrows lifted towards her hairline in response.

"What if you believed that a crime might be in progress?" He nodded. "That woman is wearing a new hat, which I know cost a fortune, and a new coat. She has come into a sum of money recently, and I believe it came from under Mrs Tattersall's mattress. Please, just take the key and have a look. If I am wrong, then there is no harm done. If I am right, then you have an accomplice for the window cleaner. Or perhaps you are holding an innocent man."

He huffed and sighed, but he took the key and rushed off to do what was needed. Mrs Penning returned with tea and cake. "Here you are. You look absolutely done in."

"I have to admit that the funeral has made me feel very much weakened. I trust in the restorative power of this wonderful tea. You are very kind to bring it to me. I am not given to moments of weakness like this. I apologise." Mrs B sipped the tea.

"No, for heaven's sake, you have nothing to apologise for. Mrs Tattersall was such a lovely woman. We are all deeply affected by her passing." She reached across and patted Mrs B's arm. "Where did your lovely nephew go?"

"Oh, his wife is pregnant, and he is the most attentive father to be. He checks in on her all through the day." She sat back, fanning her face with her hand. "My, my; I am quite overheated. Is it particularly warm in here?"

The crowd began to thin out an hour later. Gradually, the women bid each other farewell, some shaking hands, other embracing, sharing their loss. Only half a dozen were left, when Arnold arrived, with two uniformed officers.

"Mrs Penning, I have reason to believe that you were involved in the murder of Mrs Tattersall. I need you to please come with me to the police station to answer my questions." He gestured to the two officers, who took her by the arms and led her away.

"You found enough to arrest her, then?" Mrs B walked to the door with Arnold.

"Yes. More than enough. Thank you, Auntie." He leaned down to kiss her cheek.

"I'll get the bus home. You go and do your duty. I shall never forgive myself for nearly missing the truth." She patted his arm.

"What made you suspect her?" He offered her his elbow.

"When she told me about the window cleaner, she was relieved, as though she had put down something heavy. I knew she had a key to the house, and she said that she had seen Mrs Tattersall leaving that morning. I believe she slipped into the house and helped herself from Mrs Tattersall's savings regularly. That day, for whatever reason, she was caught. The window cleaner gave her a good scapegoat, and I fell for it. It was so simple to move the chest of drawers and leave the window open. Honestly, Arnold. I have been so stupid. I could kick myself. That blanket was the best clue of all, though." She shook her head, angry at herself.

"I would not have even thought of looking in her direction without your suggestion." He smiled down at her. "Uniform will take her in. Come on, I'll drop you home."

Together, they walked out of the church hall and into the evening sunshine. Mrs B could go home, safe in the knowledge that she had done the right thing by her friend.

22.
Mrs B and the blue ribbon

"Mrs B? Mrs B?" Mrs Lennet leaned in through the back door.

"Mrs Lennet? Good afternoon to you. Are you well?" Mrs B dusted her hands on her apron. "I am in the middle of making my pie for the village fayre. The pastry is in the pantry. It is the perfect time to stop for a cup of tea." She filled the kettle and set it on the top of the oven.

"Thank you. I will admit that I am absolutely in need of a cup of tea. Patricia is driving me insane, and the village fayre is tomorrow. My husband has been called away and will be unable to declare the fayre open, and on top of that, I am feeling quite unwell. Thank you, a cup of tea would be wonderful." She slipped into a seat at the kitchen table.

"Oh, my goodness, Mrs Lennet. Tell me first, in what way are you feeling unwell?" She sat down at the table opposite her guest.

"I, well... it's a little personal. May I trust I

can rely on your discretion?" Mrs Lennet's eyes slipped sideways, but caught Mrs B's swift nod. "I am suffering, hot sweats, as though I am on fire. I imagine I am infected with a fever." She fanned her face with her hand.

"You are hot and sweaty, particularly at night. Your temperature soars without warning. You feel entirely out of control?" Mrs Lennet nodded. "And you are no longer visited by the curse of women each month?" Mrs Lennet's eyebrows leaped towards her hairline. "It's the change. Perfectly normal. You are not unwell. You are a woman." Mrs B patted the other woman's hands and went to the kettle, which was whistling. She brought the teapot back and set it between them to brew. "Now. Tell me about Patricia!"

"Oh, Mrs B. Of course, you're right! I am so stupid." Mrs Lennet shook her head. "Patricia. Yes. She is doing nothing to help. She sits with her feet up, eating chocolates and shouting her demands. I am exhausted."

"Right. Leave Patricia to me. Anything else?" Mrs B poured tea into their cups. "Your husband may not be there to open the fayre, but you will, or if you are uncomfortable with that, the reverend Chambers will step in, I am certain." She pushed a cup of tea towards Mrs Lennet. "Drink your tea, and please stop worrying. It will be perfectly fine." Her smile was genuine and warm. "Trust me."

****

"Good afternoon, Patricia. I hope you remember me?" Mrs B smoothed her skirt over her knees as she sat down.

"Mrs B? Oh my, what on earth are you doing here? Did my mother-in-law send you?" Patricia ran a nail file across her fingernails.

"No. She asked me not to come. I, on the other hand, was determined. I felt it necessary to tell you the truth that they have been hiding from you." She stood up. "However, I see how things are with you, and I may have misjudged the situation. You may, as they told me, need your rest." Mrs B stood up and checked her jacket was properly fastened.

"What is it they are keeping from me?" Patricia sat up straighter, her perfectly plucked eyebrows pushing together.

"No no. I was wrong to come to see you today." Mrs B smiled a gentle smile.

"Tell me! You are entirely infuriating!" Patricia pushed her legs off the sofa.

"Oh dear. I had no wish to upset you. It's only that your husband confided in his mother that sitting on the sofa has made your calves and ankles swell a little. He misses the way they were before." Mrs B rolled her lips together. "Please ignore me. I am a stupid old woman."

"Fat ankles. Oh, for heaven's sake." She almost jumped from the sofa. "I love that man, but he is a complete imbecile." She pushed her hair back out of her face. "I was always intending to go to the village fayre, anyway. I love the local yokels and all that. It's such a scream." She marched from the room with determination in every step. Mrs B allowed herself a small smile.

****

The pies were lined up, as were the marrows and the jars of pickles and the jams and marmalades. The Reverend Chambers made an opening speech, which was far too long. Mrs Gartree won the prize for her plum jam. Mrs Goffey won second prize for her pie, which upset her when Mrs B took first.

The beer tent did a roaring trade, and everyone remarked on how happy Richard and Patricia looked together.

"You are a marvel, Mrs B! Patricia is off the sofa. I have stopped worrying about the mysterious ailments I was suffering, and you won the pie contest." Mrs Lennet's smile was warm and genuine. "Ah, Mrs Goffey, how lovely to see you. I understand your pie was rather wonderful. The judge told me he struggled to decide." She smiled her warmest smile.

"Indeed! I am not entirely certain that the competition is fair. It seems to me that those who are friends with the highest in the locality gain an advantage." Mrs Goffey stamped away; her head held high.

"All entries are entirely anonymous. I can assure you." Mrs Lennet's hand fluttered to her throat. "I am so sorry, Mrs B. The accusation is unfair and unfounded."

"Perish the thought, Mrs Lennet. Mrs Goffey is cross, but that is nothing new!" Both women laughed. When they turned and saw Mrs Goffey's face contract into a snarl, they struggled to contain their giggles.

The Lennet's car drove up the driveway, slowing to a stop where Mrs Lennet and Mrs B were standing. Mr Lennet opened the door before the driver could get there. "Sorry darling. I tried to get here to open the fayre. Oh, Mrs B, good afternoon to you. I see you have a blue ribbon. Congratulations!" Mrs Lennet nodded to Mrs B and allowed her husband to lead her away to greet the rest of the villagers.

Mrs B stood back. Arnold and Barbara joined her. "Well done, Auntie. I always thought you made the best pies." Arnold kissed her cheek.

"Now then, you two. I suggest we find our way to the refreshments tent. There is tea and cake waiting for us." Mrs B linked an arm through each of their elbows and they made their way through the crowds. "Nothing like a cup of tea."

In the tent, Mrs B was making a choice between a Victoria sandwich and a chocolate cake. She overhead Mrs Goffey telling Mrs Gartree that she had been cheated out of first place for her pie, by Mrs B's friends in high places. The anger that rushed through her was for her own impugned integrity, but also for Mrs Lennet, who also stood accused.

Arnold collected the tea and cake for them all, carrying the tray towards an empty table. Barbara followed him, both of them unaware of the argument which was about to take place.

"You have no business saying that. Mrs B is the most honourable person I have ever met. You, however, are a rude and obnoxious woman who cannot make pastry." Mrs Gartree's voice rose and her lips pulled back from her teeth in a snarl. "You are a poor loser, and worse, a sniper. Good day to you."

Mrs B laughed to herself, and made her way to the table, where Arnold was already pouring tea for the three of them. "Auntie! I wondered where you had gone to." He pushed a slice of chocolate cake towards her.

"I was being nosy and listening in to a conversation." She confided.

"Ah, you know, eavesdroppers seldom hear good things about themselves." Barbara laughed. Mrs B joined in, but she knew something that they did not.

23.

Mrs B and the surprise

The windows shone. Mrs B rubbed and polished. When Arnold stopped his car outside in the lane, she was smiling and waving before he was out of the car.

"Arnold! Hello." She held the front door open.

"Auntie. How are you?" He leaned down to kiss her cheek.

"How lovely to see you. I was just about to make a cup of tea. Perfect timing." He followed her into the kitchen. "I thought you would come over tomorrow. What a lovely surprise."

"The thing is, Auntie. I have some news. Mrs Penning has admitted it. She will have to go to court for sentencing, and she will go to prison." He accepted a cup and saucer from her.

"I find no joy in that. She killed my dear friend, but her desperation drove her to it." She rolled her lips over each other. "Perish the thought that we should forget that anyone can make a mistake." She sipped her tea. "I made a mistake thinking that the window cleaner had been involved after all."

"The thing is, Auntie. I was called in to see the Chief Inspector. He's really quite scary." He laughed. "I received a commendation for the investigation into Mrs Tattershall's death. The thing is that it was all your work, not mine. I told him exactly what happened." He met her eyes. "The Chief Inspector has asked to have a meeting with you."

"Me? Oh." She lifted her cup to her lips but put it down again without drinking. "Why?"

"I think he would want to tell you himself. It's certainly above my remit to speak on his behalf." He laughed and accepted one of the biscuits Mrs B offered.

The knock on the front door startled her. "Well, there we are, another visitor." She stood up and went to see who was there. "Hello?"

"Mrs B? My young Detective Sargeant gave me your address. I hope that you will allow me to have a few minutes of your time?" He had to stoop to keep his head from hitting the door frame when he stepped inside.

"William Hunton?" She stood with her hand at her throat.

"Yes. Oh my. The years have been kinder to you

than to me, I think. How are you? How is Letty?" He smiled widely at her. "It is so very good to see you." She led him through to the kitchen. Arnold jumped to his feet and stood to attention. His courtesy waved away by Chief Inspector Hunton.

Mrs B poured a cup of tea and pushed a jug of milk and the sugar bowl to him.

"This is a surprise. Letty is well, thank you. She had a son, who is a promising Detective Sargeant currently." She smiled, pushing the plate of biscuits across the table.

"Ah yes. Down to business first. I understand that Mrs Tattersall was a dear friend of yours. I offer my condolences." They nodded their understanding together. "Your skills have helped us to solve the crime, and as you will be aware, money is tight. It might be very helpful to the local police force to ask for your help from time to time. Would you consider assisting us?" He bit into a biscuit. "These are delicious."

"Well now. I am not sure how much help I would be. If you think I might... I would be very proud to assist." Marmalade the kitten wound his tiny body around her ankles. She reached down to run her hand over his flank. Her smile was wide. "I do love puzzles."

"Wonderful. This is going to be so helpful." He directed his attention back to Arnold. "You will liaise between the investigating officer and your aunt when required." His voice was back to his normal order barking tone. He turned back to Mrs B. "Thank you for the tea. May I take another of these marvellous biscuits?"

Mrs B fetched a piece of greaseproof paper and wrapped the rest of the biscuits on the plate for him to take with him.

"It has been lovely to see you, Will." She walked him to the door and passed him the package.

"I will be back to visit soon, if I may?" He took both her hands in his before accepting the package.

When she had closed the front door behind him, Arnold met her glance with raised eyebrows. "Will you tell me how you know him?"

"Perish the thought. He was a wonderful friend many years ago. He is; however, your superior officer, and it would be inappropriate for me to undermine his authority in any way." She patted Arnold's hand. "Have another cup of tea, dear."

24.

Mrs B to the rescue

"Mrs B! Mrs B!" She was polishing the last desk in the front office of the Little Mellington Police Station. The sight of the distraught vicar with his hair sticking up at strange angles was enough to have the young officer at the desk at sixes and sevens.

"Sir, please take a seat." He spread his hands in the air. "Please."

"Reverend Chambers? Whatever is the matter?" Mrs B put down her duster. The young constable breathed a sigh of relief.

"It's my wife. Please come. I don't know what to do!" His hands grabbed handfuls of his hair. "She's not making any sense."

Mrs B nodded and rushed to meet him, pulling the door closed behind her. "Come along Reverend Chambers." She pulled on her coat and bustled out of the police station. The vicarage was on the other side of the road, next to the church. The front door stood open. "Mrs

Chambers? Are you at home?" The sound that greeted them was mostly a wail. "Oh dear, Mrs Chambers." Mrs B knelt on the floor next to her. "What happened?"

"Mrs B? Thank God." Her breath was coming in short gasps and pants. "The baby is coming."

"Reverend Chambers, I am not a midwife. Mrs Chambers needs some professional help." Mrs B turned towards him; her eyes were wide with fear.

"The doctor's on his way. You are, however, the calmest and most resourceful person I could think of. Please help her." He sank into a chair.

"Mrs Chambers." Mrs B grabbed her hand. "Hold on to me. Look into my eyes. We can do this together." Mrs B shook her hand until she had the other woman's attention. "Now then. What do we know about having babies? Between us, I mean." Mrs B laughed. A gentle sound. "Tell me what you need me to do."

"I'm already calmer. These pains are like waves. What I need you to do is help me keep going through the ups and downs." Mrs Chambers wrapped her fingers around Mrs B's.

In the living room, with the afternoon shadows gathering around them, Mrs B supported the woman who had become a friend. Her arm holding tightly around the shoulders that heaved with effort. Each contraction that hit her body seemed to last longer, to consume more of her energy. Together, they breathed through it all.

"You are doing so well. Reverend Chambers, your wife might need a glass of water, perhaps?" The vicar sprang to his feet, grateful to have a purpose.

"While he's gone, listen to me. The baby is too early. Promise me you will do everything to save the baby. No matter what. If it means a choice between me and the child." Her eyes locked with Mrs B's. "Choose the child."

"There is no way that it will come to that. You are worried, but you will be fine." The front door opened, and the doctor arrived. He brought with him professional competence and confidence. Mrs B shared a smile with Mrs Chambers. "The doctor is here. It will be fine now." Mrs B rested back on her heels. The weight of responsibility lifted from her shoulders.

"Good God. What are you doing on the floor, woman? Come along. You should be in bed." Both women turned to glare at him. "It's a simple enough request."

"Doctor, I have no experience with these things, but perhaps asking Mrs Chambers to climb the stairs might be a little unfair." Mrs B held out her hand to Mrs Chambers, who was recovering from her most recent contraction.

"You are absolutely correct." The doctor smiled at both the women. "You have no way of understanding this process. Now if you would leave me to my patient." He left his bag on the armchair and leant down to Mrs Chambers. "Come along now."

"Nooooo!" Mrs Chambers screamed. "I need Mrs B to stay." She scrabbled to reach for Mrs B's hand. "Please stay with me."

"Of course, your friend can stay, if you wish. We need to check how far along you are and how the baby is doing. Best place for you is your comfortable bed." He patted the back of her hand.

A contraction gripped her, and her fingers wrapped around the doctor's hand. Her breath came in gasps. "You're doing wonderfully. I'm sure the doctor agrees." At that moment, the doctor was cradling his hand.

Mrs B stepped out into the hallway to allow the doctor to examine Mrs Chambers. "Mrs B? Thank goodness. Is everything alright?" The vicar seemed almost as distraught as his wife.

"Reverend Chambers. I am no expert, but the doctor is with her, and I am certain that she is in expert hands." A squeal from the living room had them both staring at the door.

"I had better get back to her. Perhaps put the kettle on? A cup of tea might be welcome. I shall come out and let you know what is happening." She patted his hand and watched him walk away to the kitchen.

"Mrs B, I am glad that you are back. If you could hold Mrs Chambers' hand and support her shoulders, we are very close to meeting this baby." He smiled up at Mrs Chambers. "When the next contraction starts, I want you to push with everything you have. All your strength." Mrs B wrapped her arm around Mrs Chambers' shoulders.

When the contraction began, Mrs Chambers began to wail. She gritted her teeth and gripped Mrs B's hand. Everything about her was pushing. Her feet braced against the sofa.

"Nearly there Mrs Chambers." Mrs B reassured.

"Very close now. Ready to go? Push!" The doctor was very close to shouting.

The first cry the baby made was small, but it lit the room up. The doctor lifted the tiny baby to pass him to Mrs Chambers. "Here he is, the little one who has been causing all the trouble." He smiled, passing the baby into his mother's waiting arms.

"Oh my! I have seen nothing so wonderful in my life." It surprised Mrs B to find tears on her face. "I think you might need a cup of tea, my dear Mrs Chambers." The doctor nodded in agreement.

Mrs B found the Reverend in the kitchen. "Mrs B? Is everything alright?"

"Reverend Chambers. Everything is a good deal better than alright." She reached out for his arm. "You are a father. Congratulations!"

"Oh. Oh, well. I am... well, of course. Is my wife well?" He was gripping the back of one of the kitchen chairs.

"Mother and baby are both doing very well. I am going to make a cup of tea for her and for the doctor. I believe that they have earned it." She checked the kettle and relit the gas beneath it. The water quickly came to a boil, and she poured it into the teapot. The reverend slumped into a chair and watched while she found cups, milk, and sugar. Once she had left the reverend with a cup, she carried a tray back into the living room. "Hello. I think you have both earned a cup of tea. I wonder, are you ready for your husband to meet your son?"

"Yes, please. Thank you, Mrs B. You have been a good friend today." Mrs Chambers was sitting up with the baby wrapped in the cardigan she had taken off earlier. His tiny hands balled into fists.

"I will arrange for the district nurse to pop in and see you later, Mrs Chambers. Congratulations. He's wonderful." The doctor packed up his bag and opened the door. "Reverend Chambers, you need to come and meet your son." He stood back to let the other man in. "I've checked him over and he's fine. Your wife did a grand job. You should be very proud of her."

"I shall leave you to it. I am so entirely happy for you both." Mrs B smiled at the little family on the floor.

The doctor opened the gate to let himself out of the front garden, then stopped and turned to Mrs B. "I'm sorry, I was rude earlier. I've never delivered a baby on my own before. Nerves! No excuse, but it's true. You were very good, very calm. Thank you." He waited for her to join him in the lane.

"You did a good job." She smiled, feeling her chest tight with emotion. "It was an astounding thing to see. Thank you for letting me stay."

"Honestly, you calmed me as much as you did the patient." He shrugged, and she realised how young he was.

"Oh no, you were entirely professional. I thought you handled it extremely well." He needed the reassurance. She watched him smile slowly to himself, taking the praise, accepting the boost to his confidence.

"You're a wonder, Mrs B!" He smiled down at her. "We should have a Mrs B statue in the village."

"Perish the thought!" Mrs B patted his arm gently and walked away.

Back at her cottage, she sat down at the table and thought about her afternoon. The miracle that she had seen and been involved in had been a revelation. The tiny kitten yawned and stretched. He padded across the kitchen floor.

"Hello little one." She picked him up and tucked him into the crook of her arm. "It's all about love, isn't it, Marmalade? That's the only thing that matters." He nuzzled his head into her. Clearly, he agreed.

25.

Mrs B's first case

"Auntie? I'm so glad that you're at home." Arnold slipped into the kitchen through the back door. "I've been sent to see you. There's a case that needs your skills." He ran his hands around the brim of his hat. "That was what I was told by the Chief Inspector."

"Oh well, in that case!" Mrs B beamed at him. "I shall have to put my hat on and feed marmalade." The little kitten padded into the kitchen.

"He knows his name." Arnold laughed. After helping his aunt into the car, he looked across at her. "Barbara is fed up with being pregnant. She's impatient for the baby to arrive. I wondered if she might come up and have a few days with you next week. Her mother is being a little difficult."

"Barbara is always welcome. I'd love her company." Mrs B smiled. It would be fun to have Barbara to stay.

The house he parked outside was tidy, the paint was fresh on the windows, and Mrs B noticed that the front step had been scrubbed recently.

It was a small house, with a patch of neatly

tended garden. Tidy, but no imagination. That was the impression Mrs B gained from the outside.

Arnold checked for the keys in his pocket and opened the front door. "Here we are." He stood back and allowed her to walk in first.

"What am I looking for?" She watched his face.

"Anything that is out of place, I think." He shrugged. She nodded.

She walked through the kitchen, living room, and then up the stairs and into the small bedrooms and the bathroom. "A man and a woman lived here. No children. They had a dog. A small one." He took notes. "The man had lost a good deal of weight recently, perhaps, and the woman was…" An image she recalled for time sitting in the bus station a few months before; of a woman in heels and too much lipstick crossed her mind. "No, I am jumping to conclusions. Let's look further."

Arnold followed her up the stairs and went through the cupboards and drawers, and then through the bathroom. She checked the kitchen and then turned to Arnold. "Right. I think there were two of them living here, and one has gone, moved away or whatever, leaving the other one here alone. If I had to hazard a guess, I would say that the woman was here after the man left." She waited for his reaction.

"Yes. The gentleman, Mr Richardson, who owned the property, stopped going to work three months ago. He continued to take money out of his savings, however, and did not inform the bank that he had moved. His wife was left here alone for that time, and then put the house up for sale. The husband had signed all the paperwork she produced, although neither the solicitor nor the sales agent met him. When the time came to sign the final papers, she said she would take them to him, and return them signed, but the solicitor insisted on meeting directly with him. Something about her reaction worried him. The woman is currently on the run." Arnold closed his notebook.

"But he attended at the bank to withdraw the money?" Mrs B sat down on the stairs to think about it and watched Arnold nod his head. "Did the staff at the bank know him personally? Sufficiently well to recognise him?"

"I would have to check." Arnold ran his finger down the page of notes. "Nothing in here to say one way or the other."

"Right then, I will need to know. Can you also find out how much younger his wife was? I think it would be a considerable age gap." She turned away.

"Yes, she is nearly twenty years younger." He read from his notes.

"Was, I believe, not is." Mrs B shook her head sadly. "If I am correct, then her husband is dead, and unless you find her, she might be too." She slapped her hands on her knees and stood up. "I shall wait to hear from you, Arnold, and in the meantime, I shall do some thinking."

26.

Mrs B's first case – part two

"Sorry to keep you waiting, Auntie. I wanted to be thorough. The staff in the bank had not met Mr Richardson before. Mrs Richardson had made the payments into his savings account. He had opened the bank account at their branch in town." Arnold made himself comfortable in the driver's seat. "Where to?"

"We need to go to the seaside. I just hope that we are in time." Mrs B handed him a postcard. There was nothing written on the back, but the picture showed Beachy Head. "Eastbourne, here we come." She smiled across at him.

"Just because of this postcard?" He tipped his head to one side in confusion.

"No, there were so many things that pointed us there. You really have to look with your eyes open, Arnold." She tutted with annoyance.

Like all seaside towns, Eastbourne is at its best in the sunshine. A light drizzle was falling when they arrived. People took shelter where they could and watched the sea. Arnold drove through the town and parked the car. "Any ideas where to look?"

"Oh yes. Come along." Mrs B pushed the door open and pulled her coat a little closer. Arnold offered her his arm, and she slipped her hand through it. The pier loomed ahead of them, the lights shining through the drizzle. "Here we are. I imagine that if we are lucky, we will find what we are looking for before the end of the pier."

The boards of the pier creaked, and the wind picked up the further from the land they walked. The tea room halfway up the pier was empty, but there were still shops and, of course, the theatre at the end. Arnold knew that there was no point asking where they were going. He would have to wait and see.

The theatre was dark. Next show, according to the sign, would be at six-thirty. Mrs B pushed open the glass door. The brass plate was cold under her hand. Arnold followed her to the side of the stage and through a door into a dimly lit corridor.

Doors led off to the left and right. Mrs B began by opening each one. Inside each one, she checked before moving on. In the third one on the left, she found what she was looking for. "Ah, here you are, Mrs Richardson. I'm so very pleased that we found you in time."

"In time for what?" She shook her blonde curls and carried on applying her lipstick.

"Well, now, I think you have a few questions to answer for the police. But worse than that, I believe that your life is in danger." Mrs B settled herself into the chair next to Mrs Richardson. "How is the show going?"

"It's alright. How did you know to find me here?" She smoothed her hand over her hair, her focus entirely on the mirror.

"There were show bills all over your house, framed. You were never a headliner, but your name was on there, was it not?" Mrs B smiled to soften the words. "All the shows promoted by Mr Johnny Edwards. He was the one who came looking for you, I presume."

"Johnny was a good friend. He always looked after his girls. All of us. He wanted me to come back. I agreed, and he said he'd speak to my husband for me. He did, and Derek agreed to let me go back to work." She ran a soft finger under her eye.

"Derek told you that? Your husband said that to you?" Mrs B leaned closer. "I would have thought that he would miss you, being away so much of the time."

"Yes, I did too, but Johnny spoke to him, and Derek moved out that day. Told Johnny to wish me luck, and he'd see me through the footlights.

Said he had no right to deprive my public of their star." Her voice was honey sweet.

"He left some of his clothes, though?" Mrs B waited for the nod of confirmation. "Did Johnny tell you that Derek had agreed to sell the house? That was very generous."

"He said I should take half and put the rest in his savings account. Derek is a very kind man, but not very exciting. Johnny put me straight back on wages. I was tickled pink. The solicitor was difficult about everything, so Johnny said to leave it for a little while and we would talk to a solicitor he knew." She checked her nails, which shone with a coat of bright red polish.

"Yes. That was when you moved back here, was it? I suppose Johnny was staying at your house to help you with everything?" Mrs B nodded along with the story. Mrs Richardson joined in. "How has it been with Johnny since you came back to the theatre?" A shadow passed over Mrs Richardson's eyes.

"He's gone to collect Phyllis. We worked together before we were married, and he wanted us to revive the act." Mrs Richardson's lower lip stuck out a little.

"Did Phyllis marry too?" Mrs B reached out her hand and held onto the younger woman's arm.

"Yes. Johnny left this morning to see if he could get her back. He always said, marry well, my lovely girls. A good marriage is an investment." She turned a practiced smile on Mrs B.

"Do you have an address for Phyllis?" Mrs B's brows were furrowed.

"Yes, she only lives just up the coast. I can show you where if you want. I have an hour before the next show." She cast an appraising eye over Arnold and smiled her best smile at him.

They parked outside a house in a nice residential area. Mrs B and Arnold asked that Mrs Richardson stay in the car for a moment, and made their way to the front door. The man who opened the door was of a thin and wiry build. "Mr Edwards? Oh, I knew it was you. I've seen so many of your shows. I wonder if you might be so kind as to give me your autograph?" Mrs B's most innocent smile adorned her face.

"Oh, yes. Of course." He patted his hands over his pockets, and brought out a very flattering photograph, which was already signed. "Here you are."

"I wonder if I might have a moment of your time too?" Arnold slapped the handcuffs onto Johnny Edward's wrists and pulled him back into the house.

In the living room, an older man seemed to be asleep on the armchair. "Check the cup!" Mrs B told Arnold.

"There's powder, undissolved in the bottom." He raised an eyebrow at Johnny Edwards, who had sunk into the other chair.

"Mr Edwards, you will need to come down to the station to answer some questions about all this." Arnold loaded him into the car.

"Go! I'll phone for an ambulance for this gentleman, and go to the hospital with him. I should be grateful if you would collect me later." She ran to the telephone box and telephoned the ambulance.

Mrs B arrived at the hospital with the bells ringing in her ears, and the teacup firmly gripped in her hand.

"Arnold? Oh, thank goodness. What happened with Mr Edwards?" Mrs B was grateful to see him. The chairs in the corridor were uncomfortable.

"Mr Edwards is refusing to admit anything except visiting an old friend." Arnold shook his head.

"Phyllis arrived twenty minutes ago. Her husband will be fine. The laboratory has tested the powder in the cup and they say it is a strong sedative. Not a name I recognised." She passed him the paper. "It's on here."

"Ah. Brilliant. Thank you, Auntie!" He offered her his arm and took her back to the police station with him.

Johnny Edwards had three things in his pockets when he was arrested: his wallet, a betting slip, and a bottle of pills. The name on the bottle matched the paperwork from the laboratory. There would be further investigations carried out, but the fact that he had encouraged both women to return to their somewhat lacklustre careers shortly before one husband went missing and another was drugged suggested that he had at least planned that much. It gave them a starting point.

It had been a long day, and Mrs B's feet were aching. She longed to slip her shoes off and put her feet into her slippers. When Arnold dropped her back to the house, she waved him off and released her feet from the tight shoes. Marmalade purred his happiness at her return. She made a cup of tea for herself and gave the kitten his dinner. She propped her feet up on a footstool and turned her face to the photograph on the mantlepiece. "We solved the puzzle, my love. Would you mind me talking to Will Hunton after all these years? I wonder. I am a little long in the tooth for it to be a worry, and so is he. Nothing worth thinking about." She sipped her tea. "I miss you." She ran her finger down the side of the face in the frame. "Every day."

Marmalade mewed at her feet, and she lifted him onto her lap. Her hands smoothed down his thick fur, and she smiled to herself. "Good boy,

Marmalade."

27.

Mrs B collects

Barbara had come to stay with Mrs B for a few days. They had both thoroughly enjoyed the time.

"You are spoiling me. I'll get used to being so well looked after." Barbara sipped from the cup of tea. "Delicious."

"Oh well, it's wonderful for me to have you here. I have missed you since you and Arnold married." Mrs B patted her hand. The bees were buzzing in the flowers, and the sun was hot in the small garden.

The car pulled up outside the garden wall, and Mrs B pushed herself out of the chair. "Hello?"

"Officer?" The young constable looked nervously over the wall. "Can I help?"

"This is the address I have." He checked in his notebook. "For Detective Sergeant Birch."

"Oh, my God. What happened to Arnold?" Barbara jumped to her feet.

"There is a situation. A bank robbery in progress and he is caught up in it." The constable blushed to the roots of his hair. "We believe he is safe, but the Chief Inspector himself told me to come and let you know, and bring you to the station if you would like to wait there."

"You can tell us about it on the way." Mrs B reached to support Barbara. Together, they climbed into the car, and the constable drove them into town. "Which bank?"

"The one at the end of the town." He pulled into the station and showed them into a small room.

"Barbara. I believe I may be able to find out a little more. Will you be alright to wait here?" Mrs B waited for Barbara's nod. "Right." She opened the door and asked the police woman outside to keep Barbara company.

The bus was pulling in when she walked out into the street. It took her to the other side of the town, and it was a short walk from there to her destination.

She stood on the pavement. A little boy pushed his way through the double doors. He collected the glasses people had left on the small tables and the window sills. "Excuse me?"

"Yes?" He had a stack of glasses in his hands.

"Do you know who Tommy McKinley is?" The boy nodded. "Is he in the pub?"

"I can't discuss our customers with anyone else. That's one of Mrs Parker's rules. I'll be in big trouble if I do." He turned away.

"Very well." Mrs B had never set foot inside a public house. This was no time to be a prim old lady. She stepped forward, her hand outstretched for the door.

"You're not going inside, are you, lady?" It scandalized the child.

"If you refuse to tell me whether Mr McKinley is inside, I have no choice." She straightened her back and stepped forward.

"Wait. I'll ask if he's in there." He fixed her with a fierce glare. "Wait here." A minute later, the doors swung open.

"You." Mr McKinley stood in the doorway.

"Yes. It is me. You told me you owed me a favour, and I have come to collect." She hugged her arms to each other.

"I'll think about it. What do you want?" He leaned against the window sill and fixed her with a stare.

"My nephew is in danger. He walked into a bank robbery. The bank in the town. I believe that you can make them let him and all the other people who are caught up in it go free." He shook his head.

"What makes you think I know who is there? Or

that they would listen to me if I did?" He turned away from her.

"You and your family are involved in everything that happens in this town. Mr McKinley. You are powerful. I know you can stop this. You promised me a favour. Please." She pushed her hands together to plead.

"I can't go down there. I'd be arrested on the spot." He crumpled his forehead.

"There is a telephone in the bank, and a telephone box over there." She pointed across the street. "I have some coins."

"If I do it. They will all be in the cells within an hour. It's a lot to ask." He ran his hand over his face.

"Ah, but they may not be. I have a plan." She smiled. "As you will see, I'm not much of an artist, but this may help." She passed him a sheet of paper, carefully folded to hide the sketch. His expression was puzzled for a moment, before he realised her meaning, and a smile spread across his features.

"Right, leave it with me." He turned on his heel. "We're straight now? I don't owe you anything?"

"Perish the thought, Mr McKinley."

......

"It was the strangest thing, Auntie. The telephone rang in the bank, and then the men untied the hands of one lady who works there. They told her to untie everyone. It took a while, and when we were all free, I was able to unlock the front door and we all left the building." He shook his head. "Nobody can work out where the bank robbers went. There were officers at every door. Very odd indeed."

"Yes, it is." Mrs B placed another cup of tea and a slice of cake in front of him. "I am just glad that you are safe."

The following day, when a young constable went up into the loft; he found the hole through the loft wall through which the men had escaped into the bakery next door. That explained the mystery. Almost.

28.

Mrs B visits

"Auntie, you don't have to go. Just because she has sent you a letter, and a visiting order. You still have a choice." Arnold accepted the cup of tea. "It might be quite upsetting."

"I will go. It's a responsibility to Mrs Tattershall. I will hear what Mrs Penning has to say." Her tone left no room for discussion.

"I will drive you. There are papers that I need to collect from the prison, anyway." Arnold drank the last of his tea and held open the door.

The building was old and smelled unpleasant. Mrs B would not have admitted it to Arnold, but she was a little uncomfortable, perhaps even scared. That was unlike her, and she straightened her shoulders. She joined the rest of the visitors, who walked through and listened to the clang of the gates closing behind them. Arnold left her to it.

"Mrs Penning?" Mrs B was surprised by the change in the woman. Her hair was scraped back, and she had lost a good deal of weight.

"Thank you for coming Mrs B. I wanted to apologise. It was an accident. I know she was your friend. The stealing was no accident. I had been helping myself for a little while. I knew it was wrong, but I had nothing. Mr Penning decided not to come back from the war. He's still alive and living in Yorkshire somewhere. I have no money. Nothing. When I saw that cash, I couldn't resist. Just a little, a ten-bob note here and there." She worried at her sleeve with stretched, tight fingers.

"You could have gone out to work, just as Mrs Tattershall did." Mrs B kept her voice low.

"Scrubbing floors? Not all of us can do that." She sniffed.

"I wanted you to know. I never meant her any harm. She went off to work that morning. I watched her go. Then I slipped in and went upstairs. She must have forgotten something, and she came back. I hid, but she noticed something was wrong, and started looking for me. Panic made me strong. I pushed her and ran. I heard the noise, her head hitting the bed. That stopped me on the stairs and I crept back up. She was already dead." Mrs Penning ran her finger under her eye.

"What did you do next? Step over her body to steal more cash, I suppose?" Mrs B snapped back at her.

"Oh, I know. Yes. I have behaved badly. You can stand in your house, with your widow's pension. You can judge me as a bad person. But do you know what my life was like?" Mrs Penning rested her hands on the table and took a breath. "I have arranged something with the police. I have told them everything. They will not ask the judge for hanging. I will live happily in here, three meals a day. No bills to pay. I have bed and board." She laughed, but there was no humour.

"What do you do all day?" Mrs B sat forward, intrigued. "You're clever. You convinced everyone that the window cleaner had done it."

Mrs Penning leaned her hands on the table. "I'm clever because I fooled you? You're a bit big for your boots, aren't you?"

Mrs B brushed the words away, like an annoying fly. "You could do something though, learn to paint or make pottery?"

"I should think I could, if I was at a fancy hotel, instead of a prison." She laughed, then leaned forward. "I know what I did was wrong. All the way from the stealing, to the accident, but I was desperate." She balled her fingers up into fists. "I talked to Mrs Tattershall about it, you know. She said she would get me some customers. She was always being offered more work than she could do."

"That would have been better than stealing." Mrs B rested her face in her hand.

"I'm not that sort of person. To scrub other people's floors, and do their dirty washing." Mrs Penning made a face, as though she had smelled something unpleasant.

"No? It seems to me that you will wash the prison floors in here." Mrs B pushed back her seat. "I wish you every joy with that." She walked away and waited for the guard to open the door.

Outside in the fresh air, Mrs B ran over the conversation in her head. She had been cruel. Not to the extent that Mrs Penning had been, but that was no excuse. Arnold had been called away, and she was grateful for the time to think. When the bus arrived, she hopped on and paid her fare. The route from the bus stop to her house took her past a small shop which sold toys. The idea that had been bouncing around in her head took her through the door.

"Good afternoon, Mrs B. May I help?" Mrs B took in the smiling woman on the other side of the counter.

"Mrs Gartree? Is that you?" Mrs B peered a little more closely.

"Yes. I have started working here two afternoons a week. I am loving it." She stood a little taller. "How may I help you today?"

"I wondered if you had any of those painting sets?"

"Oh yes! We have. I will fetch a selection for you to look at. They range from the basic paints and brushes. Then more fancy ones. Oh, and these are ones where you paint the colours in the box with the number in it. It's a new idea, called painting by numbers. It comes with everything that you need." Mrs Gartree laid the boxes on the counter.

"That is perfect. It might help her. Could you wrap it?" Mrs Gartree nodded and fetched paper and string. "You have been very helpful. Thank you, Mrs Gartree. You are looking very well." The two women exchanged smiles, and Mrs B wrote Mrs Penning's name and the address of the prison on the front.

"It was a pleasure to see you, Mrs B." Mrs Gartree smiled and waved.

Mrs B went straight to the post office and sent off the parcel before she could change her mind. It was rare for Mrs B to lose her temper and it had left her feeling uncomfortable with herself. If the situation had been different, she would have gone back to make a proper apology. Mrs Penning's imprisonment made that more difficult. The gift maybe would have to express regret on her behalf.

Marmalade was waiting impatiently in the

kitchen. "Hello Mr Marmalade. I suppose you would like something to eat?" She stroked her fingers through the white and ginger fur. "Come along then." She put down the food and watched the little kitten eat. "I have behaved rather rashly. I should have been quiet and let Mrs Penning say her piece." She huffed a sigh. "I am too old to still be learning to control my temper." The kitten sat back and looked at her. "Good boy Marmalade." She reached down and stroked him. "I think I need a cup of tea."

Within a few minutes, Mrs B was sipping from a cup of tea, while Marmalade curled into a contented ball and fell asleep purring.

29.

Mrs B meets a new friend

Barbara was pacing the floor when Mrs B arrived home from work. "Oh, Auntie, I thought you would never arrive." She stopped and held the back of a kitchen chair, her breath short.

"Are you? I mean, shall I run for the doctor?" Mrs B watched the young woman who had become so very dear to her.

"Yes, please!" She began to walk again, and with a last look across the kitchen, Mrs B ran for her bicycle and pedalled down the hill.

"Doctor!" The young man's frown cleared when he saw that it was Mrs B. "Please hurry! My nephew's wife is in labour in my kitchen." His eyebrows shot up in surprise and he grabbed his bag.

"Come along now. I'll take you in the car. Where is your nephew?" He collected items from around the room and slipped them into his bag.

"He's a police officer, at Potterton." She followed

him out of his surgery into the reception area.

"Leave his details with Sandra here, and she will contact him." Mrs B scribbled his name and Potterton Police Station on a piece of paper, and chased the doctor to the car. They roared up the lane, and she had to run to keep up with him through the garden.

Barbara, on the other hand, was completely relaxed and sitting on the kitchen floor, cradling her newborn daughter.

"She seemed to be in a hurry to put in an appearance." She laughed. The tiny fists waved with determination.

"Oh my. You were all alone. Oh Barbara, she's beautiful." A tear slipped unimpeded down Mrs B's cheek.

"She's rather marvellous, isn't she?" Barbara smiled.

The doctor checked that they were both well, and cut the cord. "Perhaps if you have a clean towel to wrap the baby in, Mrs B?" He asked.

"Oh yes, of course. I am doing nothing helpful, just gawping! Hold on, I will only be a moment." She ran up the stairs and returned with a soft cotton towel. "Now, how about a cup of tea?"

"Yes, please." Barbara smiled across the room. Mrs B filled the kettle and smiled out of the window.

"There have been so many very special moments which have happened in my kitchen, but I think this is the best of them." She laid out the cups and saucers, and waited for the kettle to boil. There was a stillness, and a peace, which she knew would be shattered soon, when she would have to share the magic of the moment with Arnold and Letty. But right then, it was perfect. Or she thought it was, until Barbara offered her the baby, wrapped in the towel. The warmth of new life and the soft skin of the tiny child changed her perception of what was perfect. The child looked back at her and she stood entirely still in case the wonder of the moment might be broken. With the child in the crook of her arm and a tiny fist wrapped around her finger, Mrs B recognised the joy of discovering a new friend.

The kettle whistled its high-pitched tone to let her know it had boiled, and the child tensed in her arms. "I had better make that cup of tea, then. Your mum will need a cup after all that. Can't have her going thirsty." She bent carefully to hand the baby back to Barbara. "She's beautiful. Thank you so much for letting me have a cuddle." A tear slipped unnoticed down her cheek.

She bustled to make the tea, humming quietly to herself and smiling widely at the prospect of the future that spread out before her.

30.

Mrs B and the power of possibility

The car passed her on the lane before coming to a stop a little further along.

"Hello!" Will Hunton, Chief Inspector Will Hunton, unfolded himself from the back seat of his car and the driver carried on without him.

"Hello. How nice to see you." Mrs B stepped off her bicycle and wasted a moment wondering if her hair was tidy.

"I wanted to let you know that we have charged Johnny Edwards with murder." He took a breath. "A gentleman walking his dog discovered the body in woodland not far from the house. We would have missed it if not for your skills. I'm grateful, and we might have been looking for another body too." His smile transformed his face.

For once, Mrs B was lost for words. She fell into step with him and they walked together up the hill. In her memory, there was another afternoon when they had both been much younger, and had walked up this same hill. That afternoon, she recalled, had ended with a soft kiss, which she still remembered.

"Arnold is shaping up to be a good detective. I presume he inherits his ability from you, rather than Letty!" He laughed. "Letty was always less serious than you were. As I remember." His voice was wistful.

"Yes, I suspect you are correct. Ah, here we are. Would you like a cup of tea?" She pushed open the garden gate, and he followed her. His large frame seemed to fill her small kitchen, even once he had folded himself into a chair at the table. "I am happy to hear that Arnold is doing well. He recently became a father, too."

"Yes, of course. You know it's a strange thing. I was remembering when we walked up the lane, an afternoon I walked up with Letty, and left her with a kiss. I imagined myself in love with her for a few days. Childhood is full of fleeting moments like that, I suspect." He nodded his thanks when she put the cup and saucer in front of him, failing to notice the slight wobble of the cup.

"That was a long time ago. Strange that you should think of it now." Whilst she busied herself with the teapot, she watched his face, softened by the memories in his mind; she wondered how she could have been so stupid, to treasure her memory of him, when he had not even thought it was her cheek he had kissed.

"Yes. You're right, of course. I hope I can rely on you to look at cases from time to time for us?" He sipped from the tea. "You haven't thought better of it?"

"Perish the thought. Of course, I would help in any way I can." She lifted her cup, but found none of the usual solace in her cup of tea.

When his cup was empty, he shook her hand and thanked her again. He wished her a good day and noticed nothing of her reserve or the disappointment in her eyes.

When she closed the door, Marmalade was waiting for her. "I'm a silly old fool." She told the kitten. "I had thought, well, nevermind what I thought. We shall be fine, just the two of us, shan't we?" The little kitten burrowed his head into her arm, reminding her of Arnold and Barbara's daughter. There was so much to look forward to, with the Christening coming up. Why then did she feel so ridiculously sad?

31.

Mrs B has an offer

"Letty?" Mrs B opened the front door.

"Hello, this is just about the most exciting this that ever happened. Don't you think?" She bustled through the house. "I bumped into Mrs Chesterton. When I told her I had a grandchild, she was green with envy. Her daughter is unmarried, and older than Arnold." She patted Mrs B on the arm. "I am having so much fun!"

"Barbara is just changing the baby. Would you like a cup of tea, Letty?" Mrs B looked past her sister to see Arnold closing the front door behind him. "Hello, Arnold dear."

"Yes, please, to the tea. I have been so busy I simply have not had a moment to sit down." She flopped into a kitchen chair and carefully placed her handbag on the table, slipping her gloves from her fingers.

Mrs B smiled into the hallway, where Arnold was making his way up the stairs to see his wife and daughter.

"I made these biscuits this morning." Mrs B put a plate on the table, loaded with crunchy sweet little mouthfuls. The kettle whistled, and she turned away to pour the tea. "Barbara has been doing so well. Your granddaughter is hungry all the time." Mrs B carried the teapot to the table, just in time to see her sister help herself to three biscuits. "I wonder where she inherited that from?" They laughed together.

"I cannot believe that they are still calling her the baby. They need to choose a name." Letty bit into the first biscuit. "These are lovely."

"We have chosen a name, actually, Mum." Arnold joined them at the table, his daughter nestled in his arms. Barbara leaned against the door frame. "If you can leave us some biscuits, we will tell you." He struggled to keep a straight face. "This little one is going to be called Jennifer." He smiled down into the sleeping baby's face. "This strange lady is your granny, and the one who makes the best biscuits in the world is Auntie B. You're a lucky girl."

Mrs B smiled across the room at Barbara. "Jennifer's a lovely name." The knock at the door was a surprise. "Can you poor the tea, dear?" Barbara nodded, while Mrs B went to the front door.

"Hello." Tommy McKinley stood on the step.

"Good afternoon, Mr McKinley. I currently have

visitors. Perhaps I could have a conversation with you later?" She looked over her shoulder.

"Yes. Half-past eight? I'll pop in for a chat." He raised an eyebrow at her and tipped his hat.

"Who was that?" Letty had always been curious.

"Mr Jensen from the village, he wondered if I'd had any problems with greenfly on the roses." She shrugged. "She's a beauty, this little one." A gentle pat on Arnold's shoulder, before she pushed the plate of biscuits towards Letty.

....

When Arnold had to leave to get to work, he took Letty with him. Mrs B kissed her sister and waved until the car was out of sight.

Barbara settled Jennifer into her cot, and went looking for Mrs B. "Are you going to tell me who was really at the door? Mr Jensen is ninety if he's a day, and as far as I am aware, he has not left his home in months."

"Ah, yes. Well, I could hardly invite Tommy McKinley in to have tea with Arnold and his mother, could I?" Mrs B reached for Barbara's hand. "I have been talking to Mr McKinley, off and on."

"Are you in some sort of danger? Or trouble?" Barbara's eyes widened.

"No, dear, not at all." Mrs B squeezed Barbara's

hand. "Everything is fine."

32.

Mrs B has an offer – part 2.

Little Jennifer gave Mrs B a perfect distraction for Barbara when she grizzled, her knees pulled up to her chest with colic. "Try a little of this. It used to work wonders for Arnold when he was a little one." Mrs B passed Barbara a bottle of gripe water. "I picked up a bottle from the chemist the other day." A tiny dribble on a spoon and some expelled wind from the baby cleared some of the discomfort. The clock ticked around towards eight-thirty and Mrs B made her excuses. "I need to check on the flower arranging rota in the church." With a smile, she left Barbara and Jennifer in the house and walked out into the garden. Tommy McKinley waited for her in the lane.

"I cannot be very long, Mr McKinley." She walked with quick steps towards so that he had no choice but to fall into step with her.

"I need your help." He came to the point with no preamble.

"My skills are more in the cleaning world, to be honest." She smiled, watching his face.

"My cousin is planning a job. I know it's dangerous. He'll be arrested, or worse. Please help me." His voice cracked.

"What can I do? This is not my territory." She shook her head.

"You can puzzle out a way to stop him. Please." Tommy chewed on his lower lip. "You're great at working out these things."

"Tell me what you can." Mrs B led Tommy into the church and they sat side by side.

"He is planning to raid a jewellery shop. The owner has been telling too many people that he has ordered a selection of very expensive items for a customer. He also told one of my contacts that he has had extra security fitted, that was guaranteed to catch anyone who tried to steal from him. I believe him." Tommy ran his hand over his face.

"Can you tell me the name of the jeweller? Perhaps I could convince him that he should move the prize, then there would be no reason to rob him." She reached across to rest her hand on Tommy's arm. "I cannot promise, but it could be worth trying."

"You would do that for me?" His forehead furrowed.

"Yes, and for the jeweller, and for your cousin. It makes sense to prevent harm." She smiled.

"Wentworth Jewellers on Gardiner Street." He watched her.

"Ah, in that case, we have a chance. Let me try." She patted him on the arm. "Come to see me tomorrow and I will have news for you, I hope."

…………..

"Good morning, Mrs B." Mr Jensen's son had run the jewellers for the last fifteen years. He had learned the trade from his father, and knew Mrs B well.

"Mr Jensen. I hope you are well?" She received a nod and a smile. "I need to speak to you on an extremely urgent matter, if I may?"

He left a young man at the counter and showed her into the back of the shop, and offered her a seat, waiting with steepled fingers.

"You know me, and that I am not given to flights of fancy." He nodded his agreement. "In which case, you may find it easier to trust my judgement and my advice." She smoothed her skirt and reorganised her thoughts. "I have heard that you have taken delivery of some very expensive pieces. I know that you have taken delivery and that you will have the pieces for another three days. Unfortunately, I am not alone in the knowledge."

"Who told you?" His hand shook as he reached across the desk to her.

"That really is not the right question. I can help you though, if you will let me." She smiled and reached to take her hand in his. "We can solve this one together."

....

At eight-thirty, Tommy McKinley let himself into the garden. "You little beauty. Whatever it was you did, it worked. My cousin is spitting fire. He's so angry, but he's safe." His smile was wide. "You and I have helped each other. Perhaps we could almost be friends?"

"I am pleased that it was successful." She held out her hand, and he took hers in both his.

"You're a good friend. Better than I deserve." He turned away to leave, and let himself out of the garden gate. "Perhaps we could help each other?" His words floated across the garden towards her. "I don't offer my friendship to many people. But you have been a better friend to me than people I've known all my life."

"Safe journey home, Mr McKinley." She smiled and waved as he reached the gate and turned back.

"Tommy, please. Everyone calls me Tommy." Mrs B nodded, and watched him walk away. He had changed over the months since the day Arnold and Barbara had married. She thought that she could see improvement.

"Mr McKinley? Tommy?" He turned. "Friends?" He nodded, stepping away with his hand raised.

....

"Are you going to tell me what on earth is going on between you and Tommy McKinley?" Barbara tucked the soft pink blanket around her sleeping daughter and sat down. "I can keep a secret, you know." Barbara waited for Mrs B to sit down opposite her. "He's dangerous. Please let me help you if you are in trouble."

"I'm not. In fact, Mr McKinley and I have been helping each other. It has been useful." She smiled and poured a cup of tea for them both. "You need to keep this entirely between us." Barbara nodded her agreement. "He's a friend. Tommy knew that a crime was about to be committed. He warned me. I warned the target. That's all there is to it." Mrs B sipped her tea.

"Not quite all, though Auntie." Arnold leaned against the back door frame. He sat down at the table. He turned to Barbara. "She turned up at the police station with thousands of pounds' worth of jewellery in her handbag and demanded that they be kept safely." He shook his head. "What I would like to know, Auntie, is how you know Tommy McKinley?"

"Arnold. Perish the thought that I would betray a confidence. You should know better than that. Now, come along. Have a cup of tea and cuddle your daughter. I have things to do." Mrs B patted Barbara on the shoulder as she left the kitchen.

The knock on the front door was unexpected. She opened it and found a visitor on her doorstep. "Mr Jensen? How wonderful to see you! It has been too long." The elderly gentleman leaned heavily on his walking stick.

"I wanted to thank you. My son told me what you did." He passed her a bouquet of roses. "Not much for what you did, but I struggle to get to the shops these days." He smiled and turned to make his way down the garden path.

"Thank you, Mr Jensen. I shall find a vase." She watched him all the way down the path and down the lane. When he was out of sight, she closed the door and breathed in the heady fragrance of the flowers. "Yes, a vase is a good idea." She carried the flowers into the kitchen. "These are rather lovely, aren't they?"

"Flowers from an admirer?" Arnold lifted an eyebrow.

"Perish the thought. Silly boy." She laughed.

33.
Mrs B and the Christening Arrangements

"These flowers are going to fill the church tomorrow." Mrs B carried armfuls of blooms into the vestry. She set up the vases, filling them with water, before she began to place each stem in. Her sharp secateurs snipping the ends of the stalks to achieve the display she wanted. "Oh my, little Jennifer. These are rather wonderful, aren't they?" The baby kicked her feet in the pram, parked by the wall, a happy gurgle echoed off the walls. "I agree. This one is much the nicest." Mrs B laughed and turned to smile down at the little girl who had captured her heart.

A sound out in the main part of the church drew her attention. She poked her head around the door. "Hello?"

Mrs Goffey was sitting quietly on her own. She showed no sign that she had heard Mrs B's greeting.

With a push to the pram, Mrs B moved the baby into the church. "Mrs Goffey? I am so very sorry to disturb you. I will leave you to have some quiet contemplation." A small sound that might have been a laugh, or a sob, escaped Mrs Goffey's mouth. She quickly covered her face.

"Mrs Goffey? Are you well?" Mrs B paused and, when she received no answer, she sat down next to the woman who she had always found difficult. Her initial reaction when she had seen the other woman had been irritation; but a reminder of where they were, and how she should behave, forced her to swallow the feelings.

"Peace and quiet are the last things that I need." She huffed. "I will soon have more than enough of those."

"In what way? What has happened, Mrs Goffey?" Mrs B reached her hand across the space between them.

"I am losing my hearing." Mrs Goffey wiped a tear away. "I have been over recent years, but in the last six months, it has almost disappeared. It's terrifying." She took a deep and steadying breath.

"But you can hear me?" Mrs B watched the other woman carefully.

"No. If I can see you, I can understand better, but soon I won't be able to hear anything at all." She pulled out a handkerchief and wiped a tear.

"Have you seen the doctor? There may be something that can be done." Mrs B realised that she was not speaking head on and turned before she repeated herself.

"It is the joy of old age." She pushed a smile onto her face.

"I could come with you. If it would make you feel more comfortable. If there is nothing to be done, I can help you work on your lip reading. You and I are both living alone. It might be interesting for us both." Mrs B crossed her fingers behind her back. Lies were not usually comfortable for her, but this was one that might help.

"Why would you come with me to the doctor?" Suspicion creased Mrs Goffey's eyes.

"Why not? Come on, let's take little Jennifer for a walk down to the surgery now. They might have an appointment for you." Mrs B slapped her hands on her knees and pushed herself up. "Come on!" Mrs Goffey stood a little stiffly and allowed herself to be guided out of the church.

"Hello. Does the doctor have five minutes, please?" Mrs B raised an eyebrow at the receptionist. The door behind her opened.

"Mrs B? How lovely to see you. How can I help?" The young doctor dropped a folder on the receptionist's desk.

"Yes please. If you could spare a few minutes?"

Mrs B held her hand out to Mrs Goffey.

"No. I have to go." Mrs Goffey backed towards the door.

"Mrs B can come in with you, if that helps?" The doctor crossed the space between them. "Let's just have a chat?" With slow, hesitant steps, Mrs Goffey walked into the surgery, grabbing Mrs B's hand, and pulling her through the door.

Mrs Goffey explained her loss of hearing, and the doctor looked into her ears, listened to her history. "This must have been very scary. I'm so pleased that you came in. There is an infection. It's deep inside. That's what is affecting your hearing. It will take a while, but I think we can get most of your hearing back." He made certain that she had seen what he was saying and went back behind his desk to write a prescription. Mrs Goffey took the piece of paper, open-mouthed. Mrs B helped her out of the office and onto the lane outside.

"I've been so mean to you." She huffed a laugh. "Not only you. I was in pain and frightened, but that really is no reason to be so unkind. I'm so sorry." Mrs Goffey held Mrs B's hands tightly.

"We all deal with fear and pain differently. It's all forgotten." She smiled across at the other woman. "Friends?"

"Yes. What friends! I am so grateful. Not that I deserve you, but I will put that right. I promise.

I will be here if you need anything. Anything at all." She patted Mrs B's arm and bustled off towards the pharmacy.

"Mrs B? Thank you for encouraging her to come in. You're a good friend. You have done a wonderful thing for her today." The doctor smiled widely. "This little one is growing fast, isn't she?"

"She is. Mrs Goffey will be alright?" Mrs B watched Mrs Goffey walking away down the lane.

"Oh yes. She will." He smiled. "We will have to have a party to celebrate you, the best neighbour in our village."

"Perish the thought, Doctor." She shook her head and pushed the pram back to her house. The next day was going to be wonderful. Little Jennifer would be christened, surrounded by family and friends. The fragrance of the flowers would wrap around them all, and the day would be one she could cherish in her memory for the rest of her days. The baby gurgled from the pram and she reached forward to touch the tiny toes. "Perfect. You're absolutely perfect." The baby gurgled back at her, presumably agreeing.

34.

Mrs B and the day of the Christening

The sun rose and Little Mellington bathed in the golden glow. Little Jennifer waved her fists and crowed, splashing the warm water. "Big day for you today, little one." Barbara washed her daughter while she played.

"Everything is ready. The christening gown is beautiful. I remember Arnold wearing it." Mrs B smiled across the kitchen. "Where is Arnold?"

"He has gone to pick up my mother, and his." Barbara's mouth rolled into a tight line. "I just hope that they are going to behave." She looked down at her daughter. "Right, Miss. I think it's time to get you dry." She lifted the baby onto the towel that was waiting on the table, wrapping the soft fabric around her tiny body. "There we are, all wrapped up and cosy." Barbara leaned down to kiss the rosy-cheeked child.

"Here they are now. I can see Arnold's car in the lane." Mrs B craned her neck to look out of the kitchen window.

"I'll take madam upstairs and get her dressed for her big event." Barbara picked up her towel wrapped baby and was up the stairs before Arnold ushered his mother and his mother-in-law into the kitchen.

"Hello Letty, Mrs Henderson. What a wonderful day, and the weather looks as though it's going to be lovely. A perfect day for a christening." She stepped back from the door, watching Letty going straight to the mirror in the hallway to check her hat. Mrs Henderson waited by the back door. Mrs B thought she looked a little peaky, and wondered, with a little guilt, if she was missing Barbara. She would miss Barbara and Jennifer when they had to go home.

Jennifer rode happily in her pram to the church, resplendent in the same christening gown her father had worn. Barbara pushed the pram, with Arnold walking proudly beside her. Mrs B fell into step with her sister and Mrs Henderson behind them, and they made their way down the hill towards the sound of the ringing bells.

Reverend Chambers held the tiny child over the font, gently pouring water over her head and smiling down into her face. Her parents and the godparents made their promises to care for her. Once the prayers had been said and the candles lit, Reverend Chambers asked for a moment of silent contemplation. "One more thing before you go." He smiled. "Jennifer Rose has today been brought into the family of the church, and her parents and godparents have vowed to protect her. There is someone else though, that her parents wish to ask for their commitment to the child." He beamed at Barbara and Arnold. "Mrs B? Will you promise, here in the church, to always be an honorary grandmother to Jennifer? Will you care for her, and offer her guidance and solace, and love, for as long as you live?" Mrs B felt the tears burn behind her eyes.

"I absolutely will." Her voice choked on the tears. She felt Arnold's hand on her arm, and smiled up at him, before she looked down into Jennifer's face, where she found love and joy smiling back at her.

35.

Mrs B and the power of change.

Mrs B straightened her hat, looking in the hall mirror, before she left for her day's work. The house was quiet, without Jennifer's gurgles and cries. Barbara had gone home with Arnold. It was all as it should be, but Mrs B missed the company. She had grown very fond of both of them.

She had a visit to make before she went to work and pedalled to the small house on the other side of the village. The curtains were open, so presumably the occupant was awake and would not object to a visitor.

"Mrs Goffey?" She knocked and pushed open the kitchen door. Mrs Goffey was sitting at the kitchen table, dabbing at her tears. The radiogram in the living room was filling the house with a beautiful melody, which Mrs B did not know. "Are you in pain, Mrs Goffey?" She reached for the other woman's hand.

"Pain? Not at all." She wiped her tears. "I am in debt." This news was delivered with a smile and a joyful twinkle in her eyes.

"You seem happy about it." Mrs B was completely confused.

"I am in debt to you. The fact is that I would not have had the operation if I had not met you that day in the church. I have been a dreadful and horrible person. You have been the most marvellous friend. Thank you. Undeserved, I know." Mrs Goffey planted a kiss on Mrs B's cheek and wrapped her in a hug. "I have been listening to music since I came home from the hospital last night. It sounds strange, but I had forgotten how truly beautiful it is. Thank you."

"Well, I am so pleased. I brought a small dinner for tonight, so that you would not have to cook. Perhaps, when you are feeling better, you might feel well enough to visit me for a cup of tea?" She unpacked a parcel of food wrapped in greaseproof paper.

"Thank you. You are the most generous person. I can only apologise for my behaviour before. You really should hate me." She hung her head in shame.

"Perish the thought! I am just happy to see you in such good spirits, and clearly making a good recovery." She patted the other woman's hand. "I shall be late if I stay much longer, but I am so very pleased for you."

Mrs B left Mrs Goffey to her music; climbing

back onto her bicycle and setting off for Mrs Chambers' house, where she was certain to find her work would be appreciated. It seemed to Mrs B that fear and pain changed people more than anything else. Mrs Goffey was a changed woman now that her hearing had been restored. Mrs Appleby, was to be her last call of the day. It seemed that she was doing no cleaning between Mrs B's visits. There must be something going on there, but maybe it was none of Mrs B's business.

Her cycle ride to Mrs Chambers' house was pleasant on the warm day, and she leaned her bicycle against the garden wall with a happy smile.

36.

Mrs B and the art of compromise

"Mrs B? Oh, how lovely to see you. For once, my little boy is awake while you're here. I would like to introduce you." Mrs Chambers bounced the baby in her arms. "This is Josiah." She raised her eyes to the ceiling and lowered her voice. "His father's choice." She shrugged and smiled.

"Well now, you have grown little Joe. It is my pleasure to meet you again." Mrs B felt the grip of the tiny fist that poked out of the soft blue cardigan. "He's beautiful, Mrs Chambers, and growing fast. You must be so proud." She smiled down into the tiny face. "Well, little Joe, I had better get on, otherwise we will still be here in an hour's time."

"Thank you, Mrs B." Mrs Chambers bustled away with her baby and left Mrs B in the kitchen. It was soon put to rights, and all the while Mrs B thought about the little boy she had seen come into the world and wondered about the life ahead of him. The world seemed to be changing so fast.

The things that these babies would see would go far beyond anything that she could imagine.

Her next stop was Mrs Appleby. The house had changed a good deal since Mr Appleby had passed away, after drinking coffee laced with digitalis. At the time, Mrs B had been disappointed with herself for not seeing what had happened sooner. By the time she had worked it out, she had cleaned away all the evidence, which was helpful to Mrs Appleby. Of course, the fact that he had been a bully had perhaps coloured Mrs B's thinking. One thing in the world that she detested was a bully.

The house was in complete disarray. Each time Mrs B came to the house to clean, it seemed that nothing at all had been done since her last visit. Plates were all over the house, with bits of dinner stuck to them. Half full cups littered every surface. Mrs Appleby was nowhere to be found, but the back door was open, and Mrs B set to work.

Each room she entered took some clearing and cleaning, but she kept at it. The last room was the main bedroom, where Mrs Appleby lay on the bed. Her face was so sad, when she turned to look at Mrs B.

"Mrs Appleby? Are you quite well?" Mrs B waited for a response, but there was none. "I'll make you a cup of tea." Mrs B shook her head a little while she waited for the kettle to boil. "Here you are, dear. Come along. This will make you feel a little better." She sat on the edge of the bed and watched while Mrs Appleby sipped. "Good girl."

"I don't know what to do. I can't sleep at night, can't think straight. Mrs B, you know what I did. I killed him. I planned it and I did it. I have no right to live." A tear slipped down her face.

"Oh, I see. Well, yes you did, and I cannot tell you I approve. However, what is done is in the past. You did it to escape a cruel and deeply unhappy marriage. I am afraid that there is very little that can be gained by guilt. It is the least productive of any emotion." She patted Mrs Appleby on the hand. "Reparation, however, is very useful. It will make you feel better and give you a way of making amends."

"Reparation?" Mrs Appleby sat up and began to drink her tea.

"Yes. In fact, I have a plan which might help you." Mrs B stood up and looked around the room. "You have a bath while I clean this room, and we will work it out together."

"You're kinder than I deserve, Mrs B." Mrs Appleby stood up slowly, as though she had grown unused to moving.

"Perish the thought. If we cannot help each other, whatever is the point of it all?" Mrs B watched Mrs Appleby out of the bedroom and heard the water running into the bath. She straightened the bedroom and left everything as it should be before she went down to the kitchen to make a fresh pot of tea. They had a great deal to do.

37.

Mrs B and the art of compromise – part 2.

"That's better. You look much more relaxed already. A good bath is a wonderful thing." Mrs B poured a cup of tea and pushed it across the kitchen table. "Now, let me outline the plan and see what you think."

To start with, Mrs Appleby was quite unsure about the plan and where it was leading, but after another cup of tea and a long conversation, she began to see that it might be the best plan she had ever heard.

Early the next morning, Mrs Appleby presented herself at Mrs Lennet's front door. Her courage almost failed her when she was shown into the huge drawing room. She remembered Mrs B's calm voice and sensible advice and held her nerve.

"Good morning, Mrs Appleby?" If Mrs Lennet was surprised to see Mrs Appleby, she was gracious enough to hide it well.

"Mrs Lennet. I understand that you need

volunteers to join the village fayre committee and help with everything." She shifted her weight from foot to foot as though she might be getting ready to run away.

"Yes, indeed, I do. I would be most grateful for the help." Mrs Lennet held out her hand to offer a seat on the sofa.

"Thank you. Also, you run the women's institute. I'd like to help with that too." Now that she had started, Mrs Appleby was unable to stop. "And the jumble sale."

"My, this is a surprise, but I must say I am very grateful. Yes, please. May I offer you a cup of coffee?" Mrs Lennet raised a perfectly plucked eyebrow.

"No, thank you. I have two more calls to make this morning. If you would let me know when I should meet you to start helping, I would be grateful." Mrs Appleby nodded and let herself out, leaving Mrs Lennet quite astonished. She could not remember ever hearing Mrs Appleby speaking more than two words together.

Mrs Chambers was delighted to hear that Mrs Appleby would be volunteering for the flower arranging and the cleaning rotas at the church. Little Josiah waved his hands and smiled up at Mrs Appleby from his pram. "Oh, and I'm usually available for babysitting."

"Oh, I'm certain Joey would love that. Thank

you." Mrs Chambers smiled and waved as Mrs Appleby closed the garden gate behind her.

Her last visit of the morning was to the Pendle's farm. Mrs Pendle was taking a break with her feet up. "Hello. It's Mrs Appleby, isn't it?"

"Yes. I'm sorry to come round unannounced. I just thought that I would like to do some knitting. I wondered if you might like some things for the baby. It has been a little while since I did any knitting, but I would like to, if you would accept them." Mrs Appleby's fingers gripped the back of one of the kitchen chairs.

"That is so kind. I am too tired by the end of the day to do that sort of thing, and, if I'm honest, my knitting is more holes than wool." She laughed. "How about a cup of tea? There's one in the pot, I think." She pushed against the table to stand up.

"No, I'll find a cup, and pour it. Keep your feet up." She poured a cup for herself and added milk.

Mrs B had been right. If she put herself out to help people, it would be a reparation of sorts. It was, she knew, not the justice that she deserved, but it was a compromise. Just like Mrs Chambers shortening Josiah's name to Joey.

Her last call was not one that had been suggested by Mrs B, but it was one that Mrs Appleby felt certain was right. Her garden was filled with flowers, and she quickly picked enough for a pretty bouquet. Once she had firmly wrapped them in a sheet from her newspaper, she carried them to Mrs B's back door, and delivered them with a smile and her thanks.

It had been a good day, and she had started to look forward to the days to come.

38.

Mrs B and her second case.

"Auntie?" Arnold let himself in through the back door.

"Hello Arnold. Perfect timing. I just arrived home myself." Mrs B was filling the kettle at the sink.

"I have been sent to fetch you. There is another case which we need you to take a look at, if you have time." He tried to hide his excitement, but it bubbled through in his smile.

"Well, in that case, we should go." Mrs B spooned some food out for Marmalade in case she was late back. He was becoming much better at using the small cat flap which Arnold had fitted in the back door, and would find the food when he was hungry.

The house they parked outside was on the more affluent side of Potterton. The roads were wider and tree-lined. Outside, everything seemed to be entirely as it should be. "Nothing has been moved, except, well, you'll see." Arnold unlocked the front door and she followed him inside.

The house inside was in complete disarray. Everything had been ransacked. "A burglary?" Mrs B walked slowly through the living room and into the dining room beyond. The kitchen was small but had every modern gadget. Upstairs, the floorboards had been prised up, and the furniture flung around. The pictures on the wall had been smashed. Mrs B ran her fingers across the canvas on one and shook her head. The main bedroom was almost untouched, but there was a dark stain on the floor. "Blood?" Arnold nodded. "What do you know about the people who lived here?"

"He was a bit of a mystery. Clearly there was money, but we have no work details for him. She was an artist. I presume some of these paintings were hers. The initials in the corner match up." He checked his notebook. "They were married two years ago. Nobody locally knew them beyond nodding good morning. It seems they moved here just a few months ago. She painted in her shed in the garden, and he went out every morning, but never discussed his work with the neighbours."

"I see." Mrs B looked down at the stain. "Who found the body?"

"Somebody telephoned the police. Anonymous tip off. The curious thing, though, is that the door was locked from the inside." He shook his head. "The key was still in the lock. We had to push the key through, and then the locksmith could open the door." He scratched his chin. "It's a puzzle, that's for sure."

"How long had she been dead?" She turned towards him.

Arnold's eyes popped open wide. "How did you know it was her?"

"It made more sense. Someone lifted all that furniture and the floorboards. That's more likely a man. He had no job, so perhaps his income was not legitimate. Whoever did the damage to the rest of the house was angry and looking for something. I just thought it made more sense." She shrugged. "How long?"

"Two days. Blunt force to her head. The bones in her hand were broken too." He looked down at the stain on the floor.

"Right or left?" He seemed confused. "Hand?"

"Ah, yes. Right." He waited quietly while she walked around the bedroom.

"Where is he?" She asked.

"We found his body out at the quarry. Blunt force trauma to the head." She nodded and reached for the dressing-table drawer, raising an eyebrow for permission before she opened it. Arnold held out his hand to show that she should go ahead. A quick look through each drawer seemed to satisfy her curiosity. She looked out of the window at the garden.

"I would like to see where she painted, please?" Arnold nodded and showed her into the garden. It was well tended, and the beds were weed free. In the shed, there were several pieces half finished, and one on the easel which looked to be complete. There was no mess in there, except the pile of oil paint tubes, knives and brushes. "How long did he die after her?"

"We think it was the same day. Water makes things more difficult." She nodded, and he waited.

"Well, it makes some sense, but I shall need to look into his life and how he made his money. I'll need his name and hers, please." She held out her hand, and he wrote the names down. "Thank you. I need to think, and then perhaps come back here."

Arnold nodded and drove her home. He knew better that to talk to her, while her brain whirred with possibilities.

39.

Mrs B's second case part 2

"Clearly, someone was searching for something. They maybe believed that it was hidden in the house. Everything was thrown about, and even the floorboards were pulled up." Mrs B sat carefully on the park bench. "She was murdered, in the house, and he was found in the quarry. Can you help me with any ideas?"

Tommy McKinley smiled across at her. "Mr and Mrs Hargreaves were not who they appeared to be. He was hiding because he stole money from some very serious people. They probably found them and wanted it back." He chewed his bottom lip. "They are not people I would want to owe money to."

"I see, thank you. As both of them are dead, presumably the money was found." Mrs B turned towards him.

"Maybe. But it could also just be to make an example, so nobody else thinks about running off with their money." He nodded to himself, as though confirming his own thoughts. "If it was me, I wouldn't hide stolen money where I lived. I would have it somewhere else, hidden, buried maybe. Perhaps somewhere I could get to quickly."

"Thank you. I cannot imagine anyone else being as helpful as you have been." She patted his shoulder as she stood up.

"Can I ask you for some advice?" He studied his shoes carefully.

Mrs B's brows pushed together. "Surely. If I can be of any help." She sat back down.

"I met a girl. People think they know me because of my family, and girls can be scared of going out with me because of that. I like this one, and I want to know what I should do to make her feel safe." He shifted his weight. "You won't tell anyone I asked you?"

"Perish the thought! I would never betray a confidence." She shook her head. "When I met my husband, the first thing he gave me was a small bunch of flowers, and the second was a promise that he would tell me the truth. I could ask him anything at all and he would not lie." She swallowed and let the memory run through her mind. "He only broke the promise once. He told me that he would come home from the war, that nothing would change." She wiped a tear from her eye.

"He sounds like a nice man." For a moment, Tommy watched her pulled herself together, then he diverted his gaze to give her some time.

"Yes, he was the best. The very best." She patted his hand. "Be the best you can be for this girl." She took a breath and stood up. "Thank you, Tommy. I'm grateful."

"Me too." Tommy McKinley watched her walk away.

"You're a good person, Tommy. Just show her the real you." Mrs B called over her shoulder as she left him behind.

"You too, Mrs B." He raised his hand and waved.

40.

Mrs B and her second case – Part 3

"Thank you for collecting me, Arnold. I need to see the house again, but I think I know what happened." She clasped her hand across her handbag.

He drove to the house, leaving her to think quietly. He had no wish to in any way disrupt her train of thought.

The house looked the same outside. Nothing had changed inside either. "Right, Arnold. Here is what I think happened. The Hargreaves were living a lie. They were not actually the people that they pretended to be. I understand that they owed a great deal of money to some dangerous people." She crossed the room to the window. "See the marks here on the window sill? A ladder leaned here. Do you see?" Arnold nodded. "That is why the door was locked from the inside. I believe the lady of the house locked herself in here whilst the house was ransacked. Whoever it was that was searching the house climbed up the ladder and through the window. You will see that the lock on the window is open?" Arnold leaned over and looked. He nodded.

"Do you think the husband did it?" He asked.

"I have no way to tell you. I do know, however, that her hand was broken, perhaps fighting back. Maybe she tried to push the window closed against him." She turned back to look out of the window. "Oh, Arnold. I have been so stupid. Do you see those allotments? Just over the fence. How did I not see them before? Come along, Arnold. We have no time to lose."

He drove as fast as he dared, finding the entrance to the allotments: small plots of land rented from the local council by residents. Each small patch was crammed with vegetables and fruit growing. They ran to the small shed, which doubled as an office.

"Which allotment is rented by Mr and Mrs Hargreaves, please?" Arnold demanded. "Police enquiry. Quickly, please!"

The elderly gentleman checked the list, running his finger down the page in front of him. "Number 23." He pointed to the left and watched open-mouthed as they rushed away.

They went as quickly as they could, dodging the runner beans which hung over the pathways. "Here, Arnold here." The allotment was as filled with healthy plants as any other. The small shed was secured with a padlock. Arnold found a small trowel and forced the hasp.

Inside, the shed was empty. "We're too late. If something was ever hidden here, it's gone."

"May I look?" Arnold stepped back, and passed her the trowel when she held out her hand. At the back of the shed was a piece of sacking, which had seemingly been thrown in the corner. Mrs B pulled the sacking out of the way and dug down into the loose soil beneath it. After two trowels of earth had been removed, she struck something hard. "You might have better digging skills than I, Arnold, and stronger muscles."

He stepped into the gloom and dug down, pulling out a metal cash box. It was large and unwieldy. He rested the box on the ground and opened the lid. Bank notes were stacked neatly inside. "Well done, Arnold." He closed the lid down and stood up.

"How kind. You've done all the work for me. I'll take the box now, thank you." The man stood just outside the door. "Now, please." He raised a gun so that they could see it clearly.

"Ah, Mr Hargreaves. How lovely to meet you." Mrs B smiled her widest and most innocent smile. "I am so very sorry for your loss."

41.

Mrs B and her second case Part 4

"I'm sorry, but it was empty. Somebody must have found it before we arrived." Mrs B stepped toward Mr Hargreaves. "Perhaps your new lady friend?"

"My what? Get out of the way, old woman! I want my box." He moved her to the side with one hand.

"Very well." She leaned back into the shed and took the box from Arnold. She had to twist to take it; the space was narrow with the door half open. When she was completely turned towards Arnold and away from Mr Hargreaves she whispered. "Be ready." Her hand fitted snugly into the handle of the box and she pulled in a deep breath. As she turned back to face Mr Hargreaves, she swung the box towards him, and brought the side of the heavy metal case into contact with Mr Hargreaves' head. He tumbled, astonished to the ground.

Arnold sprang from the shed and closed handcuffs around Mr Hargreaves wrists before he had the chance to regain his senses. The gun landed on the soft ground, where carrots and parsnips competed for space.

"Jolly good. I think a cup of tea is in order." Mrs B smiled down at Mr Hargreaves. "Not for you, though." She straightened up and directed her gaze to Arnold. "He needs to be charged with murder. The man who was found in the quarry, and his wife. I think his new lady friend will be waiting a while for him to come back, but I imagine she will move on fairly quickly."

"You can't prove I have a girlfriend." Mr Hargreaves was sitting up, snarling his anger.

"Oh, I believe I can. She wears very bright red lipstick. She also has very little experience or interest in laundry. That would lead me to believe that she is younger than you by a few years." She smiled gently at him.

"You're an interfering old woman. I cannot believe that the police have stooped so low as to rely on the opinions of an old crone like you." He spat his accusations.

"Uncalled for, but you are entitled to your opinion. Also, you're right. I have interfered in your life. I have been to your house and seen the stains on your carpets where your wife died." She raised an eyebrow. "Did she know about your girlfriend?"

"No." He closed his eyes, and she waited for them

to open again. "I loved my wife. Perhaps I enjoyed a little entertainment elsewhere, but I loved her. She was already dead when I came home." His face twisted with pain. "There were always other girls, but I loved her. When I found her dead, I went after them. Yes, you're right. The man in the quarry was the one who I believe killed my wife. He deserved what he got. She really deserved none of it. The truth is, she should have married someone better. She married me, and because of that, she is dead." His voice caught on the words.

"I think you should talk to this officer. He will take your statement." She stepped aside as Arnold pulled Mr Hargreaves to his feet. "I am so very sorry for your loss." She stepped back from the path. "Your runner beans are really looking very good."

"Not mine. She grew everything here. She built things. I knocked them down." He hung his head and allowed Arnold to lead him away. She followed behind them with the box and waited for Arnold to help him into the back seat of the car.

"You go ahead, Arnold dear. I need to have a walk to clear my head, and the journey home will do just that." She patted his hand and walked away from him, her back as straight as a poker, and her handbag dangling from the crook of her elbow as always.

42.

Mrs B gets ready for a dinner date

She had already tried on two sets of clothes and hats to match. The morning had been spent working hard, which was a good thing. As soon as she had stopped, the worries about what to wear and whether she should be going at all reared up, and had her jittering all over the house.

"Mrs B! Mrs B! Thank goodness you are at home." Patricia slumped down on a chair at the kitchen table. "I need your help."

"Patricia? Whatever is the matter?" Mrs B reached across to the younger woman.

"I am having this baby. Right now. The driver is completely useless. He brought me here in a panic. Oh. Ow. This hurts!" She gripped the table as a pain made her body tense.

"Is the car outside?" Mrs B stood on tiptoe to see out into the lane.

"Yes. I told him to wait." Patricia was breathing

heavily.

"Come along, then. We need to get you some help." Mrs B put her hand under Patricia's elbow.

"I really think I am not able." Patricia braced herself against the table.

"You? Not able? Goodness, I imagine you are able to deal with almost anything. That husband of yours jumps when you shout. Your mother-in-law lives in terror, hostage to your every whim. I imagine walking the ten feet to the car with my help should be easy." Mrs B raised her eyebrow in a challenge.

"You are a very annoying old woman." Patricia pushed herself away from the table. "In terror?" A grim smile played around her lips.

"I know I am annoying. You keep moving, or I can be much more irritating." Mrs B supported Patricia's weight. "Good girl. Keep moving. One step at a time." They reached the back gate before the next contraction. "Hello, can you help, please?" The driver rushed to open the door, lifting Patricia off her feet and into the car. "Now, straight to the doctor's surgery, please."

"Owwww." Patricia gripped the soft leather of the upholstery.

"Nearly there. Hold on, dear. You are doing very well." Mrs B smiled gently. "I have had a good deal of experience with these things lately. You are doing exceptionally well." She patted Patricia on the arm. "Look. Here we are. The doctor will be able to help us."

"Mrs B? This is becoming a habit." The doctor met her eyes over Patricia's head. "Come along inside. We are going to meet your baby very soon I think."

Mrs B leaned against the door frame and listened to the sounds coming from inside. It seemed Patricia's baby was on the way.

The driver joined her on the doorstep. "You're kind. She's a difficult woman, mean and not polite about you at all."

"Oh, I am fully aware that I am not her favourite person. However, today is a difficult day for her. Perhaps inadvertently, she has saved me from making the mistake of believing that the dress I wear makes any difference at all." Mrs B smiled at him as a wail pierced the air from inside. "It appears that the child is no happier than the mother."

"Mrs B? Patricia has asked for you." The doctor held the door open and stepped aside.

Inside the room, Patricia was on a couch with a soft blue blanket pulled across her, and a towel wrapped bundle in her arms. "I know I have not always been very polite to you, Mrs B, but you came up trumps for me today, and for this little boy. Thank you." She smiled up at Mrs B. For a moment, she looked a good deal younger than her years. Without the lipstick and the attitude, she was a different person. "I need the driver to take me home. My husband will be delighted that we have a son. He was hoping for a boy." She ran a finger down the child's cheek. "Could you help me? Perhaps if you took the baby?" Mrs B gladly took the tiny bundle from his mother.

"Oh, my dear, he's quite wonderful." Mrs B rocked him gently.

"I am ready to go home. I will be more comfortable there, and we can book a private nurse to care for the baby." Patricia was already refreshing her lipstick.

"I'll ask the driver to help you." Mrs B leaned forward to pass the tiny boy back to his mother.

"No, that's fine. You can take him to the car. The doctor says I have to be checked over before I go. I imagine it will be a few minutes." She waggled her fingers at Mrs B and the baby. "Doctor? As quickly as possible, please?"

The driver gazed down into the baby's face. He was clearly smitten. "He's a little dazzler, isn't he?"

"Indeed, he is. Ah, here she is. Patricia, your son is waiting for you. I will leave you to your family. I am certain that this young man's father will be delighted to meet him." She passed the baby into his mother's arms and stepped back to close the door.

"I thought it would be better if you came home with me, helped me to settle in." Patricia furrowed her brows.

"I'm afraid I cannot. I have dinner plans, and I must change. Congratulations, my dear, and welcome to the world, little one." Mrs B closed the door and waved to Patricia, who sat open-mouthed in the back seat.

A short walk back to her cottage found Mrs B smiling to herself, and choosing a dress in pale blue fabric. She always felt comfortable in blue. The face that smiled back at her from the mirror was more confident than she had felt for a long time.

When Will knocked on the door, Mrs B was ready to go, and looking forward to her dinner. It had, after all, been a busy day.

43.

Mrs B goes out to dinner

The restaurant looked very expensive, even from the outside. A bubble of nervousness took root in Mrs B's stomach. She would have no idea what to order. The waiters would look at her simple blue dress and know that she was in the wrong place. That she did not belong there.

They followed the waiter to a table, where crisp white linen was laid with sparkling silver and crystal. "Madam?" The waiter stood to her side, lifted the napkin from in front of her, and flapped it theatrically. She sat back in surprise, and he laid it reverently across her lap.

"It all seems a lot of palaver. Is this somewhere that you come to often, Will?" She watched him smiling across at her.

"I know it's all a bit flashy, but they do the most wonderful beef dish and I hope you will like it." He smiled across at her. "Or anything else that you feel like." The waiter presented a menu that was bound in leather.

"Good grief. This looks interesting." She opened the outer cover and found the menu inside. More choices than she could imagine were written there. She read each one with great care. "I think I shall be guided by your choice and go with the beef." She smiled. "Although they all sound delicious." She passed the menu back to the waiter. Did she imagine the ever so slight roll of his eyes? For a moment, she told herself that she was finding offence where none was offered. "Did I say something to offend you, young man?"

"Sorry? No, not at all." The waiter stuttered his way through the words.

"Why then, would you roll your eyes in that way?" She turned in her seat to address him directly. "Did I do something that you found irritating?"

The diners at nearby tables had stopped eating and were watching the conversation. "I meant no offence."

"I think that is untrue. You thought that I would not comment on your behaviour. You imagined that I would be quiet, and accept your assessment that I am not worthy to eat here." She reached out and patted his arm. "You're right. I should eat somewhere where I am welcome. Which I do not feel here." She stood up and collected her handbag from beneath her chair. "Will, I am sorry, but I am not comfortable here.

If you wish to stay, I will make my own way home." She gave him a gentle smile across the table.

"Not at all. If this restaurant is not prepared to treat my friends properly, I am not prepared to eat here." He stood up and placed his napkin on the table.

"Sir, is there a problem?" The manager arrived at the table.

"Yes indeed. I believe you have a problem with your staff. I will not allow my friend to be treated with such disrespect. You need to choose your staff with more care. I wish you a good evening, and better staff." He held out his arm, and Mrs B rested her hand in the crook of his elbow. "Where would you like to eat this evening?" They moved away from the table.

"You cannot walk away from a table in this establishment and ever book again." The manager pulled himself up to his full height.

"I would not wish to eat in an establishment, sir, where a customer would be treated so poorly." Will smiled down at Mrs B and they walked away together.

Outside, Will opened the door of the car for her. "I am so sorry. I wanted to impress you."

"You did. It takes courage to stand up to bullies." She waited while he shut the door and walked around to climb into the driver's seat. "Are you still hungry?" He nodded. "Fish and chips?"

"Sounds brilliant. Can we eat them out of the newspaper?" He laughed.

"Yes, I think they taste better that way." She smiled across at him.

When they had collected fish and chips, wrapped warm in newspaper sheets, they found a bench by the river, and sat together. Each mouthful of salty vinegar doused chips and crispy batter filled with flakes of cod made them smile.

"I've never eaten better chips." His face was wreathed in a smile which he threw at her. "Perhaps it's the company."

"I'm not certain. These are rather lovely chips." She laughed at his expression. "I'm sorry I spoiled your dinner plans."

"You really didn't. My plan was to eat with you. And here I am." He reached across to hold her hand. "I'm sorry I chose a stupid restaurant."

Later, when they walked back to his car, she realised that her hand felt completely comfortable resting in the crook of his elbow. Life was changing, and Mrs B would have to consider what those changes meant. She planned to think about that in the morning. For now, she was completely content to be enjoying the company of Will Hunton.

When he left her at her door, he left her with a kiss so tender it woke up places in her heart that had been sleeping, and he also left her with things to think about.

44.

Mrs B receives news

The sun was shining. Mrs B rode her bicycle down the hill to the police station. She had a busy day ahead. The back door to the canteen was open, and she propped up her bicycle. "Good morning, Kathleen. It has been such a long time. Are you too busy to have a cup of tea?"

"I'm never too busy for you. I've an iced bun fresh in this morning, too." She poured two cups of tea and brought them over to a table.

"Thank you, Kathleen. It's lovely to see you. How have you been?" She patted the other woman's hand.

"I have not had a moment to think today. Something big has happened. First thing this morning, everyone was here, as usual. Then, all of a sudden everyone had to leave. The whole place is empty." She sipped from her cup. "You will buzz through this place today." She smiled and patted Mrs B's arm.

"Well, I must get on. It has been lovely to

have a chat." Mrs B smiled across the table and collected her cloths and polish from the cleaning cupboard. Kathleen had been right about the offices being empty. There was not a single officer to be seen.

She began with all the toilets, leaving them smelling fresh and clean, then swept the hallways. The offices were much quicker to clean without people to dodge. She straightened the paperwork and polished the desks. In the last office, when the desk was clean and the piles of paper were tidy, she leaned down to pick up a hand-written note which was on the floor.

"Officer seriously injured. Potterton." Mrs B laid the paper on the top of the pile. Could it be Arnold? Her hand fluttered to her throat. He was a young officer and would maybe be involved with dangerous situations. She needed to get to Barbara in case she heard the news and was worried.

Mrs B pedalled away from the station to Mrs Gartree's house. "May I leave my bicycle with you?" She propped it up against the wall. Mrs Gartree nodded and waved as Mrs B ran to catch the bus as it pulled up.

The bus stop was just up the road from the house. Mrs B marched up to the door. "Barbara! Hello, are you here?"

"Hello Auntie. We are in the garden. Come

through." Mrs B found Barbara and the baby sitting on the grass in the sunshine.

"Barbara. I hope you don't mind me popping in unannounced." She bent down to tickle little Jennifer's toes. "Hello sunshine. You are the loveliest little girl."

"Barbara?" Arnold's voice rang through from the house. "Are you here?"

Mrs B's hand rested on her throat. The relief at knowing he was safe made her realise that she had been holding her breath.

"Arnold, we're out in the garden. Auntie came to visit. Come on out, and I will make some tea." Barbara stood up to meet him.

"Hello Auntie. It's lovely to see you." He rested his hand on her shoulder. "I've only popped home to let you know I will have to work late. There's been an incident. It's good that you have Auntie here to keep you company." He smiled down into his daughter's face.

"What was the incident?" Barbara watched his face change.

"We are still investigating, but someone attacked a senior officer. He's in the hospital with head injuries." He sat heavily on the small bench.

Mrs B watched him. Something about the way he sat made the pit of her stomach cold with fear. "Was it someone you know?" She took a step forward, her hand outstretched.

"Yes. You know him too. Chief Inspector Hunton." He turned to look at her. "Auntie? Are you quite alright?"

"No. Arnold, please take me to the hospital." He looked up at her sharp tone. "Right now, Arnold. I will explain on the way." She walked to the garden gate. "Sorry Barbara. I have to go."

The tears were hot behind her eyes, but she would not allow herself to cry. Before anything else, the important thing was to find out how Will was. Her hand lay on her lap. The same hand that had been tucked into his elbow the night before. She touched her lips, where he had kissed her.

"Arnold. I should have told you before. Will and I knew each other when we were younger. I only saw him again when he came to my house when you were there. But I have spent time with him. He has become...very dear to me." One tear slipped out of her eye.

"Auntie. I'm so sorry. I'll come with you to see him." He swallowed hard.

He held her hand through the corridors and up the stairs. There were two uniformed officers outside the ward. They allowed Arnold through, and his aunt with him.

Will was lying in the bed in a separate room off

the ward. There were bandages around his head, his arms were outside the sheets, and his eyes were closed.

She sank into a chair by the bed, holding his hand. Tears dripped from her chin in silence.

"Will?" She watched his face for any sign that he had heard her. There was nothing. "It will take time. There is plenty of time. When you wake up, I will be here." She patted the back of his hand and straightened her back. "I'll be waiting."

45.

Mrs B investigates

"I need your help. Please." Mrs B spread her hands on her knees.

"I'll ask around. Honestly, it's a huge risk for anyone to attack a copper. It would have to be someone with a really good reason." Tommy patted her on the arm. "He's special to you. I'm glad." Her head snapped back in surprise. "I know it hurts, but that's only because you love him." Her chin dipped down towards her chest. "No. Don't you feel bad about this. Love is love. You taught me to show who I really am to people who I care about. You've changed how I see life." He shrugged. "Not the time. I know that. I'll see what I can find out. Keep your chin up, my friend." He left her on the park bench, his head down into the collar of his coat, against the chill wind that was blowing.

Barbara had decided to stay with Mrs B while she was spending so much time at the hospital. It was reassuring to the whole family to know that when she came home; it was not to an empty house.

"Perfect timing. I just made tea." Barbara set the cups and saucers on the table. "Any change today?" Mrs B sank into the chair and shook her head. A cry from upstairs sent Barbara to settle her daughter.

A short, sharp knock on the back door had Mrs B back on her feet.

She opened the door. "Tommy? Come on in, there's tea in the pot."

"I have information. Hunton was with some people. There was an argument. I don't know much more. The man I spoke to was in the building, but not in the room. He heard shouting, then the others all left. He found Hunton on the floor." Tommy chewed on his lip. "You remember the people I told you about? The ones Mr Hargreaves owed money to?" She nodded. "He was with them."

"Why was he with them?" Her voice was low, but he heard the fear in it.

"Perhaps there was a genuine reason. I really don't know. Maybe he can tell you when he wakes up." He shot a reassuring smile across the table. She nodded slowly to herself and poured him a cup of tea.

"Can you tell me who was there? Names?" She

watched him flinch. She was fully aware of how much she was asking.

"I would be dead if anyone ever found out. Worse, you would be dead if you went looking for them. I can't put either of us in that much danger." He reached across the table and held her hand. It was a gentle gesture and tears threatened again. She swallowed, and he watched her grapple with her emotions.

"You never told me about what happened with you and that girl." Her brows pushed together, and she sipped from her tea.

"Ah. She liked your suggestion that I promised not to lie to her. I haven't lied to her once. She reminds me of you. Her name's Maisie." He took a sip. "Nobody knows about her, except you. I know that you would never tell anyone. I trust you."

"Perish the thought, Tommy. I would never betray a confidence or a friend. If you can think of a way that you could tell me the name without putting yourself or your friend in danger, I would be grateful." She wrapped her hands around her cup. "It's a cold night out there. Drink your tea before you go back outside."

"I'll give it some thought." He drank down the hot liquid.

"I have every faith that you will." She patted his hand. "Thank you, Tommy." She passed her hand over her tired eyes. "I am very grateful. Whether you feel you can help me or not."

46.

Mrs B receives information

"Hello." Tommy was waiting by the church gate.

"Tommy. Good morning. You're out early this morning. I have to clean the church. Can we talk while I polish?" She leaned her bicycle against the wall, and he followed her inside. He watched her whisk her cloth over the wooden pews.

"Can you stop for a second?" Tommy clenched his hands. "This is you. The church, you believe it all." She stopped and turned to smile at him. She nodded. "We had a different religion."

She sat down on the pew she had been cleaning. "Come and tell me about it."

"Family first. No questions, just loyalty. I'm a McKinley, that means something. Mostly it means my dad tells me what to do, and won't listen to any arguments." His smile was grim. "The second thing is, no grassing. Ever. If I tell you what happened, it's breaking the rules." He huffed out a sigh.

"I understand. Truly I do. I know that you're fighting with yourself on this. Whatever your decision, we'll still be friends." She ran her duster over the rest of the pew.

"Alright. I'm going to tell you some things. But you have to promise me that you will not go poking about. The people involved make me look like a choir-boy." He held on to her hand. "Promise."

"I will promise." She sat down next to him.

"My friend was there. Not in the room, but in the building. He heard shouting, arguing. Whatever was said, Anthony Newton was furious. It is never a good idea, ever, to make Anthony Newton angry." He paused, waiting to be certain that she understood. Her nod showed that she did. "He heard sounds like furniture being tipped over, and then nothing. Mr Newton left with the two guys who arrived with him, and my friend found your friend on the floor with a bad bang on the head. He ran to a phone box and called for an ambulance. That's it. Remember, you promised. No taking on the Newtons."

"Perish the thought." She shook her head. "What did your friend hear them talk about? Does he know why they were meeting together? Was he trying to arrest them on his own?" She was twisting the duster in her hands, round and round.

"He was in the other room. I really don't know any more. But to be honest, nobody would try to arrest Anthony Newton on their own. You have to understand, the Newtons are different. It's like they have a guardian angel watching over them. No arrests. They're never there when the police arrive. Perhaps they did have someone watching over them. Not an angel, but…" He looked down at his hands.

"You're suggesting that he was taking bribes?" He kept his eyes down and refused to meet hers. "No. I cannot believe it."

"I'm only telling you what I heard. Just remember your promise." He shrugged.

"Tommy. I am sorry. I have no reason to doubt your friend, and it was rude of me to do so. Thank you for telling me. I know it was difficult." She patted the top of the wooden pew; her head tipped sideways. He smiled back, but his eyes were sad. "You are a good friend." He patted the back of her hand and stood up.

"I have to go. Remember what you promised." He walked to the door and lifted his hand to wave. She waved too.

Her cleaning was finished. The bus would not wait and she needed to look hard at Will Hunton, to see if she could make sense of what she had learned from Tommy. Perhaps he was mistaken. Or she was.

Mrs B had always been of the opinion that a bus ride was a good opportunity to clear her mind and think more clearly. She smiled at her indistinct reflection in the bus window, while the fields and hedges went past.

47.

Mrs B and the truth

"I'm so pleased that you arrived. He woke up an hour ago, and he's been chatting up a storm." The nurse bustled away. "I'll bring you both a cup of tea. I'm sure that you could do with one."

Mrs B slid into the chair by his bed, where she had spent so many hours over the last few days. He turned towards her, and his face lit up. "Hello. They told me that you have been sitting here waiting for me to wake up. I am so sorry to have worried you." He reached for her hand and she allowed it to be held.

"How did this happen? You could have died, Will." Every part of her felt like she was pretending.

"A stupid accident. That's all it was." He smiled, but it was only with his mouth. His eyes were blank.

"No. Someone hit you on the head. My information is that his name was Anthony." She watched his eyes pop wide open. "Yes, so please can you tell me the truth now? What on earth were you doing with such terrible people?"

The nurse brought cups of tea, which gave him a moment to collect his thoughts. Mrs B thanked her and took a sip while she waited for him to consider his position.

"I was around the same age as your nephew is now when I married. She was a pretty girl, Margie. We got along alright for the first few years. I had imagined that children would come along, but there were no children. Work was going well. I seemed to have the luck when it came to making arrests. I was promoted, over and over." He took a breath, closing his eyes for a moment. "Then one night I came home and Anthony Newton was sitting in the kitchen. Margie was, it turned out, his half-sister. They had the same father. Her mother was dead by the time I met her." He rested his head back against the pillows. "Every arrest had been set up for me. They had steered my career until I could be useful." He bit down hard on his lip. "I lost my temper, threatened to arrest the pair of them. They laughed at that. They would have said that I was on the take, that I had known all along that she was Anthony Newton's half-sister."

"So, you turned a blind eye. You warned them when an arrest was coming so that they could be out of the way?" She watched his eyes.

"Yes. I did, in the past. When I went to meet him the other day, I told him I would not help him any more. With Margie gone, and the chance of a new life. That was what the problem was." He touched his head.

"I have to think about this." She slid her hand out of his. "I know that it was not your fault. But I would have preferred to hear it from you, not to have to find it out myself." She patted the back of his hand. "I will see you soon, Will."

"Is this the end?" He reached for her hand.

"As I said. I need to think about it." She blinked away the tears that threatened. "Feel better soon, Will."

She walked slowly out of the ward, listening to her shoes on the hard floor echo around the high ceilings. The bus ride home gave her time to think about what he had said, and how he she felt about it.

She collected her bicycle and rode up the hill. Barbara had fallen asleep on the sofa. Mrs B laid a soft blanket over her nephew's wife, and went into the kitchen, where Marmalade waited for her. She stroked her fingers through his fur and closed her eyes. "It has been fun to think that I might have had a different life, Marmalade, but that's all it was. Only a thought. Just a possibility." She wiped the tear that fell. She sat on the kitchen chair and the kitten curled up on her lap. "Good boy, Marmalade." He purred loudly, and she smiled. "Good boy."

48.

Mrs B and the big thank you

Mrs B had almost caught up with the work she had missed. It went against the grain to let her customers down, and all the hospital visiting had taken her attention. That she had been visiting someone she barely recognised, only added to the concern she had carried with her all day. By starting early, she had managed to get through more than usual, and her customers were happy. The hill seemed a good deal steeper than it had when she left for work.

Marmalade was delighted to see her, and even more so, to curl up on her knee for a cuddle. He purred deep and low, and Mrs B smiled. He was a wonderful companion, better than she ever could have imagined. His ears pricked up just a moment before there was a knock on the back door. Gently, Mrs B lifted Marmalade down onto the floor and went to see who was there.

"Hello?" It was a strange situation. Mrs B had never had a conversation with a bouquet of flowers before. She laughed.

"Afternoon, Mrs B. These are for you." Richard's head poked around the side of the blooms.

"Do come in." Mrs B held the door open wide. "How is Patricia, and your little boy?"

"May I be honest?" He passed the flowers to her and sank into a chair.

"Always the best way to be, in my opinion." She waited for him to settle himself. "I just made tea. Would you like a cup?"

"Thank you. That would be wonderful. My mother tells me that you are very helpful to talk to. I am beside myself with worry, and nobody seems to have an idea how to help." He accepted a cup of tea and two biscuits.

"I will help if I can. Happy to." Mrs B sipped from her cup and hoped that none of the family were unwell.

"Patricia seems completely uninterested in the baby. She has hired a nurse, who is very efficient, but I feel there should be more love. I try, but I am at work so much of the time. My mother has been wonderful, of course, but she and Patricia have never been the best of friends. Our daughter, I think you met her?" He raised an eyebrow, and Mrs B nodded. "She is quite jealous of the new baby, I think. I am torn between the whole family. Only my father seems entirely unconcerned." His chin sank onto his chest.

"Well. I believe it is quite normal for the first few weeks to be tiring and emotionally draining. If Patricia has a nurse, then she might feel a little shut out of caring for her own son. Perhaps with your mother being so good with babies and with the nurse there, she feels a little that she has no role? Could that be so?" Mrs B's brows furrowed together. "It would be easy to suggest to your mother that she take your daughter for a day out and give the nurse a day off. You would be just the three of you then. Perhaps that might help with getting to know each other. It might cheer your daughter up too." She sipped her tea.

"It is worth a try. Thank you. I will put it into action today, perhaps for Saturday, as I will be at home." He smiled widely.

"It might also be a good idea to remind Patricia how much you love her, just for her, not as a mother, but as your wife." Mrs B tipped her head to the side. "Remember how cross she was about your dancing lessons?"

"Yes. That is another sterling idea. My mother was right. I am hugely grateful. For the tea and the advice." He sipped again. "Oh, for heaven's sake. I forgot the reason I came to see you. I wanted to thank you for looking after Patricia the other day, when the baby was born. You were wonderful then, and again today. We're calling him Gerald, by the way." He smiled at the thought of his son. "I hope that you will join us at the Christening?"

"Thank you, that would be most kind." Mrs B pushed the plate of biscuits across the table and watched two more disappear.

"I feel so much better, just for talking it through. Thank you again." He stepped out of the back door with a last wave.

She sat down to finish her tea, and was surprised to hear a knock at the door. Perhaps Richard had forgotten something. "Tommy? Are you quite alright?" His face was pale and sweating, and when he opened his jacket, his shirt was stained with blood. "Come in."

He sat down on the chair just recently occupied by Richard. With care, Mrs B eased the jacket from his shoulders and unbuttoned his shirt to take a look. He made a noise through gritted teeth that told her the movement had caused him pain.

"I need to clean this wound, otherwise we risk an infection. I can clean and dress it. In the past, I have stitched wounds when I worked at the hospital, but that was some time ago. More than that, you will need to see the doctor." He nodded, the sweat standing out on his forehead. "Did you get this wound on anything that could be rusty?"

"Kitchen knife." His breath was laboured.

"Stay there and I will fetch what I need." He clung to the edge of the table when she cleaned the wound with iodine. Now that she could see clearly, the cut was deep and a few inches above his hip. It was too far over, she hoped, to have caught any vital organs. "I think it needs a few stitches. Shall I fetch the doctor?" He shook his head. "Very well. I cannot do anything about the pain." He nodded his understanding, and she fetched a needle, which she held over a flame on the gas cooker to kill any germs. Once it had cooled, she threaded the needle and began to stitch the skin together. "Best I can do. I think. More iodine. It will hurt." He gripped the table and grunted through the pain. "I am going to put a dressing over this and you will need to eat something, and then sleep." She took his shirt away and came back with gauze and bandages. "It is not the neatest dressing, but it will serve."

Mrs B left him to recover and warmed some soup on the cooker. "Eat this. It will do you good." She passed him a spoon and buttered two slices of bread. When the bowl was empty and the plate only had crumbs left, she helped him up the stairs to her spare room, and left him with strict instructions to sleep.

Back downstairs, while she wondered what on earth had made someone inflict such a wound on him, she made use of her time cleaning his shirt. Her thoughts turned to her own supper, which she had given away, but while his shirt dried, she found some cheese to have with another slice of the bread.

Every hour, she checked on him through the night. His temperature stayed normal, and he slept well. She found that reassuring and hoped that she had done the right thing.

When the grey of the first light began to chase away the darkness, she put the kettle on to make another cup of tea. She would need to have a conversation with Tommy. It was none of her business to ask why someone would hurt him, but it was reasonable to check if it was likely to happen again.

49.

Mrs B asks for redemption

"Tommy?" She carried the tray into the bedroom. "I brought some breakfast. I made scrambled eggs and toast. A cup of tea. Come on now. Wake up." There was no response, and the panic rose in her chest. "Tommy?"

"Mmm." It was the most wonderful sound she had ever heard.

"Come along. Wake up! Your breakfast is getting cold." She pushed a smile onto her face.

"Did you say scrambled eggs?" His eyes were still closed.

"Open your eyes and see." He did as she asked.

"Breakfast. Thank you." He sat up in bed, winced slightly at the pain, but smiled up at her when she put the tray on his lap.

"Eat." She nodded towards the dressing. "Are we likely to see more of this?" She watched him think about the question. "Maybe what I mean is, are you safe?"

"Who is ever safe?" He bit from the toast. "I know what you did for me last night. You saved my life, maybe. I owe you. I know I said it before." He shovelled eggs into his mouth. "Thank you."

"Will you trust me enough to tell me what happened?" She leaned her hands against the foot of the bed frame.

"I trust you." He watched her for a few moments. "Alright. The friend who told me about your friend with the head wound? They worked out he was the only one in the building, so he must have called an ambulance. He was in a bad way after they caught up with him." He shrugged. "Lucky to be alive. He came to see me, to tell me not to repeat what he had told me. I told him I had told a friend. Only one, and I knew it would go no further. He was frightened. That's all this is." He bit into the toast in his hand. "He's not a bad man, but they scared him."

"Will he tell them that you know?" She chewed her lower lip. "Will they come after you?"

"He swore to them that he told nobody, phoned the ambulance anonymously from a telephone box. He would be dead if they thought he might have told a friend." Tommy carried on chewing and took a sip from his tea.

"I'm glad that you came here last night, and that I could help. I wish you had no need. You need to rest now. I will bring you some lunch when

I come back from work." She took the tray back downstairs and washed up the dishes.

Mrs B checked her hat was on straight, and cycled down to her work at Mrs Appleby's house. It needed very little, just a clean through of the kitchen and the bathroom. It seemed that her suggestion to Mrs Appleby had been working well. Perhaps life was back on track. The whole idea played on her mind while she cleaned. She needed time to think. Once the house was clean, she cycled to the church and sat in the hushed atmosphere. She had suggested reparation to Mrs Appleby. Was that possible for Will Hunton?

Mrs B closed her eyes and cleared her mind. Was it even possible to redeem himself? Perhaps he was not interested in putting things right. He seemed to be more concerned with protecting his reputation.

Redemption. Was it his, or her own that she wished for? It could only be her own. She needed forgiveness for her stupidity. Perhaps everyone can be allowed to dream that someone will care for them, even that they have held a memory carefully through their life. Real life, though, was not made of dreams. She would make her own reparations wherever possible. By helping others, she would find peace of mind, to replace the turmoil of the past week.

"Mrs B?" Reverend Chambers stood at the door. "I

am so sorry to disturb you, when you were so lost in your thoughts. Is there anything that I can do to help?"

"Thank you, dear friend. I am perfectly well. I was just thinking about how life is filled with mistakes and misjudgements." She smiled across the church at him. "Even when we start with good intentions."

"Indeed, so. I hope that you would call on me, if ever you were in need of a friend." His eyebrows raised in question.

"Thank you. I am grateful." She made her excuses and returned home. The ideas in her head might need some fine tuning, but she believed they might be made to work.

50.

Mrs B receives an invitation to a funeral

The postman dropped three envelopes through the letter box, and they landed on the mat in Mrs B's hallway.

Her breakfast was nearly ready, she was only waiting for the tea to brew. Marmalade was making short work of his food, and she collected the envelopes.

One was her electricity bill, which she checked carefully. The second was a letter from her aunt, who was making less sense with every letter. Mrs B would reply to the letter with news and friendly chat. She shrugged. The last one was in a thick, expensive envelope. It slipped open easily and inside was a stiff card. The writing on it was in a heavy copperplate hand. 'You are invited to a funeral. 9th September. 2pm.' On the rear of the card was the name and address of the church.

Mrs B checked the small diary in her handbag. She had nothing booked in for that time. She could go if she wanted to. It was such a strange idea. It had no name of the deceased, or even a note of the family. She put it down on the kitchen table. Once she had poured the tea and spread some butter on her toast, she tried to remember ever having received an invitation to a funeral. Usually one heard from the family, or from a friend. She had to admit, though, that it had piqued her curiosity.

The 9th was only two days away. She looked out her dark suit and shoes, and hung them ready on the wardrobe door.

On the morning of the 9th, she was still intrigued enough to brush her suit and pin her hat on, before she caught the bus to Potterton for the funeral.

The service began, as all funerals do. People gather to say goodbye, small conversations of no importance are shared. Everyone waits for the family to arrive. They lead the mourners into the church and then the service starts. This funeral was at least normal in that regard.

The deceased was named Carol. Mrs B could not recall anyone of that name. No member of the family was familiar, either. It was a puzzle.

After the service, she followed the rest of the mourners out of the church to where the family waited. Everyone shook hands with the tall man in a dark suit. She watched him. His eyes were hooded, and the skin below them was dark with lack of sleep. She stepped forward, and he reached for her hand. He held it in both of his.

"Thank you so much for coming. I have been looking forward to meeting you." His mouth curved into a smile. "Perhaps you would spare me a few minutes at the wake?" Mrs B nodded and moved on.

She moved through the small group of people and accepted a cup of tea and a sandwich with a polite smile.

"Mrs B? Perhaps we might have a chat?" He held out his hand, offering her a seat.

"I am afraid you have an advantage over me. I have no idea who you are." Mrs B sipped her tea before setting it down on the table next to her.

"My name is Anthony Newton." His voice was low. "This is my wife's funeral. Carol was stupid. She was also a thief. The man she left me for was a fool. He took my money and my wife." Mrs B's brows creased in confusion. "You found the money they took from me in a shed on an allotment, I hear." He rested his elbows on the arms of the chair and steepled his fingers together.

"I did. The police are holding the man and the money. I thought her name was Mrs Hargreaves. I am so sorry for your loss." She pushed against the arms of the chair to stand up.

"I wanted to ask you. If you might be prepared to work for me from time to time. You found the money. None of my men could." He shrugged.

She started to think about a reply, which would not tell him that she knew about his reputation, but would politely turn down his offer, but was distracted when she saw a familiar face across the room.

"I am so glad that we had this chance to chat, Mr Newton. Honestly, I would be of little help to you, as my days are very much booked up. I will need to get going now. Thank you for your invitation." She pushed herself up from the chair and walked towards the door. The man crossed the room to meet her halfway.

"Will. I am so glad to see that you are back on your feet." She smiled. It was genuine.

"Are you?" His eyes met hers.

"Tell the truth and shame the devil?" She lifted one shoulder. "I am pleased. I can be disappointed in you, and wish you a speedy recovery at the same time."

"You are a better friend than I deserve." He looked down into her face. "May I walk you out?"

"I am perfectly happy to walk out alone, just the way I walked in. I trust that you will be safe here?" He nodded, and she smiled, walking away from him. Her eyes stung with unshed tears in the bright sunshine outside while she waited for her bus.

51.

Mrs B takes her own advice.

Marmalade's meow was better than any alarm clock. Mrs B opened her eyes. The soft sheets that she had washed and ironed for herself, and the smooth blankets were cosy against the chill of the morning. The persistent call from the little kitten brought a smile to her lips, and she pushed back the covers. "I will be down to make breakfast shortly, Marmalade."

He was waiting in the kitchen, a picture of patience next to his bowl. His tail wrapped around his feet. She picked up his bowl and filled it. He padded his feet up and down, impatient to be eating.

Her breakfast took time, waiting for the kettle to boil and for her toast to brown. Her working day would be long, but she would come home to an empty house. That had not mattered to her before. Not until she had been offered the chance to change it.

The tea was hot, and it warmed her insides.

What would she advise someone else in her situation? She took a moment, eyes closed, her breath measured.

Of course, she knew what it was that she had been missing. She had forgotten to be grateful. She had, after all, a great deal. Her nephew and his wife and daughter for a start. Her friends, and her faith. Work that kept food in her cupboards and a roof over her head. Marmalade had finished his breakfast. He lifted his little pink nose towards her, looking for a stroke. "I forgot to be grateful for you, Marmalade. How could I forget that?" She picked him up and ran her hand over his fur.

Her first call would be to Mrs Pendle. It was time to focus on her friends and seeing what she could do to help them. Wallowing in her own problems would not solve them, it would only make her miserable.

The sky was bright blue with fluffy clouds. The smell of autumn hung in the air, and the leaves were just starting to turn. Her bicycle wheels swished their way through the dampness left by earlier drizzle on the road. The smile on her face felt a little more like it belonged there.

"Mrs Pendle?" She poked her head around the back door. There was nobody in the kitchen, but it was a mess, so that seemed like a good place to start. The pans and plates were soon washed and the whole kitchen put to rights in less than an hour. In the living room and bedroom, she followed her usual routine. Only when she had finished the bathroom did she hear someone coming into the house.

Mrs Pendle tracked mud across the freshly washed kitchen floor, and sank into a chair in front of the fire. "Oh, no! I'm sorry. The floor looked lovely, and I've ruined it." Tears began to flow unchecked down her cheeks.

"Mrs Pendle? Let me help you." Mrs B eased the boots from the sobbing woman's feet. "Now then, shall I take this little one and make you a cup of tea? You look like you could use one." Mrs B lifted the baby gently and felt the damp, cold clothing. "I am going to change the baby, and then we will sort you out. Put your feet up. I will only be a moment."

Once the child had been changed and fed a bottle, Mrs B fetched a cup of tea and a sandwich for his mother. "Are you feeling any better?"

"I'm drowning. That's what it feels like." She ran her hand over her face. "My husband had an accident. One of our sows backed into him. His foot is broken. He is in the hospital and I am here on my own. The baby was up all night, and I'm almost out on my feet."

"Bath for you, and I shall have something for you to eat before you go to bed. I am no pig farmer, but if you tell me what to do, I will manage." Mrs B helped her out of the chair and guided her to the bathroom. She ran the taps and peeled the clothes away. The water was hot, and she watched Mrs Pendle's eyes closing. "Have a soak and I will make you some food." She gathered the filthy clothes and left Mrs Pendle to soak.

The sink in the kitchen was full of soaking laundry. Mrs B shook her head. It would take a good deal of work to get them anywhere near clean. The vegetables she had chopped into a pan were bubbling. The soup would be good for Mrs Pendle. Once she had eaten and explained what was needed for the pigs, she slept. The baby took another bottle, and a fresh change, and followed his mother's example.

Mrs B visited the sows, tipping food over the side of their pens, mostly into their troughs. They seemed unworried if they had to snuffle around on the floor for any scraps that had missed. The animals seemed happy enough. A quick visit back to her own home meant that she could feed the cat before she returned to Mrs Pendle's farm.

The clothes that she had left soaking took a good deal of scrubbing, but when she checked, and checked again, she was happy to see that everything was clean. The fire in the kitchen was hot and the clothes soon dried enough to be ironed.

When the baby woke, she was able to bring him downstairs and give him another bottle before spending a happy half an hour rocking him to sleep. "You're a good little one, a sweetie. You remind me of Arnold at your age." She smiled down into his face, watching the baby's eyes slowly close.

Upstairs, she tucked the tiny boy into his cot, the soft blankets warm around his sleeping body.

Back down in the kitchen, Mrs B made herself a cup of tea. The chair by the fire was comfortable enough. She had certainly spent less comfortable nights.

She had been remiss, and she knew it. Her attention had been distracted and, as a result, she had missed Mrs Pendle's troubles. She had advised Mrs Appleby to make life better for herself by helping others, yet she had failed to take her own advice and had let down a friend in the process.

When the morning woke her, the first order of the day was to make a bottle for the little one, and a cup of tea for his mother. Once they were both comfortable, she cycled across the village to fetch Mrs Appleby to help.

Within an hour, after several visits, Mrs B had secured promises of help from half the village. This was what she should have been doing.

Mrs Pendle was in good hands, and Mrs B needed

to sleep. She cycled home, and was surprised to find someone waiting for her in the garden.

52.

Mrs B refuses

"Good afternoon." Mrs B opened the gate.

"Mrs B. We need to talk. This is urgent." Tommy was transferring his weight from foot to foot.

"Oh my, come on in, Tommy." She unlocked the back door and let him in. The cold water ran into the sink, and she filled the kettle. "Right, tell me what has happened while we wait for the tea."

"It's Tony Newton. He wants you to help him. There is money that went missing when his wife left. More than was recovered." He watched her warm the pot and pour the boiling water over the leaves. "He is determined."

"I told him that I would not work for him, and I meant it." She set the teapot on the table and fetched cups and saucers. "He cannot imagine that he can force me to."

"I think he imagines a good deal worse than that." Tommy accepted a biscuit when she offered.

"Oh. I see. Can we think of a way to stop him and his imaginings?" She poured the tea and took a sip. "You and I have been in tight scrapes before, Tommy McKinley. We most likely shall be again." She smiled across the table at him. "He may be a tough nut, but he cannot make me do a good job."

"All I am saying is not to underestimate him." He took another sip of tea. "If he comes, he will be hard to turn down. We will need a plan just in case."

"Good advice, fairly given. We shall drink our tea and plot together." She pushed the plate of biscuits towards him. "How is young Maisie?"

53.

Mrs B to the rescue

The scent that came with the end of the summer was strong in the air as she pedalled home. After work, she had called in to see Mrs Pendle and had found that Mrs Chambers was there with her little one. It was a joy to see how the village had come together to help Mrs Pendle in her hour of need.

The car that followed her up the lane was an expensive one. The engine whispered discretely. When she reached her cottage, she pushed her bicycle into the back garden and rested it against the wall.

"Mrs B?" She recognised the voice that called out to her. She wanted, more than anything, not to be right. "Please, can you give me a moment of your time?" She turned and took a look over the top of the wall.

"Mr Newton? What brings you to Little Mellington?" She leaned against the wall and watched him carefully.

"I want my money back. You're the only one I believe can find it for me. Please, could you help me?" His smile was one he clearly believed he was going to win her over.

"I thought I explained that I would not be able to do that." She watched his face carefully.

"I wondered if you might be unwilling. I am a reasonable person, a sensible businessman. That's why I have taken out some insurance." He smiled, no humour, just a lifting of the corners of his mouth. "I am used to getting my own way." She felt her brows push together. "I believe you are good friends with Will Hunton? He took a nasty knock to the head a few days ago." He held his hands up. "My fault, I'm afraid. However, you can stop all that nastiness happening again. He is my insurance." His smile was closer to a sneer than anything else.

She watched him, her glare steady. "How can I be sure that you can even find him to carry out this dreadful threat?"

"Oh, I'm so pleased that you asked that." He clapped his hands together like a small child on Christmas morning and opened the door of the car, stepping out to join her on the lane. He pulled open the back door so that she could see inside. Will was sitting with his hands tied in front of him, next to an angry-looking man. "Mr Hutton will be staying with me, as a guest until you find the money for me. Please do not refuse. That will force all sorts of unpleasant things to happen." He pushed the door shut and turned to Mrs B. "I am presuming that we have an agreement?" She nodded. "Wonderful! In which case, here are the details." He passed her a folder. "Feel free to let me know when you find it. Or if you need any information. You can reach me at the Royal Oak in Potterton." He opened the door and slid in behind the wheel. "Good day, Mrs B."

She watched him drive away. After all her planning, she had not imagined this eventuality. Will had looked scared. She closed her eyes. He had been taken because of her.

"Well, we certainly didn't see that one coming, did we?" Tommy McKinley stepped around the corner. "Let's have a cup of tea and see if any of those papers tell us anything interesting."

She nodded to herself. His sensible attitude was refreshing. They needed to start looking and stop worrying. Will Hunton was perfectly safe as long as she was working hard on finding the money, but she imagined that Mr Newton would be patient only for a short while.

54.

Mrs B begins her search

"Tommy. If you had money to hide, and you were on the run from a really scary person, where would you hide it?" She sipped from her cup. The tea was perfect. Hot enough to warm her throat on the way down, but not too hot to scald.

"I'd want it close, but not where I lived. I told you that before, right?" She nodded. "Probably a few different places, so if someone found it, they only found a fraction. I'd be careful about it though. Indoors, maybe, as I would have more control. But nobody's house." He met her eyes across the table. "He might have had different ideas from me, though." His shoulders lifted in a shrug.

She went to the cupboard and pulled out a map of Potterton, and to another for a dinner plate. With care, she positioned the plate with the property close to the centre and drew around the edge of the plate with her pencil. "If you are correct, then this is where we should look."

"We can cross out all the houses unless they're

empty. Anywhere that anyone else can go to, like a park or a library, would be too hard to watch. Somewhere that's private, but in public view. Oh. I just listened to myself. That's crazy talk." He dropped his head into his hands.

"No. Maybe not so much as you think. Look. Come on, Tommy, search this area with me." She ran her finger over the map. "These are houses. This is a church. A school. More houses. What's this?" She looked across the table and smiled. "Where better to bury something than a cemetery?"

"Oh, you little beauty. Yes. Let's go." He was already on his feet.

"No Tommy. You cannot be seen with me. Mr Newton is, I imagine, a vengeful soul. Thank you for your help. I will, I am certain, need more of your assistance, but I will not have you help me publicly." Mrs B pulled on her coat and tucked a scarf around her neck. "Marmalade likes to eat at four thirty. I will see you as soon as I can." She rested her hand on the door handle, turning to smile at him while she fussed with her scarf.

"Who are you kidding? I'm coming with you. We will be back before the cat needs to eat." He was already shrugging his own coat on. She shook her head. "I'm driving and you're on the bus. I'll get there before you." He laughed. The worry that he carried around his eyes fell away, and he looked younger. She could see what he would have been like as a child.

"Come on then. I tried, Tommy." Her shoulders dropped a little, and she climbed into the car beside him. "We have to be back for the cat, Tommy." She smiled across at him and he started the engine.

"You worry too much." He laughed.

"How is your scar feeling where I stitched you up?" His laughter died. "You do not worry enough."

55.

Mrs B goes searching

The cemetery was behind houses, not the houses where Mr Hargreaves had last seen his wife, but not far away. They walked slowly, unsure of what to look for. After an hour, they had found nothing.

"These recent graves have no stones. Perhaps if we could find out the names of the people buried here, it might give us an idea?" Mrs B strode towards the small office near to the gate, returning just a few minutes later with a map. "I believe that perhaps Mr Hargreaves had a sense of humour." She held out the paper to Tommy. His brows pushed together while he read the list. Mrs B, however, had no time for him to think about it. She was walking fast, striding towards the area of the graveyard where burials were currently being made.

Once she located number eight hundred and forty-seven, she made certain that she took a note of where she was. It would be necessary to come back later, when nobody was around to check on people digging up a fresh grave. Everything that she believed in balked at the thought of desecrating a holy burial, but this was a chance to rescue Will. She might need to compromise on the difficulties she would feel.

"Oh my. Yes, indeed. He had a sense of humour." Tommy stood behind her. "Are you thinking that we might come back here this evening?" He lifted his eyebrow.

"To be honest, Tommy, I am very uncomfortable with the whole idea, but it seems that you agree. I shall bring back a few flowers to plant as an apology. The poor man who is buried here was not involved and should not be disturbed, but perhaps, if we are right, we can leave him more peaceful without the stolen money in his final resting place." She folded her hands in front her of her and whispered a prayer.

"We had better get back to feed your cat then, and wait for the cemetery to close." Tommy smiled down at her.

The paper in his hand had a muddy smudge under the name of the man buried in the grave in question. Mr Newtown. It was close enough.

56.

Mrs B's night out

"Do you have anything less formal?" Tommy stood at the bottom of the stairs.

"This is my first trip to a graveyard after dark. I was unsure of the protocol." She shook her head slightly.

"Try these." He passed a bag to her, and she peered inside.

"Trousers? I have never worn trousers." She thought about it. They might be the more practical garment. "Very well." Upstairs again, she tried them on. They were a revelation. Of course, they were too long for her, and she needed to roll up the legs to stop herself from falling over, but she now understood why men strode about so much. It was so easy without the difficulties of skirts. "Thank you, Tommy. I think I shall need to purchase some for myself."

"They suit you. Shall we go?" He pulled his coat on and opened the front door for her.

They left the car around the corner and walked to the back fence of the cemetery, where Tommy had spotted an easier place to climb over than the front gates. She watched where he put his feet, and his hands, and with one hand in his, she made it over the fence in once piece.

They moved quietly along the grassed walkway. The hedges on either side shielded them from any onlookers, but made it darker than she had expected. When she was certain that she was in the right area, Mrs B pulled a torch out of the bag, which she had across her back. "Eight four three. We're close. Here it is, eight four seven." She dropped to her knees and allowed the bag to slide to the ground, pulling out her gardening trowel and the plants that she had brought with her. "I would imagine it would only be a shallow dig, if it is here." She whispered over her shoulder to Tommy. Her trowel slid easily into the earth. Nothing. Each time she pushed into the soil and found nothing, she moved another three inches away from the grave number. When she reached the next marker, she shook her head. "Sorry Tommy, there's nothing there."

"Ah, but I think our Mr Hargreaves was a tricky so and so. Look." He shone the torch on the next grave. The marker showed three hundred and forty-eight and the one after that showed three hundred and forty-six. "I think he might have switched the numbers."

"Yes. Brilliant Tommy. Let's check." She turned and pushed her trowel in again. On the first push, they both heard a clunk when it hit something hard. Together, they cleared the thin layer of soil and pulled out a shallow biscuit tin. Tommy opened a corner and his eyes popped open. "Cash?" He nodded and slapped the tin closed. She moved further down the grave and found another box.

With the practiced movements of an experienced gardener, Mrs B planted her flowers, and they retreated from the graveyard. Each of them carrying one of the biscuit boxes.

"A good night's work, Tommy. I think we deserve a cup of tea." Mrs B declared when they climbed into his car.

"Yes, indeed." Tommy smiled across at her and they drove home to find that Marmalade was most put out at being left waiting.

57.

Mrs B goes on the offensive

"Hello?" Mrs B stood near the bus stop. It was evident to her that this exact situation was how she had met Tommy. Although she had no hopes of friendship with Anthony Newton, the feelings she had about entering a public house were the same. It was entirely inappropriate and would never happen. She shifted her weight from foot to foot. The young man who was about to enter the building paused with his hand on the door.

"What do you want?" His brusque manner was a shock to her.

"I need to speak with Mr Newton. He asked me to contact him here." She pointed to the sign above the door. "The Royal Oak."

"Wait here." He pointed to the pavement.

"Thank you so much. I am so grateful for your help." She smiled as sweetly as she could. He shrugged, and pushed open the door, leaning his shoulder into it. The warm fug from inside floated across the pavement towards her. The door bounced back against the frame. When it opened again, Mr Newton emerged.

"Well, well. You have news for me?" He had been drinking. His eyes were glazed and his hand reached out for the support offered by the door.

"I have the money. I found it." She kept her voice low. "I will give it to you in return for Will Hunton."

"Oh, very good. I knew you would do it. Lovely! I am very happy." He was loud, and she flinched from the sound.

"Perhaps you might call by my house to drop off Will and collect your money in the morning?" She nodded and stepped away from him.

"No. Let's go now. Come on. I'll grab someone to drive." He leaned forward from the waist. "I've had a few drinks, so I'm not certain that driving would be a good idea." His tone was conspiratorial.

"Only if we collect Will Hunton on the way." She straightened her back and met his somewhat glazed expression with her own firm stare. "The money is hidden. You will not find it unless I tell you where it is. I shall not tell you until Will Hunton is returned to me unharmed."

"You demand a great deal for a little old lady." His lip lifted in a sneer and he staggered a little.

"A little old lady who found your money when

nobody else could." She reminded him.

He threw back his head and laughed. "Fair enough. You know that I can pick up Hunton any time I want, I presume?"

"I will not even tell you what I can do. If you pick up Will Hunton again, or threaten him, or if he catches the sniffles unexpectedly, you will find out. Now, come along, Mr Newton, if you will. I have a very busy afternoon, and you are taking up my time." The young man who had been dragged from the pub to drive the car hid his laughter by turning his face away, but his shaking shoulders gave him away.

"Fetch the car, Ronnie." Mr Newton pointed at the young man.

"No need, but thank you for the offer. I have already arranged a lift. I will be expecting you once you have collected Mr Hunton." She walked around the corner and turned right. Tommy was in the car waiting, as agreed.

"How did it go?" He put the car into gear, and they moved away from the pavement.

"I think that he imagined that I would bring the money in a shopping bag." She shook her head a little. "You will need to drop me off and get going. I don't want you to bump into Mr Newton at my house."

"It's fine. OK. I will park at the church and walk

back up. He will have no idea." She nodded across at him.

As good as his word, he dropped her to the house and was back in five minutes; he was a little out of breath, and pink in the face, but he beat Anthony Newton to the cottage, which was the only thing he minded about.

When the knock came, they were expecting it. Tommy stayed in the living room while Mrs B opened the door.

"Mr Newton? Where is Will Hunton?" He lifted his foot to step inside the house. "I'm sorry, Mr Newton, I did not invite you into my house."

"Will is in the car. I want to see the money that you found." They had been expecting this.

"Very well. I have one of the boxes that I found. A sample, if you like? The rest is hidden. You can have it as soon as I have Will back safe." She pushed the shopping bag by her feet into the gap created by the open door.

"You are not serious." He reached down into the bag. "It's in a biscuit box, for goodness' sake."

"Yes, it is. Safe and dry. No nibbles from the wildlife." She smiled as widely as she was able.

"Fine." He threw his hands in the air. "You are the most infuriating woman I have ever met." She stayed at the door while he walked back to his car. "Hunton! Get out of the car!"

She held her breath, watched the door open and Will unfold from the seat within. He looked well. The bandage was gone from his head, and apart from looking a little pale, he seemed untouched by the ordeal.

"Will?" She watched his eyes. His smile.

"You did all this to get me home. Thank you. I had no reason to think that you would." He stepped towards her, but Anthony Newton's hand snapped out, barring his way.

"You wait. Give me the rest." His arm might have been against Will's chest, but his eyes never left Mrs B.

"Here you are." She reached behind the door and unhooked the bag from the back of it. She held it out. "Will, come inside. It's getting a little chilly." She opened the door a little wider.

The two men walked together towards her. She held out the bag, which Anthony Newton took, and Will slipped in through the door.

"I am very rarely impressed. You are an exception, however. Thank you." Mr Newton raised his hat and nodded his head. "Good day to you."

Mrs B pushed the door closed and leaned against it. Her heart was pounding in her chest.

"You got your man back safely, then?" Tommy poked his head through the living room door.

"Tommy McKinley? Whatever next?" Will Hunton held on tight to the door frame.

"Tommy has been a good friend. You owe him your thanks." Mrs B took a deep breath.

"The two of you need to have some time to chat." He smiled down at Mrs B. "Always a pleasure." He sketched a salute at Will Hunton. "Chief Inspector." Tommy let himself out of the back door and he was gone.

"He was right. It is time we had a talk." Will reached for her.

"I had better put the kettle on, then." Mrs B told him with a pat to his arm.

58.

Mrs B tells the truth

"Thank you. You brought me home." He slumped into a chair in the kitchen. His face dropped into his hands. "I was honestly not certain that you would."

"I would have hoped that you would have more faith in me." She tipped her head to one side and watched him. The kettle screeched to a boil and pulled her from her reverie.

Once the tea was made and the cups and saucers waited on the table, Mrs B slid into the chair opposite Will. "We need to talk about this. There are some questions I need answered first, though." She checked the tea and poured two cups. "Here, have a drink. This will make you feel better." She pushed the cup across the table.

He sipped. "Lovely. Thank you. That is exactly what I needed."

"Right. I need to know. Is your connection with Mr Newton over and done with?" Mrs B sipped from her cup.

"Yes. Whilst I was staying with him, we talked at length. He threatened to go to the press with information about my marriage. I told him not to bother. I plan to retire. That way, I will be of no further use to him and no further danger to you." He reached a hand halfway across the table. "I have no reason to think that you might even think of me that way, but it was the only way I could think of that would take the power he held over me out of his hands."

"Yes. You thought your way through it. I am impressed." Her hand moved towards his. "I realised a few things, Will, while I was trying to work out how to find Mr Newton's money. I was angry with you." She shrugged and picked up her cup again, clattering it down into her saucer without a sip taken. "That is untrue. I was furious. I allowed myself to imagine that you and I might have had a future together." She closed her eyes. "Ridiculous. I made myself foolish for you." She wiped across her face to catch the tears with her fingers. "I have very little left, but I have my dignity."

"You have a great deal more than that. A wonderful mind, and a generous heart." He opened his hand. "The happiest I have been in years was the time we spent together. I had such hopes. All the time I knew that the secret that hung over me: my connection with Newton would prevent us from being together." He laid his hand flat on the table. "I was weak. When I should have told you the truth, I hid from it." He closed his eyes. "I am sorry."

"It seems to me that you are giving up before we have even discussed it." She smiled across the table at him.

His hand found hers, and they sat at the table while they drank their tea. The clock in the kitchen ticked. The hands moving around until their tea was cold, yet still they sat. There was nowhere else that they wished to be.

59.

Mrs B takes a chance.

The sunlight woke Mrs B, and she was pleased to find that she still had a smile on her face. Will had left late in the evening. They had talked very little. She knew that the conversation would have to come. It would be uncomfortable. Even knowing all of that, she looked forward to it.

Marmalade met her at the bottom of the stairs. He had plenty to say about life. He trotted towards to kitchen, mewing as he went, his tail swaying behind him.

The day ahead was booked with work. The police station, and Mrs Appleby would need a visit. She would call in to see Mrs Pendle, to make certain that everything was going well with her. First things first, though. Breakfast for her and for her kitten. Once he had eaten, she watched the little cat walk away. He was growing into a very dear companion for her. Her cup was empty and the kitchen clock had ticked around to eight o'clock. It was time to go. "Be a good boy, Marmalade."

She called to him as she pushed her feet into her shoes.

She parked her bicycle against the wall of the police station and slipped into the canteen. "Good morning, Kathleen." She waved to her friend, who was busy with a queue of customers. The cupboard where she kept her cloths and polish was under the stairs. She took what she needed, but heard a familiar voice, which made her pause. Out in the hallway, she saw Arnold chatting to another officer.

"Hello, Auntie. Have you got five minutes to have a cup of tea with me? I need to talk to you." He was happy to see her nod her agreement, and they walked back into the canteen together. Mrs B was pleased to see that Kathleen had finished serving, and he quickly ordered two teas and carried them to a table. Kathleen followed him with two plates.

"I just had a delivery from the baker. Iced buns are the best when they are fresh." She put the plates down. "Oh my, sorry, I have to go. There are so many customers today." She bustled away, leaving them to chat.

"How are you, Arnold?" She took a sip from the cup.

"Well, thank you. I stopped you, because I have some news, and I wanted you to hear it from me." She waited while he gathered himself. "It's the

Chief Inspector. He has retired with immediate effect. Perhaps that injury was worse than we thought." He took a sip from his cup. "I know that you and he were very close."

She took a breath. He had done as he had promised. Her breath came a little more easily. Perhaps she had been waiting to see if he would live up to his word. Arnold was waiting for a response from her.

"Sorry. Well, you might be right. He is a few years older than me. I would imagine that he would have retired soon enough, anyway." She took a small bite from the iced bun.

"I'm not certain who will take over from him. Someone will have to. I'll let you know as soon as I know. I have to go." He picked up his iced bun and waved it in the air, leaving her to her thoughts.

The question which was racing around her mind was whether Mr Newton would accept that Will would be no further help to him.

All through the station, the talk was of the Chief Inspector. She moved through the building, her hands working automatically while her mind was free to consider the possibilities.

Mrs Pendle was looking much better, and Mrs B was pleased to see Mr Pendle propped up on cushions in front of the fire. "You're back home. That is good news." She watched him bounce the baby on his good knee.

"Thank you for looking after my family. I am so grateful." Marmalade's mother threaded her way around Mrs B's ankles. Mr Pendle watched her carefully.

"We are friends, I believe. Why on earth would I not help a friend in need? Perish the thought, Mr Pendle." She patted his arm and left him with his son.

Mr Newton was waiting in his car in the lane. "Good afternoon, Mrs B." He turned to look through the window, his hand on the steering wheel.

"Mr Newton." She nodded her greeting.

"My brother-in-law appears to have gone through with his resignation. That makes me very angry. There is, of course, nothing that I can do about it, which makes me crosser still." He chewed his lower lip. "I will find a way around it, and you can be certain that I will be in touch." He drove away without another word.

Mrs B shook her head. He was a dangerous enemy to have, and she would have to think carefully about what could be done.

"Mrs B?" She looked around to see who was calling her. There was nobody that she could see.

"Hello?" She turned a full circle.

"Hello. He's trouble. I heard your man chucked

in his job, that's why I came to see you. It might be the smart move, but watch your back. The Newtons are furious." Tommy stood up behind the wall so that she could see him.

"I think you may be correct, Tommy. Are you in the mood for a cup of tea and a chat?" She raised an eyebrow.

"I'll meet you at your house. It's not safe for you to be seen with me. Not with all this going on." Tommy disappeared behind the wall again, and Mrs B set off up the lane.

60.

Mrs B under pressure

Mrs B made it home before Tommy arrived. She put the kettle on, certain that he wouldn't be far behind.

When she heard the back door open, she was expecting to see Tommy's cheerful smile, but the face that greeted her was Anthony Newton's.

"Well, Mr Newton, this is the second time today." She tried to keep the nervous tremor out of her voice. "As you said earlier, Mr Hunton has retired. He really cannot be of any further use to you. I found your money, Mr Newton. I cannot imagine that we have anything further to discuss." She twisted the tea towel between her hands.

"Do I make you nervous?" He lifted an eyebrow. "I should." He smiled, but his eyes were cold.

"What is it that you want, Mr Newton?" She straightened out the tea towel she had been twisting and laid it over the back of the chair.

"I want you to look into something for me. It's important." He sat down and pointed to the chair opposite him, which she sank into. "My daughter. She's gone missing. She's seventeen. It's been three days. I am terrified. Her mother and I separated when I met Carol." He dropped his face into his hands. "I'm begging you.

She's my treasure. She's the most important person in the world to me."

"I'm so sorry. Tell me about her." Mrs B dropped the cloth on the table and reached across to him, although she stopped before she touched him.

"She's lovely, kind and gentle." He took his wallet out of his pocket and showed her a photograph.

"When was she last seen?" Mrs B rested her hands on the table.

"She's been seeing someone. A man. He's taken her away." He put some effort into pulling himself together. "She was supposed to come and see me. She wanted to catch the bus, and her mother agreed. The bus should have got her to me at half-past two, but she never arrived. Please. I know you hate me, but this is my daughter."

"Don't be ridiculous. I don't hate you. You have to stop this drama. The important thing is to find your daughter." The back door opened, and Tommy walked in.

"McKinley? What are you doing here?" Anthony Newton glared across the kitchen.

"He is my friend, and he was invited. Neither of which are claims that you can make." Mrs B shrugged, shaking her head. "If you want my help, you need to stop all this nonsense."

Mr Newton thought about it for a moment. "Sorry." He held out his hand to Tommy. They shook. "I'm beside myself with worry about my daughter."

"Give me her address, and I will make some enquiries." Mrs B pushed a piece of paper across the table and watched him write the details.

"Please bring Maisie back to me." He stood up from the table. "If you need anything, you know how to reach me." He left the house, and the back door swung closed behind him.

61.
Mrs B makes some choices

"Tommy. Is Mr Newton in his car?" She folded her hands on the table in front of her.

"He is." He turned back from the kitchen window.

"Please tell me that your Maisie is not Maisie Newton." She raised beseeching eyes to him.

"Ah." He fiddled with his sleeve.

"Tommy McKinley. How could you not tell me?" She ran her hand over her forehead.

"She is perfectly safe. But she's afraid." He sat down in the chair across the table from her. "Her mother is unkind. Angry and unhappy. Her father lives over a pub, surrounded by thieves and thugs." He hung his head. "Please don't ask her to go home."

"Perish the thought. You know me better than that. But her parents, despite their shortcomings, and I believe that there have been many, are still human beings, no matter how flawed or damaged they are." She pushed herself up from the table. "Can you tell me where she is?"

"She doesn't want to go home." His tone was petulant.

"She will not be an adult until she is twenty-one. Legally, she is still a child." She reached across the table. "Tommy, we need to tread carefully. She is sad, and probably lonely, but her parents are her legal guardians. If we are to resolve this, we must do so by negotiation." She patted his hand. "Can you take me to her? I think it is time that I met your Maisie."

"You will not tell them where she is?" His face creased with worry.

"Perish the thought that I would ever betray a confidence. I promise you, Tommy, I will not push Maisie to do anything that she does not choose." There was sadness. He saw it around her eyes. "Can you take me to see her?"

"She will be angry with me." He studied his hands.

"I will explain. Better that I find her, and try to agree a better resolution of this problem than one of her father's thugs, surely?" Mrs B pulled her coat on. "No time for waiting, I'm afraid."

Tommy drove through Potterton and beyond, into the next village and then the next town. "This is the place. She rented a room here." He parked the car.

The front door creaked and opened into a damp hallway. Tommy led the way up the stairs and knocked on a door. "Maisie?" They heard someone moving inside the room. The door opened just an inch.

"Tommy?" Her eyes were enormous. She opened the door. "You brought someone with you? Tommy, how could you? You promised." She was angry and clearly frightened.

"This is Mrs B. I told you about her. She wants to help." Her eyes searched his face, finally allowing the door to open enough to let them in.

"Miss Newton, please. I think I have an idea, a way out of this. You do not, I know, plan to live the rest of your life here. May I sit down?" Mrs B clutched her handbag with both hands. The room was dirty, in need of a coat of paint, and had a musty smell about it. Maisie held out her hand towards the only chair in the room. "Thank you, dear. I understand." She took Maisie's hands in hers. "You and Tommy had such a similar childhood. Both of you grew up in similar families, with the same threats and worries. It may be that you will be in love forever, but if you want to live a life without looking over your shoulders, you will need to convince your families that you are safe and they are, too."

"She's right." Tommy shrugged. "She usually is."

"What if I convinced your father that I could

keep you safe? Would you like to come and stay with me for a little while? You will be more comfortable than you are here." Mrs B reached forwards and took Maisie's hands again.

"Can you?" Maisie gripped Mrs B's hands.

"To be absolutely honest, my dear, I am not certain, but I will do my very best." Mrs B turned to look at Tommy. "Are you certain of your feelings for her? This is going to be difficult for both of you."

"I love her." The simplicity of his words, and the strength of feeling that they carried, surprised Mrs B, and from the look on her face, Maisie too.

"Very well. Maisie, you will need to wait here, and Tommy will come with me. I am going to attempt to convince your father that you will be safest and happiest if you stay with me for a while." She patted the young girl's hands. "Wish me luck?" Mrs B stood up, and was surprised to find Maisie's arms wrapped around her.

"Thank you." Maisie squeezed more tightly.

"Oh no, it's far too early to be thanking me! Come along Tommy, you need to drive me to meet Maisie's father."

62.

Mrs B has a meeting

Mrs B left Tommy in the car and walked to the front of the Royal Oak. The young boy she had met there before was outside. "Hello. I wonder if you might ask Mr Newton to come outside to speak to me?" He looked her up and down and seemed to reach a decision, disappearing inside the pub.

"Did you find her?" He stopped just short of grabbing her shoulders.

"Yes, indeed I did. You and I need to have a conversation, please, if you will, Mr Newton. Perhaps we might have a cup of tea." She pointed across the road to a small café.

"Was she alright, unhurt?" Mrs B nodded and crossed the road. The bell above the door of the café jangled to announce their arrival. They sat down at a small table.

"First of all, she is perfectly well." She watched him breathe a sigh of relief. "It appears that there have been some very unpleasant arguments with her mother. She no longer wishes to live there. She also does not wish to live with you over a pub, where she is surrounded by men of whom she is afraid." The young girl arrived at the table with a pad and the stub of a pencil. "A pot of tea for two please dear."

"Her mother was always a bit fiery. She drove me mad when I was with her. Maisie would be safe with me. She knows that." His brows pushed together.

"She knows nothing of the sort. I have a feeling that there is more going on, but I am unable to find out what. I have, however, made an offer to Maisie. Whilst I know that this was done without your authority, she is so very upset that I thought it better to give her an option, rather than have her run off again." The girl brought the pot of tea on a tray with cups, saucers and a milk jug. "Thank you, dear."

"Just tell me where she is, and I will bring her home." He laid his hands flat on the table.

"She will run away again. Worse, we will have lost her trust. I might not be able to find her next time." Mrs B poured a cup of tea for him and offered milk and sugar.

He took a deep breath and huffed out a sigh. "What did you offer her?"

"That she come to stay with me. She would be perfectly safe. No arguments with her mother.

She can come to church with me, and help with the flower arranging." She sipped from her cup. "It will probably be extremely boring for her, but that might be a good thing. She might wish to return home to her mother, or to you."

He took a sip, watching her over the rim of his cup. "You remind me of my mother." He smiled at her surprised expression. "She was a tough negotiator, not as polite as you. She had eight children and no money. My father spent his life in and out of jail. Life must have been hard for her, but she kept pushing forward." He sipped from his tea again. "I think she would have liked you."

"She sounds like a remarkable woman. Your daughter perhaps takes after her grandmother." She watched him think about it, concentrating on keeping her breathing steady.

"You may be right." He drank the rest of his tea. "I will visit once a week. If I see anything that suggests she is not being well cared for, she will be coming home with me."

"Very well. I will do my very best to help her." She finished her tea. "When will I expect your visit?"

"I will surprise you." He smiled, but his eyes were cold.

63.

Mrs B's houseguest

"Good morning, Maisie dear. I've made you some breakfast. We have a busy day today." Mrs B rapped on the bedroom door.

They shared breakfast and Mrs B fed Marmalade. He had decided, after initially being quite timid around her, that he liked Maisie.

"Why are we busy today? It's Sunday, nobody works on a Sunday." Maisie bit into the toast.

"I promised your father that you would attend church. Then we need to rush home and make a roast dinner, as we have guests coming." Mrs B took a sip from her cup.

"Who is coming to dinner?" Maisie smiled. Mrs B could see why Tommy was so in love with her. She was beautiful, but also charming. Her eyes lit with delight at the thought of guests. "Is it Tommy? Is he coming to dinner?"

"Yes, he is, and also your Uncle Will." Mrs B smiled across the table. "Pop upstairs and find a nice dress. We need to leave in ten minutes." Maisie ran for the stairs. Mrs B sipped the last of her tea. She was becoming very attached to the girl.

The walk to the church was pleasant. Maisie chatted happily all the way there. Reverend Chambers turned to greet them. "Good morning, Mrs B and this must be Maisie."

"Good morning, Reverend Chambers." Mrs B led Maisie in and they sat together. The service started with a welcome and a hymn. They stood to sing. The notes wheezing from the organ pipes. The villagers lifted their voices in song, but one by one, they stopped. They listened in awe to a voice of such sweetness and power, more so than they had ever heard. The notes she sang lifted to the ancient rafters, filling the space with such strength and joy that they discovered that they had tears in their eyes. At the end of the hymn, a hush fell over the congregation.

Reverend Chambers stumbled through the prayers, and the readings, clearly distracted. The second hymn started with everyone singing, but quickly became a solo, with Maisie singing and the rest of the congregation listening in silent awe.

"Please be seated." Reverend Chambers looked from face to face. "I had a sermon ready to go, but honestly, perhaps we need to think about the gifts that the good Lord bestows upon us. The wonder of young Maisie's voice has shown us how she has been blessed. Each of us has a gift or an ability, and just as Maisie has shared with us today, we can all help each other by using our own abilities." He smiled widely. "I wonder if we might ask Maisie to sing for us again."

Maisie looked around her, then at Mrs B. "You have a beautiful voice, dear. Go and sing."

Maisie stood, a faint blush painting her cheeks, and held the hymn book open in front of her. The organist began to play. When she opened her mouth to sing, the people of Little Mellington sat in rapture, listening to the notes that soared through the small church.

It took a long time for Mrs B and Maisie to leave, by the time everyone had congratulated her on the wonderful singing. They walked back up the hill together. Maisie was excited, her steps halfway between walking and skipping.

"Have you ever had singing lessons, Maisie?" Mrs B tipped her head to one side.

"No. I've never really sung much. I used to sing when I was at home, but it annoyed my mother." She smiled at Mrs B. "I'd never met those people before, but they were so happy to hear me singing. They were very kind."

A car pulled up next to them on the lane. Maisie looked in through the window. "Hello Maisie."

"Tommy!" She squealed. "I have missed you."

"I will walk up. You jump in with Tommy." Mrs B leaned in to the window. "Straight to the house, please, Tommy." She fixed him with a firm stare.

"Of course, Mrs B." He reached for Maisie's hand.

Mrs B watched the car pull away and smiled to herself. She trusted Tommy, even if she did not know Maisie very well.

Will's car was parked outside the house when she arrived. "We are a little late, I am afraid. Maisie was quite a sensation. Not to worry, we can chat while the dinner cooks." She smiled up at him, and felt his hand on her back as he stepped back to let her through the gate.

"Mrs B! Mrs B!" Mrs Goffey was rushing up the lane towards them. "I must speak to you."

"You had better come in and tell me all about it while I peel the potatoes." Mrs B held open the gate and waited for Mrs Goffey to join her.

64.

Mrs Goffey's surprise

"Please take a seat, Mrs Goffey. I hope that you will forgive me if I peel the potatoes while we chat?" Mrs B lit the gas oven, pulled potatoes out of the cupboard, and set out a piece of newspaper on the table to catch the peelings.

"I have something to tell you. It's very important." Mrs Goffey folded her hands over each other on the table. "As you will have noticed, Daphne was visiting for the weekend. She is working as a secretary. Perhaps you recall my telling you?" Mrs B nodded and waited for Mrs Goffey to continue. "She works for a man who is well respected. He makes programmes for the wireless." She nodded, her pride in her daughter clear.

"Yes, it was lovely to see your daughter at church this morning." Mrs B carried on peeling the potatoes.

"She is driving at this very moment to see her employer." Mrs Goffey paused. "He is in the process of making a religious programme, which will be broadcast once a week. Daphne listened, as we all did, to your friend Maisie singing today and she immediately knew that she was exactly the person that they have been looking for." Mrs Goffey leaned across the table, lowering her voice for confidentiality. "Daphne has always had wonderful taste in music."

"Are you telling me that they will want to have Maisie sing on the wireless?" Mrs B laid down the potato and her knife. "That is very exciting. I will speak to her parents and see if they are prepared to allow her to perform." She reached across the table. "It is very kind of you and of Daphne, of course, to wish to offer this opportunity to Maisie. I am grateful." She patted Mrs Goffey's hand. "Truly."

A smile lit up Mrs Goffey's face. "I am pleased. I will tell Daphne when she comes home." She gathered her handbag and buttoned her coat. "I will wish you a good day, Mrs B."

"Thank you, Mrs Goffey." Mrs B smiled across the table at Mrs Goffey, reaching to clasp her hands.

The pile of peelings grew on the newspaper while Mrs B imagined Mr Newton's reaction to the news. Dinner would be a little late, but she could hear that Will, Tommy and Maisie were chatting and happy. She could afford a little time to think about how best to help her young friends.

65.

Mrs B arranges an audition

Dinner had been comfortable. Whatever ice there might have been between Will and Tommy had been broken before they sat down to eat roast beef.

"You should have heard Maisie sing today. She was really rather marvellous." Mrs B sliced into a crispy roasted potato.

"Why have I never heard you sing?" Tommy's brows pushed together in confusion.

"My mother always told me not to make a racket when I sang at home. Today, with all those kind people around me, they were singing all around me. It was just like I let go." She helped herself to a little more gravy. "This is delicious."

"Perhaps, if I might suggest? I will ask Mr Phelps if he might spare you an hour. He can play the organ whilst you sing. Tommy could hear you. It would be a wonderful experience for him." Mrs B patted her hand. "In any case; I believe that you and Tommy have things to discuss."

"If you need to go down and arrange it with the organist, we will do the dishes." Will smiled happily. "After a dinner this wonderful, it is the very least that we can do."

Tommy and Maisie walked to the church and met Mrs B on the steps. "Mr Phelps was delighted to play for you. He's waiting inside."

Will stopped the car outside the church. "Are you going to tell me where we are going?"

"Oh, yes indeed. We need to go to the Royal Oak in Potterton." She smiled across at him. "Thank you Will. You're a good man."

Mr Newton was not pleased to be asked to come with them with no further information, and surprised when Will parked outside the church. He lifted an eyebrow but followed them out of the car.

The notes that drifted out of the church door were pure and beautiful. Mr Newton tipped his head to one side and stepped through the open church door. He stood just inside, listening to Maisie sing. After a few minutes, he turned to Mrs B. "You knew that she could sing like this?"

"I found out today. She has a gift and an opportunity, which is why I asked you to come and listen to her." Mrs B hid her smile at his expression, caught between surprise and rapture.

"Mr Newton? I'm Gerald Morley." He held out his hand. "I run a programme on the wireless. You might have listened to it?" Anthony Newton shook his head. "No matter. I came here to listen to your daughter sing, and I am not disappointed. She can be singing on the wireless within the week." He turned to look at Maisie. "Keep singing, Maisie. You're doing really well." He turned back to Anthony Newton.

"Do you know who I am?" He leaned into Morley's face.

"I believe I have heard of you." Morley's eyes widened.

"Good. Write down the amount you will be paying my daughter each week, where she will have to work, how many hours. All of that. I need to have a conversation with some people out here, then you and I will discuss it." He fixed Morley with a look; which made him sit down suddenly. He strode out of the church, and with Maisie's notes twirling through the air around him, he beckoned Mrs B and Tommy towards him.

66.

Mrs B makes a deal

"Please tell me what you are thinking of? Why would you invite that slimy thing in there near my daughter?" Anthony Newton's voice was low and dangerous.

"I have a few things to tell you." Mrs B held out her hand to quiet Tommy's reaction. His chest puffed out in indignation. "Maisie and Mr McKinley here are in love." She watched Anthony Newton rear up and move towards Tommy. "She is in an innocent. Mr McKinley has made sure that she stays that way. He has protected her. She could have taken a bus anywhere, been alone in a big city. He kept her safe. His intentions are honourable and include marriage." She watched his nostrils flare, and his breathing hitch.

"No. A McKinley will not marry my daughter." He moved towards Tommy.

"They could have driven north, gone to Gretna Green and come back married. Tommy's choice not to. She loves him. She would go anywhere with him." Mrs B reached for Newton's arm. "My understanding of the situation is that she is safer with him that without. She has an amazing talent. The entertainment industry is, however, a murky one by all accounts. Perhaps between Tommy and yourself, you can give her the protection that she needs, and still allow her to sing as she should."

Newton turned to Tommy. "You love her?"

"I absolutely do." Tommy held out his hand to Maisie's father.

"I knew your mother. You look like her." He nodded. "You know the stories, I am sure, but you and I should sit down and talk them through?" Anthony Newton took the hand that had been offered in friendship.

"Thank you. It would be a pleasure, Mr Newton." Tommy's smile was nervous, but it was there.

"Right, you and I need to have a discussion with Morley, I believe." He turned towards the church. "And it's Tony, not Mr Newton."

Mrs B watched them walk into the church while the melody of Ave Maria drifted out, with Maisie's voice lifting the notes up into the rafters of the ancient church.

67.

Mrs B is accused

"Mr Morley?" Tommy McKinley stepped into the church, keeping his voice low. "This is Maisie's father. I believe you met earlier?"

"Morley. You know me, and my reputation." Morley nodded his head. "Good. No need for me to explain then. You need to listen very carefully." He waited for agreement to flit across Morley's face. "My daughter is my treasure. She is my everything. If you lay a single one of your grubby fingers on my child, I will remove it from your hand. Do you understand?" It was clear from the pale, sweaty skin on Morley's face that he was all too aware. "If anyone who works for you, or is in any way is connected with you, touches my girl, I will come after you. Mr McKinley will be watching. He will tell me what happens." He nodded to Tommy. "Now show me those figures that you have for me."

"I promise you, Mr Newton, I have no intention of anything like you are suggesting."

He stuttered and stumbled over the words but pulled paperwork from his briefcase. "She will be perfectly safe." He held his hands out in front of him, then curled his fingers under his palms, perhaps remembering Anthony Newton's threat.

"I think you can do better on the starting offer for her wages. Also, it seems that she would not be able to accept any offers to work elsewhere, whilst under contract to you. Perhaps I have misread that section." Newton raised an eyebrow. "Perhaps you could make that section clearer."

Morley took the contract and changed the clause that restricted her work and increased the payment details. He passed the paper back and waited.

"Yes. That will do." Newton nodded, a smile spreading across his face as Maisie joined the group. "Maisie love, do you want to sing for Mr Morley? It would mean living away from here, away from home." He watched her eyes. "Mr McKinley has agreed to travel with you, and make sure that you are safe. Mr Morley has guaranteed that you will be well looked after. I will expect a letter every week, telling me everything that you are doing." He waited for her response, and her squeal of joy and the hug that she wrapped around him left no doubt. "Very well, you sign here, and I will sign here and here." He pointed and waited for her to sign. "Will you sing again for me?" She ran back to the organist and filled the building with her joyous notes.

"Morley. When does she have her first appointment with you?" He watched Morley check his diary.

"Wednesday, and then Sunday." He nodded to himself.

"Give the address to Mr McKinley and he will make sure that she is there on time." He shooed the pair of them out of the church and turned to watch and listen to his daughter. In the back row of pews, Mrs B sat listening. "You set this up?"

"Not at all. My neighbour's daughter works for Mr Morley and told him about Maisie." She shook her head. "She is rather wonderful, isn't she?"

"You're a crafty old woman." He smiled. "I misjudged you. Tell me something?"

"If I know the answer." Mrs B turned slightly to look at him.

"Do you think Maisie is my daughter?" He kept his voice low and his eyes focused on hers.

"I have never considered her not being." She watched him.

"Her mother told me that there was someone else." He shrugged. "It was when I left her, perhaps just anger and spite talking." He shrugged. "Do you think you would be able to find out?"

"Heavens. How on earth would I do that?" Mrs B sat back against the hard wooden pew.

"You're part witch or something. Scariest woman I've ever met." He smiled. "Now, I am off to see if my daughter and her fiancée would agree to dinner with me tomorrow. He patted the seat. "My brother-in-law is a lucky man to have you in his corner." He walked up to the front of the church and spoke to Maisie, then nodded to Mrs B, slipping his hat back on as he left.

"You did it, Mrs B!" Maisie hugged her tightly. "He's agreed to me singing, and to Tommy and me getting engaged. You are amazing." She kissed Mrs B gently on the cheek. "I need to find Tommy." She ran from the church, leaving Mrs B sitting and thinking. What on earth did Mr Newton expect her to find out about Maisie, and was it wise to even start?

68.

Mrs B does her research

"Mrs B? I hope you are not unwell?" The doctor hovered in the doorway.

"No. I am in the best of health, thank you, Doctor. I just wondered if you could please spare me five minutes?" Mrs B stood up.

"Of course. Come on in." He stood aside.

She sat down. "I need some information. Of the scientific variety." He raised an eyebrow. "Is there any way to determine if someone is the father of a child?"

"No. Not yet. Although science is advancing all the time. We can tell that someone is definitely not the father. To explain it simply, blood is grouped. From the blood groups of the parents, there are only certain groups that their child can be." He tipped his head sideways. "Is there something that you need to tell me?"

"No. Well, perhaps." She took a deep breath. I have been asked if Maisie, my houseguest, is her father's child. I have not the faintest idea how to move forward."

"Mrs B. You might have better luck with talking to the mother. You're very good at winkling out information. She is the only one who will know if it is a possibility." He lifted his shoulders.

"Thank you, Doctor." She beamed across the desk at him, and was gone before he could make a reply.

Mrs B hopped off the bus with a spring in her step. The house that she was looking for was only a short walk away. Number thirty-one had a short path to the front door. She knocked and waited.

"Yes?" The woman was rake thin and wore more make-up that Mrs B had worn in her whole life.

"I'm so sorry to bother you, Mrs Newton. Maisie asked me to pop in to see you. I know that she sent you a note to let you know her exciting news, and that she will be singing tonight. I wondered if you might like to come with me to watch.

"And you are?" Mrs Newton leaned against the door frame.

"Oh, I beg your pardon. I should have introduced myself. I am Mrs B. Maisie is staying with me for a little while." She smiled and waited.

"She should be here with me." The scowl

descended across her features.

"Perhaps. Sometimes everyone needs a break from families or friends. She will most probably need a break from me very soon. I suspect I am not the most exciting housemate." She laughed and watched the disgruntled expression begin to crumble.

"Come in then, don't stand on the doorstep." Mrs Newton walked inside. They sat at the table in the kitchen. "Maisie has been difficult since my husband left. She never went without, but he's a difficult man and she was unhappy about his new wife." Mrs B nodded slowly.

"That must have been difficult for both of you. She's a lovely girl, a credit to you." Mrs B took a breath. "I am certain that you miss her. She is young and headstrong, but I know that she would love you to be there tonight. She's nervous."

Mrs Newton clenched her hands into fists. A muscle in her jaw worked. "Fine. I'll go. She's annoying, but I love her."

"I have been offered a lift. Perhaps we could collect you on the way?" Mrs B asked.

"No, thank you. I have a car. I will meet you outside though, if that's alright? One other thing?" She received a nod from Mrs B. "Will my husband be there?"

"I believe he will." Mrs B laid her hand flat on the table. "She will be pleased to see you both there, I suspect."

"I will not sit with him. I will sit with you." There was something brittle in the way she spoke. She reached for a pack of cigarettes and lit one up, dragging the smoke deep into her lungs. She tapped the ash from the end.

"That is perfectly fine. I will meet you outside. Thank you, Mrs Newton. We aim to be there for a quarter to six. She will be singing at seven, or soon after, but I dislike being late."

It was agreed. Mrs B climbed onto the bus to go home and found a seat. The houses passed her, but she saw nothing. The first step in her plan was completed, and her plan for the next was already taking shape in her mind.

69.

Mrs B enjoys the music

Tommy had managed to find a parking space directly outside the theatre. "Are you ready, Maisie?" He reached across and held her hand lightly.

"I'm shaking inside, more than I ever have, but I'm as excited as I am scared." She turned to face him. "What if I mess it up?"

"You won't. But if you do, I will still love you." He lifted her hands to his lips. "Come on, we need to get you inside so that you can run through the songs before everyone else arrives."

Mrs B climbed out of the car. "Good luck, my dear. I'll wait out here for your mother. I know that everyone in Little Millington will be listening on the wireless tonight. We are all behind you." She hugged Maisie's thin frame tightly. One more smile and they were gone.

Ten minutes later, Mrs Newton arrived, and they walked inside together. Very little was said between the two of them. The truth was that they were both nervous. Mrs B hoped with every part of her that Maisie would be able to sing as sweetly as she had in the church. She also hoped that the plan she had been turning around in her mind would work.

To begin with, Mr Morley made some announcements. The people in the audience sat up a little straighter. He introduced a man who sang in a deep baritone. A strong voice which rang around the building with confidence. Everyone sat still and listened as he carried them through the music. Their claps were heartfelt when the song came to an end. Mr Morley came back then and thanked him. A knot tightened in Mrs B's stomach, knowing that Maisie was going to be nervously waiting for her turn. She turned to look at Mrs Newton, who was sitting on the edge of her seat.

Maisie's steps were confident, her soft blonde hair falling in waves to her shoulders with each step. The music began, and she pulled in a breath. Mrs B and Mrs Newton both breathed with her. Mrs B was surprised to feel Mrs Newton's hand in hers. Whether she had taken it or Mrs Newton had taken hers, she could not tell.

Maisie's mouth opened, and the audience held their combined breath, waiting for her first note.

70.

Mrs B finds some common ground

Maisie lifted her voice; filling the theatre and carrying the whole audience with her, on the notes she sang. The power and passion with which she filled the song, bringing tears to the eyes of those who listened. When the song came to an end, the sound of clapping and cheering was thunderous.

Mrs B's hand felt the squeeze of Mrs Newton's fingers. Her expression, when Mrs B checked, was one of astonishment. She turned to meet Mrs B's stare. "She's amazing! How could I not have known that she had this talent?" Her eyes shone with tears. "Why did she hide it from me?"

"Sometimes we find it hardest to share our secrets with those we love the most." Mrs B patted the other woman's hand. "Most hairdressers walk around with a head full of secrets, because people tell them things their husbands, children and closest friends would not guess." She shook her head, as though she lived in a state of constant surprise when confronted with the human race.

"You're right." She nodded slowly. "A stranger is easier, I suppose. My husband always said I told him nothing." She smiled. "He was right about that."

"How so?" Mrs B turned towards her, tipping her head to one side and listening to every word while she watched every expression that might give her the information she needed. She could not afford to upset Mr Newton, not if Maisie was to be allowed to have a chance at the career she wanted.

"He could be a vicious man, sharp tongued. Too quick with his fists too. I never should have married him. He made me unhappy for years. Maisie too." She shook her head at Mrs B's gasp. "No, he never hit her, but he's mean. Be careful if you're around him." She smiled, the lines around her eyes creasing her make up.

"You did a wonderful job, bringing her up, especially if it was under such difficult circumstances. She really is a joy." Mrs B smiled widely and tried to imagine what life had been like for Mrs Newton.

The next singer was the last on the programme, and they sat still to listen. Although Mrs B would not remember any of the performance, her mind whirred with thoughts and ideas, and ways to keep Maisie and Tommy safe.

The audience filed out, chatting excitedly with each other about the wonderful singer they had heard. They told each other that they would go to see her again if they could find out where she would be performing next. Mrs B sat patiently with her companion and watched Mr Newton sitting on the other side of the theatre watching them. She was grateful that he kept his distance.

When Maisie and Tommy finally emerged, she was dancing with every step. Mrs B had never seen anyone so proud as Tommy McKinley was in that moment.

"You were wonderful, Maze." Her mother patted her on the arm, when a hug would have seemed more appropriate.

"You sang like an angel, dear. Your mother and I listened together." Mrs B put an arm around the girl's shoulders.

"Perhaps I could take you all out to dinner? We should celebrate." Mr Newton stepped into the group.

"No. I have to get back." Mrs Newton collected her bag and jacket. "Lovely job, Maisie. I'm proud of you." Mrs B caught an expression of regret as it crossed her face. Maisie was lost to her. The career that had been launched would take her beyond her mother's imaginings.

Mrs B watched her leave. Whatever could she do to protect Maisie from her family?

"Mrs Newton?" Mrs B hurried after her. "I wanted to thank you for letting me share the moment with you. Your daughter is wonderfully talented. Thank you." She extended her hand. Mrs Newton took it. "I wondered if you might like to come to my house, pop in for a cup of tea." Mrs B smiled. "The kettle always seems to be on."

"Thank you. I would like that. While we are on the subject. Thank you for looking after my Maisie. I know that you helped her to get this job. You're a nice person. I'll be there for the tea." She shook Mrs B's hand. They shared a smile and Mrs Newton left. She stood a little straighter than she had before. Mrs B watched her leave.

She would need to give some thought to how she could best help Tommy and Maisie.

71.

Mrs B makes tea

The knock at the door was unexpected. Mrs B was in the middle of dusting the living room. She opened the front door and found Mrs Nerwton on the step.

"What a lovely surprise! Mrs Newton, come on in. I was just about to stop for a cup of tea. Your timing is perfect." Mrs B smiled and held the front door open.

"I took you at your word. I hope that you really meant for me to drop in on you." Mrs Newton followed her hostess into the living room.

"I'm so glad that you did. I'll fetch us a drink." Mrs B came back to find Mrs Newton looking out of the window. Once the tray was on the table, she joined her visitor at the window. "Maisie is doing so well. I cannot imagine how proud you were the other day." A tear slid down Mrs Newton's face, and she swiped it away.

"Me and my husband, we messed it all up. I can see that now. We loved her, but in the wrong way.

We both wanted to keep her safe, but we went the wrong way around it." She took a breath. "You have given her what we couldn't. When you live in a world where everyone is dangerous and the only way to stay safe is to be scarier than everyone else, it's hard to see anything but danger." She shook her head.

"I did nothing but give her a place to stay. She made the choices. I suspect she would have done so anyway. I have an idea that Maisie generally finds a way to make her own decisions." Mrs B chuckled. "I like her."

"I'm glad." Mrs Newton moved away from the window and sat down. "The whole thing is a mess. Anthony is an idiot, but he was my idiot. When he left, I was furious, humiliated. Not only that. I was lonely." She accepted the tea that Mrs B offered and sipped from the cup. "I met him when I was at school. He was everything to me. There were always other women, but nothing serious until he met Carol." She sipped from her tea. "I don't know why I'm telling you all this." She shook her head.

"I think it must have been very scary, being left alone for the first time. Maisie is a lovely girl, but headstrong. You must have missed having another grown-up you could confide in." Mrs B watched her visitor carefully.

"You're a good listener." She smiled for the first

time. "I know that Maisie will be safe with you, and that's an enormous weight off my shoulders."

"Thank you. That's kind." Mrs B patted her hand. "What will you do now that Maisie is going to be all over the country?"

"I am thinking about going to an art class. Anthony always used to laugh at me for drawing. It's something I always enjoyed, though, so I'll give it a try." She wrapped her fingers around each other.

"Mum?" Maisie peered around the door frame.

"Maisie, how lovely to see you! I'll make some fresh tea. Come and sit with your mother." Mrs B picked up the teapot.

"No. I have news to tell you both." They both turned to look at her. "Mr Morley has arranged an audition for me. They are looking for a singer. I could be in a film!" Her eyes sparkled with the news. "I might not, of course, but it's a chance."

"Wonderful. Oh, this calls for a celebration." Mrs B hugged Maisie tightly. Tommy was waiting for her in the kitchen. "Maisie just told us her wonderful news."

He sunk into a chair at the table. "Oh, Mrs B, I am in so much trouble."

72.

Mrs B sorts it out

"Tommy, for goodness' sake, whatever sort of trouble are you in?" Mrs B sat down opposite him.

"It's the worst kind." His eyes met hers across the table. "I overhead the man who is running the audition talking to Mr Morley. He's... well, I am struggling to tell you politely."

"Then tell me the truth, Tommy. You're frightening me." Mrs B reached for his hand.

"He was talking about Maisie, like she was a cheap tart. I won't tell you the words he used. I wanted to knock his head off, but Maisie already knew about the offer, and she's so excited. So, either I do the right thing and knock him into next week, and she will be devastated, or I stand back and let that nasty weasel of a man near my Maisie. I don't know what to do." His eyes closed to keep his misery inside. A groan escaped his lips. "This is before I have to explain either one of those choices to Mr Newton."

"Can you not be there with her?" Mrs B watched

his expression.

"Morely told him I would be watching and he would be stupid to think about going anywhere near her. He laughed. Actually laughed. He said he would get Maisie to tell me to wait outside, that he had done it before." He spat the words.

Mrs B thought about what he had said before she spoke. "There is another option, of course." His head snapped up so quickly it took her by surprise. "You could allow me to go with her to the audition. I can stay with her all the time and stand between her and any danger. She will never know, and he will never get near her."

"But they won't allow you there when she is doing her audition." He chewed his lip.

"They will if Maisie's father insists on it. After all, she is underage." His eyes opened wide. "I will tell Maisie that he will withdraw his permission unless she allows me to stay."

"Genius! That's what you are!" He jumped to his feet and grabbed her hands. "I will never be able to thank you enough."

"No need for thanks. Let's just keep Maisie safe and happy between us." There was a knock on the back door, and she opened it. Patricia stood on the step. "Patricia, do come in. I was just about to put the kettle on. How is your lovely son?" She turned to Tommy. "Tommy dear, would you pop into the living room and see if Maisie and her mother would like a cup?" He nodded, and left them to talk in the kitchen.

"I won't beat about the bush, Mrs B. I see you have visitors. I need your help. My husband has been acting very strangely, and I have no idea what he wants." She slid one glove off a perfectly manicured hand.

"In what way is his behaviour strange?" Mrs B filled the kettle and put it on the stove.

"He gave the nurse I employed the day off three Saturdays in a row and insisted that we take care of the baby ourselves. He kept saying that it would be good for the family. It was exhausting. Then he wanted me to dance with him. All I wanted was to go to sleep. I thought perhaps he had been drinking, but he assured me that he was as sober as a judge." She accepted the cup of tea that Mrs B offered her. Her mouth was a tight little pout.

"Patricia, he loves you. He was worried that neither of you were bonding with the baby. That's all. He came to see me. It's my fault! I suggested he spend some time with you and the baby as a family." Mrs B laughed; her hands flat on the table. "You two need to talk to each other. I am very fond of both of you, and there is always a cup of tea here for you, but you love each other. It should be so easy." She wrapped her fingers around Patricia's hand.

"Yes, it should be." She caught her lower lip between her teeth. "It isn't always, though. I will talk to him. So simple, but I really had never thought about it. Thank you, Mrs B." She squeezed Mrs B's hand and let herself out of the back door, leaving the cup of tea untouched.

"Yes, please, they would like tea." Tommy popped his head around the kitchen door. "Is there anyone who doesn't come here for help?" His eyes sparkled with good humour. "I'm looking forward to watching you take on that slimy slug tomorrow."

73.

Mrs B's brush with stardom

Maisie was delighted to have Mrs B come along with her for the day. "Can you imagine? What if they say I can have the job? We could go to the picture house in Potterton and see me on the screen!" She hopped from the car. Tommy reached for her hand.

"You are going to be as wonderful as you always are, my darling Maisie." Tommy smiled, carried along with her enthusiasm.

The main doors were made of polished wood and led into a wide reception area. Maisie stood still, just inside the main doors. "Oh." Tommy stopped and turned to her. "I can't do this."

He turned, his jacket swinging open. "Maisie Newton? Can't do this?" He shook his head. "No, I have never heard of that happening." He leaned down to kiss her cheek. "You are the most amazing, stupendous, fantastic woman I have ever met. If these people do not offer you a job in a movie immediately, they are more foolish than an apple pie with gravy." Her huge eyes looked up into his.

"Fantastic?" He nodded. She sucked in a deep breath. "Right then. What are we waiting for?" She marched to the desk and announced her arrival. Mrs B nodded slowly to Tommy. She was proud of him.

"Ah, Miss Newton! What a pleasure to see you again. I hope that you are going to sing for me today. We are planning a screen test, just the way I explained to you. I would like you to read some lines, sing a little, and then I will ask you to talk a little about yourself. It's very simple." He reached for her hand.

"Mr Rampsey, thank you so much. I will do my best." He patted her hand gently. If his hand held hers for a little too long, perhaps it was no surprise.

"As I explained yesterday, we usually use a closed set for these things to prevent any distractions." He tucked her hand into the crook of his elbow. "We should get started."

"Excuse me, Mr Rampsey?" Mrs B leaned between them. "Miss Newton is underage, and therefore, she is only here for as long as her father gives his permission. He has instructed me to be wherever she is for her screen test, or he will not allow her to test." She bit her lower lip. "Sorry to be the bearer of bad news." She smiled up into his face.

"A closed set means nobody." He glared at Mrs B.

"Oh dear. I'm so sorry Maisie. Your father will not allow this. I explained this morning. He was absolutely determined on it." She shook her head. "Far be it from me to cause a problem. Mr Rampsey. I will sit very quietly in the corner. You will not know that I am there." He was unhappy, but left with nothing he could argue about. He shrugged and gave in with a bad grace.

Mrs B was as good as her word. Her hands folded in her lap, she sat in the corner and watched Maisie sing a little, read some lines and answer questions. She sparkled. More than that. She lit up the room.

Mr Rampsey asked if Maisie might like to join him for dinner that evening, but Mrs B stepped in, reminding him that she was underage, and would be making no dinner arrangements. Other than that, he behaved, and Maisie did a wonderful job.

If the camera had caught a tenth of the charisma which Maisie exuded, then she would be on a screen very soon indeed, Mrs B surmised.

They climbed into Tommy's car, his smile filled with relief and pride.

"I was right." He smiled across at Maisie. "You are fantastic."

"I love you, Tommy McKinley." She slid her hand

across the seats to hold his.

"You are both entirely remarkable young people, but if you could please drop me off at Mrs Pendley's house, I need to get to work." She watched out of the window from the back seat, listening to Tommy and Maisie chatting as he drove back towards Little Mellington.

74.

Mrs B referees

"I am not entirely sure why I need to come with you, Tommy." Mrs B held firmly to her handbag.

"Well, that makes two of us. But no matter how much Mr "call me Tony" Newton pretends that he's my friend, if he says you and I need to go to a meeting with him, we go." He nodded across at her.

They walked to the Royal Oak and crossed the road to the small café, where they ordered tea and waited for Mr Newton to arrive. They both had nearly finished their tea before he arrived.

"Thank you for coming." He signalled to the waitress to bring another cup. "I have some things to talk to you about, McKinley, which are maybe quite strange. I was late getting here because I was trying to work out if I should do this or not."

The waitress brought another cup and a fresh pot of tea. "Thank you, dear." Mrs B poured them all a cup. "I always find that if you have something uncomfortable to say, it's best to just say it." She pushed the cup across towards him.

"Right. Good advice. That's why I wanted you here. You are here to keep it calm. In case either of us thought about being stupid." He took a deep breath. "Me and your dad, Tommy, we grew up together. He lived three doors down the road from me when we were kids. He played football in the same team as me. Then we started to grow up, and neither of us were too careful about the rules. I won't lie; we weren't friends. Then he met Jeannie. The first time I saw her was when he brought her to a dance. She was so pretty, and she only had eyes for him. No matter what I did. I found out where she worked and I waited for her. She told me; so gently that it felt like needles in my eyes. She was in love with your father, and though she was flattered by my interest, there was no interest on her side." He raised his eyebrows. "I went on a bender, drinking far more than I should for months. When I sobered up six months later, I was engaged to Maisie's mum." He ran a hand over his face. "I was so sad when Jeanie died. It was the end of my marriage. I stayed for a few more years, but I was gone and we both knew it." He heaved a sigh and looked across at them both. "I understand why Maisie loves you. She has always been very like me. You're very like her."

"I had no idea. She was a very special person,

but then, she was my mum, so I'm bound to think that, I suppose." Tommy took a sip from his cup. "I still miss her. I suppose we have that in common."

Anthony Newton shrugged. He had spent most of his life in love with a woman who had loved someone else. He took a breath and sipped from his tea.

"You have something else in common, you know." Mrs B smoothed her hand over the tablecloth. "You both want the best for Maisie. Perhaps that is enough common ground to start with." She rested her elbows on the table. "There will be difficulties, of course. Tommy's father may not be overjoyed at this turn of events, but families get through far worse things."

"I have asked Maisie to marry me. She said yes, but she wanted you and her mother to approve. To be frank, I thought that there was very little chance of that. Thank you for telling me." He held out his hand. Mr Newton took it in his own and they shook. It was awkward, and they were both struggling with the new information.

"If I may?" They both nodded. "You are very similar in many ways. That you both care about Maisie is clear. Perhaps that is what you should work on together." They stood, and Mr Newton paid for the tea.

"Tommy, will you fetch the car, and let me talk

to Mrs B for a moment?" Surprise registered on Tommy's face, but he did as he was asked. When he was far enough away that he could no longer hear, Mr Newton leaned closed to Mrs B. "Any news for me on that other matter?"

"I am making progress, but I have nothing to report yet." She shifted her weight carefully.

"You would not keep anything from me, would you?" He was so close to her that she could feel his breath with each word.

"Perish the thought, Mr Newton." She pushed her most confident smile onto her face, keeping her feelings almost entirely hidden. "As soon as I know anything, if there is anything to know, you will be the first to know."

"I will be the only one to know, Mrs B." He turned at a sound behind him. "Here's Tommy with the car. Thank you for coming." He opened the door and smiled across to the driving seat. Mrs B climbed in, and took a deep breath.

"Are you alright? What did he want?" Tommy's breathing was faster than it should be.

"He was just reminding me that Maisie should be well cared for." She turned away from him and watched the houses go past her window. She had hoped that Mr Newton might agree to leave his worries about whether he was Maisie's father behind. Clearly, he had no intention of doing that, and she would need to think again.

75.

Mrs B and Grizelda

"I am certain that the show will be another huge success. I am so sorry that I will not be able to attend." Mrs B gave Maisie a last hug.

"I'll miss you, but you can come to the next one. Maisie squeezed back. "By the way, thank you for looking after me with that horrible sleaze of a film producer. I couldn't say anything to Tommy because he would hit him or something!" Her smile, when she stepped back, was entirely innocent, but Mrs B realised that she had been underestimating Maisie. It was a relief. "I know that you have to work. I've taken up enough of your time." She smiled; her face once more cloaked in innocence. Mrs B shook her head. It would be interesting to know what went on behind those curls.

"Bye Mum." Maisie squeezed her mother and jumped into the car.

Tommy drove away, leaving Mrs B waving from the gate, and Mrs Newton wiping a tear.

"Mrs B? Please help. Someone has stolen Grizelda." Mrs Pendley puffed up the hill to the cottage.

"Mrs Newton, I have to go and look for Grizelda. Please make yourself at home." Mrs B stepped out into the lane.

"Absolutely not. I'm going to help you search." They fell into step with Mrs Pendley, and marched through the village, checking over every fence and into every garden.

"Could she not have just got out and wandered off?" Mrs B caught Mrs Newton's surprised expression, but the hill was steep and talking made it seem steeper.

"Not unless she could use bolt cutters to cut through the chain on the gate." Mrs Pendley's expression was grim.

"We should ask Mr and Mrs Anderson. They might have seen something." Mrs B pointed to the farm gate as they drew level.

"I was thinking the same thing." Mrs Pendley pushed the gate wide enough for them to walk through and closed it behind them. "Can you ask, Mrs B? I'll just have a quick check in the barn." She turned into the shadowy building, leaving them in the bright sunshine of the farmyard.

"Mrs Anderson? Hello, I wonder if you could help? Mrs Pendley is looking for Grizelda. She is missing. Have you heard anything?" The woman turned towards Mrs B and Mrs Newton, surprise followed by fear crossed her face.

"Nellie Anderson, as I live and breathe. I haven't seen you in a while." Mrs Newton rested her fists on her hips.

"Mrs Newton? Is that you? No, it has been some time." Her voice shook with nerves.

"Found her." Mrs Pendley led her prize pig out of the barn behind them. "You tell your husband to stay off my farm, or he'll meet my husband's shotgun next time. You hear?" She led the pig towards the gate. "Come on, sweetie. You must be hungry. Let's get you home." The animal snuffled gently at Mrs Pendley's hand.

"Nothing changes, does it Nellie? You tell your no good thief of a husband that if he touches another pig on my friend's farm, he'll have to deal with my husband, never mind hers. You hear?" Mrs Anderson nodded, and watched Mrs B and Mrs Newton walk out of the yard.

"I am very impressed, Mrs Newton. You are quite terrifying." Mrs B walked next to Mrs Newton down the hill.

"I remember them both. They had to leave Potterton a few years ago. Fell out with the wrong people." She laughed, bending double and holding on to the wall. "I had no idea we were looking for a pig. I thought it was a kiddie that had been taken." She spluttered through her laughter.

"Oh. Oh my!" Mrs B laughed too, realising that she had failed to explain that Grizelda was, in fact, a prize-winning sow.

They soon caught up with Mrs Pendley and explained the joke to her, between gales of giggles. Soon the only one not laughing was Grizelda who was busy pulling grass and wildflowers from the hedgerow.

"Thank you for your help, and for telling her off, Mrs Newton. I'm going to take Grizelda home and give her something to eat before she demolishes your garden." Mrs Pendley waved and left them at Mrs B's house.

"I think we deserve a cup of tea after all that, Mrs Newton." Mrs B led the way into the house and put the kettle on. "I rather wanted to ask your advice."

They carried their tea out to the garden, where the sun was still pleasantly warm. "What can I do to help?" Mrs Newton settled back into her chair.

"I lost my husband in the war and I have been alone since then. I have had no regrets. However, recently I have been seeing a man, as a friend only, but I suspect he wishes it was more than that. I have no experience to know what to do. I have only ever been with my husband, and then only for a short time before he was drafted into the army. What should I do?" She picked up her cup of tea and sipped from the cup.

"Well, well. You are a dark horse. I would never have suspected. Yes, you are right. I have a little more experience of the world that you do." She leaned her chin against her hand. "Before Tony, there were other young men. I was a pretty girl when I was younger." She smiled, a wistful look crossing her face. "I was engaged to another man before I met Tony. I thought he was a lovely man, played the piano like a maniac, but he left town in a hurry, owed a lot of money by all accounts, and left me behind. When I met Tony, I thought, why not? He was going places and earning good money. I did love Tony, but not in the same way as my first love."

"So you think that I could be happy with this man? Is it possible? I would have to tell the new gentleman everything. There could be no secrets, I suppose." Mrs B trapped her bottom lip between her teeth to think about the situation. "Not that I've many secrets, but we all keep some things hidden."

"Do you have any sherry?" Mrs Newton leaned her elbow on the table.

"Yes, I think so." Mrs B pushed herself out of her chair.

"Thank goodness. I am fed up with tea, and I think we could both do with a proper drink."

Mrs Newton smiled across the table and sat back while Mrs B went into the house in search of the sherry.

76.

Mrs B has a frank conversation

The two small glasses sat next to each other on the table. Mrs B refilled them.

"Delicious. Thank you." Mrs Newton sipped from the glass. "I was thinking, on the subject of men. You should be cautious about telling too much of the truth. It is a lovely idea to be so open with someone, but some things are better kept under wraps." She smiled, a knowing smile on her lips. It reminded Mrs B of Maisie's feigned innocence.

"What sort of things should I keep from him? I'm such a fool about these things." Mrs B's hands fluttered to her throat.

"For goodness' sake, don't tell him too much about your husband, or compare them." She laughed. "I told Tony very little of my life before I met him." She shrugged. "I behaved badly. Often. I loved him, but he never loved me. It hurt my pride being second best. But I know I hit back and hurt him, too." She ran a finger under her eye, swiping a tear away. "Maisie was in the middle, while we were ripping chunks off each other. We damaged her. I am the worst mother ever."

"No, you are not. Good heavens, she is a happy, well-adjusted young lady. Mr Newton and you were both unhappy, perhaps, but that is not your fault." Mrs B reached across the table. "I am so sorry that you had such a difficult time."

"I am so pleased that I met you, and that you are Masie's friend. Thank you." They sat for a while, watching the sun go down, and Mrs B considered. If Mrs Newton had told her that Masie's father was not Mr Newton, what benefit would be gained by any of them by telling him? As it was, no such statement had been made and it was clear and evident that both Mr and Mrs Newton loved Maisie. No, she would go to see Mr Newton and tell him that as far as she could determine, Maisie was his daughter. That was the only reasonable path forward.

On the bus in the morning, she found that she was a little nervous, but Mr Newton always made her feel that way. She would get the meeting out of the way and be home before lunchtime. Mr Newton, once summoned from the Royal Oak, arrived at the tea shop. She told him that, despite all her best efforts, everything that she had found out suggested that Maisie was indeed his daughter.

"Thank you. I'm pleased. I just thought, well, it

doesn't matter now. She's a good girl, and she's doing well with this singing thing. I suppose I was right that her mother was only trying to hurt me. Thanks Mrs B. You've been a good friend." He threw some money on the table for the tea and reached across to shake her hand.

Mrs B boarded the next bus, but in the back of her mind was a worry that she was not seeing the whole picture.

77.

Mrs B calls in on Arnold

"Auntie?" Barbara opened the door. "What a lovely surprise." She shifted Jennifer from one hip to the other. "Come on in."

"I am so very sorry to come in unannounced. I was on the bus home, and I was thinking about you, and about Arnold, and little Jennifer." She followed Barbara into the house.

On the floor in the living room, Barbara laid the little one on a soft blanket on her tummy. Her little feet kicked, and she gurgled quietly to herself.

"She's getting so big." Mrs B ran her finger along the baby's soft cheek.

"Yes, she is strong, too. I think she will be crawling soon." Barbara stood up. "I'll make us a cup of tea, and you can tell me what has been going on. I hear you have Maisie Newton staying with you."

Mrs B raised an eyebrow, but she made no

comment. "You are such a pretty little thing." The little girl pushed herself up from the blanket.

"Here we are." Barbara set the tray down. "Look at her, another five minutes and she'll be across the room."

"I knew that Arnold would not be able to visit comfortably while Mr Newton's daughter is staying with me. The fact that she is engaged to Tommy McKinley would only make that worse." Mrs B sipped from the cup that Barbara passed her. "I knew that, but I really could not refuse to help her." She raised her eyes to meet Barbara's. "I have missed you, though."

"I hear that she has a wonderful singing voice." She smiled.

"You hear quite a lot." Mrs B smiled.

"Oh yes. Arnold talks of very little else." Barbara laughed. "He also tells me that you are good friends with Tommy. I'm glad. I always thought he could be a better person if he was away from his family." She bit her lower lip. "Be careful, Auntie. Arnold says the power struggle between Mr Newton and Tommy's father is coming to a head. Please, be somewhere else when it happens." She reached for Mrs B's hands.

The bus ride home gave Mrs B some time for thinking. Barbara had given her information, which she had not heard before. Or perhaps, if she was to be more accurate in her thinking, she had given Mrs B some ideas on where her thinking should go.

When the bus stopped, Will was waiting for her. "Hello Will, how lovely to see you."

"I bumped into a lady near your cottage and she said she saw you board the bus earlier. I thought I might as well wait for you." His eyes crinkled with a smile.

"I thought perhaps you felt unable to come to see me with Maisie Newton as my houseguest." She smiled up at him.

"You are the most straight-talking person that I know." He fell into step beside her. "I was sorting out some things in my life. There were things that I needed to tidy up before I came to talk to you about our future."

They reached her garden gate. "Sounds like hard work. Shall we have a cup of tea, and you can tell me all about it?" She reached up and kissed his cheek gently.

78.

Mrs B is called away

"Mrs B? Thank goodness." Maisie was waiting in the kitchen when they let themselves in. "Something has happened. Tommy dropped me off here and told me to stay inside. He raced off as though someone was chasing him." She was pacing the floor. "Somebody who works for my dad turned up at rehearsal today. He told me that Tommy's father had heard about us, and he was going to the pub to have it out with my dad." She slumped into a chair. "My father won't accept that. It's an insult." She dropped her head into her hands.

"Surely, they can understand that people lose their tempers. They will sort it out." Mrs B reached for Maisie's hand.

"No. You don't understand. Tommy will be in danger. Please, Uncle Will. Please, can you stop them?" Her eyes were red rimmed with tears.

"Maisie's right. I should try to stop this. It

could be an extremely dangerous situation." Will jumped to his feet.

"You are definitely not going alone." Mrs B fixed him with a stare. "I may be able to talk sense into one or all of them."

"I'm coming too." Maisie jumped to her feet.

"No. I promised your father I would keep you safe. Tommy would be furious if I put you in danger, and rightly so." Mrs B reached for Maisie's hands. "We will drop you down to Mrs Gartree's house. You might be able to keep her company."

Despite Maisie's protests, Mrs B knocked on Mrs Gartree's door and asked if Maisie might be able to spend a few hours there.

Outside the pub, three large men stood guard. Mrs B asked one if Mr Newton was available. He dismissed her request, moving her gently but firmly away from the door.

A car stopped across the road. "Oh my. Come away." Will pulled at Mrs B's arm. "We are too late." He stepped in front of her, shielding her with his body. "Alan McKinley." He shouted across the street. "Come away. It's not too late."

"Hunton? Are you telling me what to do?" The man turned towards Will. He was heavy set and angry. He advanced towards Will. The sound of running footsteps distracted him,

Tommy raced around the corner. He was red in the face and his breathing was ragged. "Dad, please. Don't do this."

"You. Of all the things that you could do. You with a Newton. I had such hopes for you. Not running around with a club singer, and a daughter of his to boot." Father and son faced each other, both were breathing hard.

"We love each other. We're engaged. If you do this, fight, beat seven bells out of each other, that won't change. I will just pack up everything and take Maisie away from here." He held out his hands towards his father.

"Why did you not tell me? I had to hear it from your cousin Joe." His brows pushed together in confusion. "You know what he's like."

"Because of this! You would have reacted this way. It was bad enough having to deal with Mr Newton." Tommy shrugged. "I would have told you. I just was waiting for the right moment."

"Might I interrupt?" Mrs B peeped out from behind Will.

"Who is this?" Mr Mckinley threw up his arms in frustration.

"I'm Mrs B." She stepped out and held out her hand. "Might I suggest that we go back to my house, and you meet Maisie?"

Alan McKinley stepped towards her with his hand still raised.

"Don't you dare." Will stepped between them. Tommy stepped in front of Will.

"Mrs B has been my friend since I came out of prison. She's stopped me going back there over and over. She has trusted me, and I trust her. Mrs B's done more for me than you have lately." Tommy's jaw lifted in an attitude of defiance.

"Cheeky..." The warning growl was left unfinished by the arrival of Mr Newton.

"McKinley? What are you doing outside my pub?" He took up a wide stance on the pavement. "I thought we had an understanding."

"We might have done until you started pushing your daughter on my boy." Alan McKinley's lip lifted; his fury was clear.

"Pushing my daughter? You are out of order." Mr Newton stepped forwards.

"Gentlemen? Please, these are your children. Are you prepared to lose your son, Mr McKinley?" Mrs B stepped between them.

"You may as well not bother. We barely speak to each other anymore. Not since my mum died." The bitterness which filled Tommy's voice shocked Mrs B. She had never heard him sound that way before.

"Tommy! You might be angry, but he's still your father." Mrs B was shocked at his anger. "Mr McKinley? Mr Newton? Brawling in the streets? I thought better of you both. Mr McKinley: Tommy speaks very highly of you. He told me that you value loyalty and family above everything. Is that what you are doing now?"

"Sorry, Mrs B." Tommy hung his head in contrition. Alan McKinley barked a laugh.

"Right. Whatever is going on, I need to hear about it. Directly from you, Tommy." He pointed his finger into his son's face. He turned to Mrs B. "You'd better come along too. It seems you're involved."

Mr Newton watched them walk away. He shook his head. He shrugged. "Mrs B strikes again." He laughed quietly to himself.

79.

Mrs B builds bridges

"Come along inside. I will make some tea. Will, show Mr McKinley and Tommy into the living room. I will bring in tea." Will did as he was asked. He was surprised that Mrs B had led them in through the front door, but he was certain that she had her reasons.

"Through here, gentlemen." Will watched the two large men take a seat on the small and definitely feminine furniture. The silence stretched between them.

"Right, here we are." Mrs B bustled in with a tray. "Tommy, I know how you take your tea, but how about your dad?"

"He takes two sugars." Tommy mumbled.

"Just like you." Mrs B passed the cups around. "Now, Mr McKinley. I am sorry, I had no intention of keeping anything secret from you. I like Tommy. He's been a good friend to me. I believe that he and Maisie are in love, and that he would have struggled to find a woman who understood his life as well as she does." She paused and sipped from her tea. "Maisie is staying with me because she ran away from home. Your son had the good sense to keep her safe. You have done a very good job with him. You should be very proud."

Alan watched her across the room. "He's like his mother. My Jeanie was a lovely woman, kind and helpful. It was cruel that she was in so much pain. Worse that we lost her so young. I haven't been at my best since then." He picked up the cup and saucer and sipped. "Nice tea."

"Thank you." She nodded. "You both need to talk to each other. I will walk down to Mrs Gartree's house and bring Maisie back. Will, would you walk with me?"

They walked slowly there and back again, allowing time for the McKinley's to talk together. "You never flinched. I was so worried that he might hit you." Will shook his head. He felt her hand on his arm and turned to look into the face he had loved for years. The calm eyes and gentle smile giving him hope that she might understand his feelings.

"Maisie dear, Mr McKinley is not delighted with the news, but I am certain that time together will help. You are a very lovely girl, and he will see how sweet you can be." Mrs B opened the garden gate and let Maisie through.

"Not to worry, Mrs B. I promise to be entirely charming." She giggled her way up the garden path.

"Tommy? Mr McKinley?" Mrs B walked through the house. "Ah, here we are. Mr McKinley, this is Maisie Newton."

"Hello. How lovely to meet you. Tommy has told me next to nothing about any of his family." She held out her hand.

"Maisie. Yes, of course. We are not good talkers. My wife was always the one who did all that." He shook her hand.

"Right. Maisie, I've explained to my dad about us. I think it would be a good idea if both of us got to know him a little better." He shrugged, trying hard to control his emotions.

"Fish and chips?" Maisie suggested, her eyebrow raised in question.

"Sounds like a good idea. Dad?" Tommy waited for his father to answer.

"Yes. Fish and chips with my son and his girl. That sounds like a good idea." He stood up. "Thank you, Mrs B, for making us talk to each other. We really haven't done enough of that."

They left, and Mrs B slumped into a chair in the kitchen. "Well, that was a worry for a while." She pushed herself up from the table. "I'm going to clean up, then I think we should have a quiet evening together."

"I wanted to talk to you once you're finished. If that's alright with you?" He pushed in the chair he had been sitting on and picked up the drying up cloth. "You wash, I'll dry."

80.

Mrs B receives a gift

Mrs B's house was exactly as it always was. Tidy and clean. She picked up the kettle and filled it up. Will shifted his weight from one foot to another. "I'm nervous. Sorry. Stupid way to start a conversation. I have a present for you. I wanted to give it to you before now, but I was stupid and scared. Anyway, putting all that to one side, I gathered what courage I had and brought the present to your house last week, but I was too afraid to bring it in." His voice disappeared into a whisper.

"Will? Drink your tea. Take two sips, and have a biscuit. Then tell me what on earth you are talking about." Mrs B took a bite from her biscuit, sipped her tea, and waited.

He dipped his hand into his pocket and came out with a fist. "Don't get upset. Or angry." He took a breath. "As I told you, I have been clearing up all the things in my life which were untidy. I wanted to come to you as a clean sheet, so to speak."

"Why would I be angry with you?" She rested her hand on top of his fist. Under her palm, she felt his fist turn until his fingers unfurled. Her hand rested on a square shape. "What's this?"

"It's a question or something." His eyes met hers.

She opened the box. Inside was a ring. "Oh."

"I knew it was wrong, sorry." He stared down into his tea.

"Oh Will. It's lovely. Thank you." She reached across the table. "It's not wrong at all."

"I'm not asking you to marry me. Not now. I mean one day? What I want to ask is if one day, you might think about being Mrs H instead of Mrs B? I love you. I cannot imagine a future without you in it." He squeezed her hand. "Should I have knelt down?"

"No. You shouldn't." She looked at the ring, settled so comfortably in the box. It was pretty. The tiny stone twinkled at her. More than that, the idea that he had been so worried about giving it to her, so afraid of her reaction. It shook her usually steady demeanour.

"Can you think about it?" His eyes met hers across the table.

"I will think of very little else, Will." She pushed the plate of biscuits across the table. "It is such a lovely ring, and a beautiful idea. I am surprised, but in a very good way."

Her mind drifted back to a day which had been so similar in so many ways. She had been a good deal younger, and carried less experience. Herbert Blandford had called at her house. He had asked her to go for a walk with him. The sun had been bright that afternoon. She remembered the fresh green smell of the grass, and the lacy shadows cast across the lane by the cowslips and the scarlet pimpernels in the hedgerow. Herbert had reached for her hand. She had been surprised by the warmth of his skin. He had asked her, his voice stumbling and catching on the words. He had promised her that he would do his best. When he had told her that he loved her, and always would, she had cried a little and smiled too. She had thought that she loved him. They had been happy enough and had made a life together. He had kept his word. He had done his best, and he had loved her. She had trusted him, and she had grown to love him. It had been nothing like the surge of joy that her heart experienced when Will's lips touched hers.

The guilt she felt over the way she felt about Will seared her soul. Every kiss she received, every touch of his fingers condemned the memory of the kind young man who had declared his undying love before marching off to his death for king and country on the battlefields of Europe.

"I need to think, Will." She swiped a tear from her cheek. "Will you wait here for me? While I think?"

"I'll wait." He watched her walk out into the sunshine and down the garden path. "I'll be right here. Take as long as you need." His voice shook a little, but he absolutely meant every word of it.

Printed in Great Britain
by Amazon